If I Loved You

Matrimony! Book One

by Jo-Ann Power
Writing as Cerise DeLand

ARE YOU SIGNED UP FOR DRAGONBLADE'S BLOG?

You'll get the latest news and information on exclusive giveaways, exclusive excerpts, coming releases, sales, free books, cover reveals and more.

Check out our complete list of authors, too!

No spam, no junk. That's a promise!

Sign Up Here

www.dragonbladepublishing.com

Dearest Reader;

Thank you for your support of a small press. At Dragonblade Publishing, we strive to bring you the highest quality Historical Romance from some of the best authors in the business. Without your support, there is no 'us', so we sincerely hope you adore these stories and find some new favorite authors along the way.

Happy Reading!

CEO, Dragonblade Publishing

Fleetside Chronicle
Serving London and environs

NUMBER 4059—Volume LXXX.
Wednesday, December 15, 1813.
Price Fourpence

WANTED: Matrimony!

Adverts for happily-ever-afters!

Frustrated in your search for domestic tranquility? Search no more!

Place your advert with the *Fleetside Chronicle*!

Find happiness in a trice!

Affordable!

Exclusive. Confidential. The strictest honour observed!

December 10, 1813

To a Lady of Distinction:

A Gentleman of pleasing manners preferring female society to solitude wishes to enter into the marriage state with a Lady of domesticated disposition and literate education. She should be from 22 to 30 years of age. She should also command from 300 to 400 Pounds. Any Lady interested with more than this sum should apply, though such fortune is not required. The qualities the Gentleman will consider the most requisite in the female are a good education in letters and arts and an amiable disposition. Personal beauty is a matter of least consequence. Social grace is of utmost desirability.

A Lady wishing for a congenial companion for life will find the Advertiser noted above as a man of sound character and sobriety. With a house in London, he resides most of the year in the country. He is 38 years of age and a man who prefers the company of his friends and associates and regards little the demands of Society.

To any qualified applicant, he will be able to give every satisfactory explanation that may be requested of him, as his proposals will be honorable and candid.

Letters descriptive of person, situation, etc. will be quickly and seriously attended to.

Direct responses to G. Hammond, Publisher, 140 Fleet St., London.

Fleetside Chronicle
Serving London and environs

NUMBER 31—Volume LXXXI
Monday, February 7, 1814.
Price Sixpence

February 2, 1814

RESPONSE to *'A Gentleman of Pleasing Manners'*:

I respond to your advertisement, sir, seeking a lady of distinction to wed.

I am 24 years of age, born in the country, raised gently with a sound education above my station in the arts, history, mathematics and useful French. I am of good health, sound constitution, and I enjoy fine company. I am the only child of my parents and come to my marriage with 400 Pounds. My father, a literate man, encouraged me in pursuit of drawing and painting. I confess I have no talents to sew or darn or embroider. But I am a good cook, my finest creations, by all who have tasted my wares, being good breads.

I seek a husband who will be my soul's companion, a man of sensibility who would share a quiet existence. I submit I am a suitable match for you, sir.

With regards,
V. A. Carr

I await your reply via G. Hammond, Publisher, 140 Fleet St., London.

Chapter One

May 12, 1814
The Great North Road

HER PREDICTION THAT traveling in the mail coach in May would ensure she'd be warm and the trip quick was very wrong. The cracked window belied her intent. So too did the ragged curtain that fell at such an angle that the wind curled in to the carriage and hit her squarely in her eyes.

Under her arm, Pip whined and burrowed more deeply into the folds of her wool coat.

"I know." Verity rubbed her eyelids with one gloved hand and, with the other, petted her little liver and white friend. "Not what you and I planned. But it seems…" she told the dog as she stretched to catch a glimpse of her coachmen who yelled at each other about reins and snow as they stomped about, "we've got a bit of bother with the horses that we cannot seem to solve. They don't like snow in May."

Who does?

She spied one coachman—the burly fellow of the two—rising from his crouch. Above the howl of the winds, she cried out to him, "Can we go on soon, do you think, sir?"

The rounded mound that resembled a snow-covered stone spun, and a swarthy face dusted in white turned toward her.

"Aye! Soon, miss!"

But that had been his answer twenty minutes ago. Or more.

Verity huddled in her worsted coat and tapped her fox-trimmed cottage bonnet low over her ears. If she'd wanted to die cold and alone, she could've stayed home and not bothered with a blizzard in May and a prospective husband in London.

Wiggling her toes in her good half-boots, she huddled Pip against her side. What fuss the men went to! *If they don't get the lines fixed soon, other travelers will find us frozen like Carrara marble statues!*

Drat! She reached in her reticule once more, unscrewed the top on her Great-Aunt Agatha's silver flask, and took a hearty swig. Pip tipped up her tiny nose at the aromas of her aunt's fine whisky.

"Not for you, my dear."

Pip sneezed and shook her little head, then dug back into her woolen nest.

Verity told herself to endure. Enjoy the burn drifting down her throat. Think of how smart she'd been to make such an intricate plan for her future. *Bollocks.* So ridiculously fine that, just for good measure, she decided not to put the cork back in or put the flask away. "If this is what saves me from another attack of congestion, it's worth it."

"Another coach!" one coachman shouted to his partner.

Lifting the ragged ends of the window curtain flapping in the wind, Verity detected movement of a dark speck along the hollowed path that in usual spring weather should have looked like a dirt road.

She caught her collar high to her throat, squinted at the approaching black lines and—*yes!* Another coach, large and blessedly mobile, carved a lane with two horses clopping readily through the drifts of snow.

Help was at hand.

If those in that carriage traveled the Great North Road often and knew where they were, and if they could summon help for her hapless driver, then she might find warmth again before she perished out here like a frost queen.

She recapped her flask, deposited it on the seat, then reached into her reticule for the box containing the other necessity of life for any lady along the famous old road. Then she waited. Reins jangled. Horses slowed, chuffed, and whinnied. A coachman hailed her own and asked the vital questions.

What happened?

How badly is it damaged?

Have you mended it?

Can it be mended?

Verity could not make out the response, but the tones that reached her ears told her what she already surmised. Repairs sounded dubious.

A rustle of doors and clank of coach steps ensued.

A huge, dark figure passed from the edge of her sight and knelt by her drivers.

"Well, then," announced a resonant voice, a baritone whose vibrance sank beneath Verity's coat to warm her cold flesh, "let me look."

Much ado of trudging feet and orders to get this tool or that occurred, and she stilled, concentrating to catch any declarations by the man with the thick, rich voice. He gave a few orders she could not discern.

Then came one she could.

"You cannot stay here much longer, man," declared the rousing baritone. "Either tie them as best you can and attempt the road or plan to unhitch your horses and ride them to safety. Do you know how far to the next village? By my memory it is Doncaster next, is that so?"

"Aye, milord."

"Three miles," said her other driver. "The Angel and Swan. Fine coaching inn, it is, sir."

"I know of it. Not far."

"John can take one horse, sir. Better than naught. But I canna leave the mail. Best you take my passenger, milord."

"Passenger?"

"Aye, sir."

"One?"

"Just so, sir."

Feet crunched the icy snow, and the flimsy door to her drafty sanctuary swung open.

Pip emerged from her covers and gave the apparition a sound talking to.

"Ah. I see," crooned the baritone who appeared before her, an inky silhouette against the iridescence of the late, snowy day. "A wolf by any other name," he said, unruffled by Pip's yips of dismay, and extended his gloved hand toward her companion. Pip, careful but not put off, sniffed at his hand, then retreated to the folds of Verity's pelisse.

Pip might be assured of safety.

But Verity still could not see him. Not fully.

Backlit by the glare of falling snow, her velvet-voiced rescuer presented her with the outline of top hat, long face, and square jaw. He filled the doorway with his tall, broad elegance bundled into a giant greatcoat. Drawing near to her, he came into more light and examined her with two large umber eyes. He blinked at her with deucedly long, snow-covered lashes, then gazed at the item in her hand. He crooked three fingers at her and the flintlock pointed at him. "Prepared, are you? Yes, well. No need for that, madam."

Behind him, his coachmen scurried around. They huddled together, frantic in their arguments. Their debate about the torn reins went on in sad refrains, to which she inferred she would not be keeping her appointment in London tomorrow afternoon.

She lifted her grandfather's pistol. The weapon was not a frilly bit, but she'd had practice with the heavy ivory and gold gun. Papa required it of her. "One does not live alone without a trusty companion, my dear one." He liked to encourage her in manly endeavors. Cards. Shooting. Target practice, definitely.

Dueling, another. Tree branches could suffice for that when glistening steel was not at the ready.

"Do put it away," her man of snow and delicious, dark delights encouraged her.

"I do not travel without protection, sir." She did not lower her aim.

He acted like a fellow used to command. His voice brooked no objections. His impressive size alone discouraged any contest. Therefore, he might be fooled to assume she'd put her weapon down, but she had no assurances of safety. She'd been promised such before and been so wrong.

"So I see, madam."

She had a greater message to convey than to correct him on his form of address.

"I assure you I have stopped to help." He took in the torn window curtain and the scarred seat cushions. The glances of his brown-black eyes told her that, in his view, the mail coach left much to be desired. "You need more assistance with your welfare. My coach is fitted with four warm bricks and woolen blankets. I do not run away with you, but offer you a respite while we attempt the best remedy to this situation. Do not argue with me. Come."

She objected to his assertive tone, but was lured by the luxury of heat and comfort. Grandpapa's pistol still held to her target.

A smile played about his lips, but did not dawn. "Very well. Keep your pistol, madam. I've no objection to it, provided you do not decide to use it on me."

"I will if I find cause." She had to threaten it. She was no desperate maiden in search of Sir Galahad.

He nodded. Flicking snow from his very fine straight nose, he tried to smile more fully. But he was strained, as if he found few things of grace in the world. "I'll have my two men vouch I mean you no harm. We must fix this, madam. I have no time to be here cajoling you!" He extended his arm further into the cabin.

She frowned at him. He wanted her hand. She gave him Pip.

The dog went, although the tiny, smart spaniel stared at Verity with wary brown eyes. Her man tucked the dog under one arm and offered his other hand. Despite her reluctance, she took it, and he grasped her with a gentleness that surprised her, given she still held her pistol. He, smart man, gave the piece frowning regard as he led her down the step to face him, two feet deep in the snow.

The heat radiating off his body drew her like a good fire. To simply stand beside him was to be shielded from the howling wind and swirling flurries. He tugged at her as she winced stepping through the drifts.

"Bollocks," he muttered beneath his breath, and shoved Pip into her arms. Her juggle of gun and dog grew precarious. But he scooped her up as if she were his booty. She grabbed at his shoulders, one hand able to clutch the silken wool cape of his coat. He charged through the snow toward his own carriage. "Open the door."

She fiddled with her possessions to do as he bade. "But sir. My reticule!"

No matter. He dumped her, dog, and pistol in a heap to the squabs.

"I must have my—"

"A moment, madam!" He shut her inside. But she heard his footsteps crunch the snow. As quickly gone as returned, he swung open the door once more and plunked her reticule beside her.

"Thank you," she said to the well-upholstered door that had shut in her face. "I appreciate your assistance…and your accommodations."

Pressing her lips together at the embrace of sweet, toasty air around her, she wiggled her derriere to adjust to the contours of the plush red leather squabs and piled about her innumerable soft, chintz-covered cushions. Her pistol had no targets in this lovely little cocoon. Smiling, she deposited it back in its wooden case in her satchel. She welcomed Pip back into her embrace, then settled into the sumptuous wealth so surprisingly afforded her.

And just as she began to regret that she'd left Aunt Agatha's flask on the seat in the mail coach, the door to her new shelter flicked open and one of her rescuer's men deposited it on the seat beside her. "'Is lordship says yer to 'ave it. Make ye feel safe, ma'am!" He tugged his forelock and slammed shut the door.

"Thank you," she told him as she raised her flask toward "'is lordship."

"YOUR DRIVERS AND mine have been able to tie the broken reins together," her rescuer announced as he climbed into the seat opposite her. He gathered his voluminous greatcoat and capes about his person and brushed snow from his broad shoulders. Sweeping off his hat, he ran long-boned fingers through his thick, wavy hair and took her in.

Lord in heaven. He was breathtaking. Big, dark, and bold. Relief ran through her at such a man's aid. Manners caught her up, and she found a reply. "Good news."

He shook his head. "Not entirely. Tied reins are not secure, and the lines need to be totally replaced. This means the mail coach will have to proceed slowly to the next inn. The best hope is that they have replacements and men to help apply them. The best plan is for you to ride with me to the inn. Not only will you be warmer, you will arrive sooner."

Dismay at being alone with such an imposing creature had her frowning.

He put up a gloved hand, and once more the expression he gave her attempted a smile. "You have no need to fear me. Take out your pistol again if you wish. Though I hope you will afford me the courtesy of not aiming it at me."

She held few coquettish concerns about her virtue. Her

mother had not educated her to be coy or foolish. Meanwhile, this fellow appeared to be a gentleman, if one judged by his hauteur and *soigné* attire. Yet traveling with him presented the disagreeable prospect of traveling alone with a stranger. "Sir, I do not know you."

"You do not know the mail coach drivers, either." This time, he did manage to form his firm lips into a look of condolence. "I am Lord Bellamy. Of York."

She had presented herself as Miss Smith to the driver. So would she to this man.

He dipped his head at her introduction. "I am pleased to meet you, Miss Smith. Now as to our journey. The next inn is The Angel and Swan near Doncaster. We shall arrive—barring any deterrents—in approximately fifteen minutes. The mail coach, later. In the meantime, if you care to open that large hamper under that cushion and your arm, my cook has sent me off with pasties and shortbreads which would feed Wellington's army. Do avail yourself of the opportunity. Otherwise, I will be offering the goods to Mr. Graymount and his servants at the Angel."

She liked hearty meat pies and shortbread. To show how much, her stomach growled. "That sounds wonderful."

He knitted his brows in a feigned horror. "Time to open up the hamper, then. You can hand over the flask of wine you'll find in there, too. Unless, of course"—his gaze ran to her reticule—"you wish to keep to your own choice."

She gave him a wistful roll of her eyes. "My Great-Aunt Agatha insisted I bring it along, and in this storm, I've been glad of it." She flipped open the wicker lid and sat back to admire the numerous tidy packages wrapped in red and white kitchen towels inside the basket. "A feast poor soldiers would relish."

He took one of the pasties from her, then held open his fingers to accept the wine flask. When he flicked open the cork stopper, he brought the flask near his nose and inhaled. "There should be silver cups inside," he said. "Will you have a drink?"

"I may take a dram after I've had one of these, thank you."

"Not eaten all day, have you?"

"No," she said to his smile at her keen enthusiasm for the meal presented. She unwrapped her prize and bit into the flaky crust. When she had swallowed a satisfying mouthful, she licked her bottom lip. "The coach left early."

"From...?"

She already had another bite in her mouth but took time to swallow the delightful glory of the pie and to ponder what particulars to reveal to him. Trying to recall the advertisement for the list of towns that this mail coach frequented was beyond her. Devoid of any other fitting answer, she told him the truth. "Bradford."

"Lovely little place. Your home?"

Her mouth full once more, she let her expression answer.

He took her statement in the affirmative. "Off to visit family, are you?"

She swallowed slowly. "No." *A prospective husband I have never met.*

He stared at her. Expecting more detail, she supposed. But she remained silent and munched her pasty.

"I apologize," he offered at long last. "I do not mean to be intrusive."

"No, sir. I understand." She wanted no conversation with him or anyone that might lead to a discussion of where she went or why.

⇶⫸⫷⇷

THE COACHING INN of The Angel and Swan sat on the east side of the thoroughfare only a few minutes south of where the mail coach had met with disaster. Verity's failure to meet his lordship's congeniality with her own meant he acquiesced, and they journeyed on in stilted silence.

Eager to be alone and end this odd encounter, she rejoiced when she spotted the rambling two-story structure. In the graying light of dusk, the snowfall had abated. But the winds whistled around the carriage and the inn and presaged a cold, forbidding night. She was happy to end her travel for today.

The innkeeper met them in the yard, arms waving them welcome, promising ale and wine and a strong fire in the common room. Verity took his hand to climb down and hurried with his assistance across the icy cobbles through the old, wide wooden door. The owner, Mr. Graymount by introduction, asked if she stopped in Doncaster or if she was to travel on with the mail. As she told him of her destination and her intention to stay with the mail, he took her to a small table nearest the large hearth and pulled out a chair for her. Pip nuzzled her arm, a sure sign the dog had to relieve herself.

Verity rose to walk outside with her when the innkeeper motioned to his serving girl to assist her. Verity was happy to hand over Pip's lead and resume her chair and the comfort of the fire.

The gray stone hearth, tall as Lord Bellamy, spread from the far wall to the other, big as one she'd seen as a child visiting with her father at the ruins of a nearby Elizabethan manor house. Lord Bellamy's two coachmen carried in her reticule and small trunk, plus their master's trunk and hamper. That last was lighter by many tasty shortbreads and three pasties—two of them gone to her, one to him. The innkeeper's offer of rooms was first on the agenda.

She, being the only woman among them, was assigned the largest room with a featherbed above the common room. Though at first she demurred, Lord Bellamy insisted that she be given the advantage. He instantly and repeatedly declared that he would take a smaller room, the attic, to be exact, and no matter it had no fire and hers did. His servants and the mail coach drivers were given the stables for the night.

Awaiting all to be settled, she sat enjoying the welcome fire. His lordship, after a long conversation with the innkeeper, came and took a seat beside her. He had divested himself of his greatcoat, and she ran her gaze over his attire. He wore a frockcoat of a woven wool yarn in shades of harvest. The browns and rust with flecks of gold showed his complexion to glowing regard. The contrast of his simply tied white stock set off the complement. The man certainly knew how to dress to burnish his image. Her fingers itched to do him justice in her sketchpad, for now, in the light of so many candles and sconces, she could celebrate the long arcs and broad planes of his classic visage. Before, in the frail light, he had loomed as a formidable enigma, strong of form and vibrant of voice. Here in the dancing flames of a roaring fire, he became flesh and blood, ruddy, stark, and beautiful.

"Will you have ale or wine? Mr. Graymount brings pitchers. His wife is his cook, and she serves us supper soon."

"I doubt I should have more spirits." She did smile at him. Sorry that she had been nigh unto rude by not conversing in his coach, she wanted to appear less a harpy. "Nor more to eat, either. You'll think I have a hollow leg."

"I was happy to share it all with you." He shifted and crossed one leg over the other, ending a long perusal of her features. He cleared his throat. "Mr. Graymount tells me you go to London."

She did care that he knew her destination now, but she could do nothing for it. Hoping only that after this night he would forget her and all her particulars, she nodded in answer. "I do. Ah, here is Pip. Thank you," she told the girl as she took the dog into her arms.

Lord Bellamy rapped his long fingers on the wooden table as if he contemplated a distressing matter. Finally, his lips crooked up in a small sign of distress. "I've spoken with Mr. Graymount about the probability of replacing the mail coach's lines. He and his stable boys have done this more than once and know it takes a goodly time to get it done. And only in light of day, too. The mail will not go through on time tomorrow. That said, I will tell you that I also travel to London, and I would like to offer you to ride with me."

She had no doubts of what her answer should be. "Thank you, sir. You have been most kind, and I am grateful. But I must continue on with the mail."

Those enigmatic eyes of his delved into hers. "*Must* you? You will be warmer in my carriage. More comfortable, too."

She counted herself fortunate—and perhaps not so—that she had learned years ago to identify the characteristics of a lecher. This man's focus held no trace now or earlier of lascivious self-interest. No desire to trap her like a butterfly pinned to a board beneath glass. Still, she would not bow to him nor give in for the sake of a few hot bricks beneath her feet.

"I heard Mr. Graymount say another traveler told him the snow has stopped to the south. In hope that is so, I resume my journey with the mail as I began it." She'd be late for her appointments in London. She'd send apologies once she arrived in Town. The first to her new solicitor would be from client to subject and excused for what it was. The second to the publisher of the *Chronicle* in Fleet Street would have to be forgiven. Her tardiness was due to inclement weather. A snowstorm in May, no less! Certainly, she had preferred to speak with those at the newspaper at length about what they knew of her chosen man before she was to meet him there. But she'd have to forgo that. Her delay here could not be helped. She'd have to be clear within her own purpose when she met him and listen well to her inner counsel before she went off to wed him, stranger that he was.

And though she had through his word and deed concluded she could trust this man with her person, she would do best to do so only for the time necessary. As it was, she held a greater concern about being in his company overlong—and it had nothing to do with any missish concern for her good name or reputation. No, in fact, she had already revealed to him her home, and from the innkeeper, he had learned her destination. While he was from York, two days and more to the east of Bradford and far from all whom she knew, he was a lord. He had lineage and interests, most likely of many years standing, that entwined with others of his ilk. The probability that he knew those she did might be small, but the *ton* met and mingled together for pleasure and business often. She dared not elaborate on her plans, lest word flow back to those she'd left behind. To her coachman, to the innkeeper, and to him, she had presented herself simply as Miss Smith. To him she was from Bradford. So would she remain. And nothing more.

Of course, Lord Bellamy deserved none of her prevarication. He seemed a kind man, generous, if unused to the need to smile. That he was extraordinarily handsome softened his correctness and made him dashing. Still and all, *arresting* was the word that came to mind.

Arresting her attention.

Arresting her imagination. Seizing her desire to pull out her sketch paper and pencils and attempt his dashing visage.

But she'd save that for later. In her room. Alone. Or better, by then, his allure would have faded away, and so would her desire to capture him and take a portrait of him with her.

But her attraction to him should fade. Die.

Few men had ever caught her fancy. To favor one at this moment in her life was most inopportune.

She was no daydreamer, but practical. No flibbertigibbet who sighed for a man who had but acted the Good Samaritan to aid her on a snowy, intractable road.

She finished her meal, and their conversation during it was spare and polite. Excusing herself and clutching Pip close, she made her way to her room. Inside, she assured herself this was a time to put aside childish things. A time for prudence. She should be focusing all her attentions on her future husband.

BELLAMY WATCHED HER go, then took his leisure draining his mug—and quieting his body's appreciation of her person. Best not to stand and allow the world to see how uncontrolled he was.

God help me. I thought I'd finished with such childishness years ago!

He clenched and unclenched his fists. *Dammit.*

He shot to his feet and grabbed his greatcoat. With a curt nod of thanks to the inn keep, he turned for the door to the coaching yard. A blast of whirling snow hit him in the face as he gained the outer stairs. Frustrated at himself about a woman as he had not been in a very long while, he charged the steps two at a time to his accommodations.

He pushed open the rough-hewn door to the attic room, then slammed it shut against the elements. The innkeeper's daughter had left two candles burning in the silver handle sconces. He ran one hand through his hair, then threw his greatcoat over the wooden rack. The room was tiny, the roof so low he had to stoop, and the bed was…what? He leaned over and fingered the stuffing beneath a quilt. Hay. He'd be well for the night. Knowing Miss Smith would be better accommodated than he had him nodding. He unbuttoned his frockcoat and waistcoat. Sat and yanked off his shoes, but decided to sleep in what remained. Idly, he glanced about in search of his valise and his tooth powder, a hairbrush. Normality.

But it was not normal for him to be concerned with a woman.

He understood stubbornness in a female. He even admired, up to a point, independence. Women needed a certain amount of that to receive proper regard and fairness in this society.

What he did not understand—nor admire—was his own fascination with the dainty bit of femininity who had just left him. Miss Smith with her pistol. Miss Smith with her personable dog. Miss Smith with eyes that reminded him of the relaxing, satisfying blue-green lagoons off Naples.

Miss Smith. A nymph. A beauty. In her attractive clothing, he could not say if she were from merchants or gentry. Yet she was from a cotton mill town he knew well. But not well enough to have ever met her or even seen her. If he had, his raging physical attraction to her told him that he would have remembered her. Everything about her. Her name, her finely boned face, her handling of a gun. But then, when would he have ever been in her company? He often had dealings with those in trade, but he did not pursue society to frivolous means. Had not. Could not. Would not. Not in the past three years. Certainly not before that, either.

Foolish line of thought. Good thing that Miss Smith would ride out of his life tomorrow.

He reached for his leather satchel and inched it nearer.

He sighed. Miss Smith. Who knew the power of color. Her barouche cloak of Pomona green that showed her complexion to a healthy peach confection. The pale fox fur of her coat collar and her French hat. Her full lips, the way she formed words, lush, distinct, silken to his ears, alluring as if she were a siren.

That she cultivated the arts of fashion disturbed him. He avoided artful women. Beauties, too. Yet Miss Smith bore a sense about her that defied such a purposeful design of her person. She was no product. Only of and by herself.

He huffed. She with her daring aim of her grandpapa's pistol. And her relish of her aunt's whisky. What pampered creature of the *ton* would show him such a strident streak?

So while he felt it incumbent upon him to protect her as far as she would permit him, she denied him. For the best, that was. For the best. So, in all she did, he wished her Godspeed.

He was now well apart from her.

He was to be married in a few days. The woman he would wed would be his helpmate, his friend. Not an attractive minx who made him far too aware of how long he'd been without the comforts of a caring woman at his table—or in his bed.

Chapter Two

140 Fleet Street
City of London

"J ESSUP!" BELLAMY CALLED to his young chaise driver. They'd sat in this traffic much too long waiting for the two over-turned curricles to be cleared off the road. "Let me out here. Walk the horses and return in twenty minutes."

"Aye. But the building you want is a wee bit down the lane, sir!"

"Just so." A stroll in the sun would do him good. *Clear my head.* He'd had nothing but trepidations about his plan since he left the Doncaster carriage inn day before yesterday. When Jessup pulled open the door, Bellamy stepped to the cobbles. "You cannot get through this mess. I will return to you."

The youth nodded and pulled his cap, then snapped the reins on the matching grays.

How quickly the weather had turned from frigid to temperate. He took the street at a clip, eager to get this done with.

Jilting a lady is not the kind of thing one does quickly or otherwise. Yet it's best. For me and her. Whoever she is.

He wove his way through the throng. It was months since he'd been in the City and to his townhouse on Upper Brook Street, but he felt oddly at ease. His butler, Withers, and his housekeeper, Mrs. Dunwoody, had all in readiness, as he'd ordered. Having retired most of his former staff two years before, he had not needed but a handful of help in this house, as he had not returned to London for any length of time in that period. Only upon his return here from Dublin last June had he hired Withers and Dunwoody. Both quiet and unassuming, the man and woman had not asked him any intrusive questions but did as they were bade and hired additional maids and two footmen as they saw fit. His letter to them this March that he wished his bedroom suite polished and refreshed for his use had inspired only one question from them. That he had quickly answered.

"Leave the mistress's suite untouched," he'd declared. For his future wife—if indeed he found the applicant he'd chosen suitable—she could choose her own fabrics and furniture. All that his first wife had chosen he had ordered carried out to the yard and burned immediately after her death three years before. He did not tell his new staff that, but had told them only what they needed to know. "The rooms are empty. Leave them that way."

He came to a stop at the number 140.

It was not as he had pictured it. The *Fleet Chronicle* was an old, well-established news sheet. Had it not stated on its masthead *Since 1721*? He'd expected a large window, a display of today's paper, a larger sign than the battered one that swung from its hooks, waving in the gusts off the Thames. Appearances often deceived, did they not?

Christ, yes. He—beyond any other lessons he had ever learned—knew that one.

He pushed open the door. The ting-a-ling of the bell above the lintel put him in a happier frame of mind. But that lasted only moments. For beyond this main room filled with two large presses, broadsheets drying on lines above his head, racks of type, and the smell of metallic ink, sweet oil, and pine, two women in the back room argued.

"I'm telling you if you increase the price of the Matrimony adverts now, you kill the goose that lays the golden egg!" an older lady put forth.

"Oh, Aunt Juno, I've got to," declared a young woman. "I've received more requests than I have room to print. Even more silly ones like this self-important chit from Manchester. She runs on and on. Rich, she says she is, like a pretentious magpie! Now I have more adverts like hers! I cannot print them all. Not at my current four pages."

"Increase to five!"

"I haven't the means, Aunt. Paper rises in cost. My stamp, too! The government taxes me three pence an issue for my four sheets. Soon to be four, if Parliament has its way. Plus I'm paying Father's debts, and—"

"The man should have been more prudent."

Bellamy winced. Had the two women not heard the door bells? He removed his hat and paced the room, and at once—one of his knees buckled.

"Well, I say!" Bellamy stooped to speak to the little boy who had nearly knocked him over. The child beamed up at him, a smile—and jam—wreathing his lips. "How do you do, young man?"

"Horth," the tiny fellow said, holding up a smartly carved bit of wood in the shape of a horse.

"He is quite handsome," Bellamy offered.

The boy showed him a mouth full of pearly teeth and giggled. Then he ran his horse on Bellamy's trousers, which now sported strawberry jam tracks up the leg.

So then! "Interesting. Dear fellow, is your mother here? Or your father?" *Perhaps in the back room?*

"Mama likes my horth." He made clomping sounds like a horth...*horse* galloping.

"And why not, eh? I like your horth, too." *Horse, Bellamy. Horse.*

The boy made odd noises while continuing to run his wooden horse over Bellamy's pants. Nothing for it, he picked up the child in his arms and met him, eye to eye, with giggles for his rescue.

"My dear Germaine," said Aunt Juno, whose deep contralto Bellamy recognized, as it was she who had advised against a price increase, "you have created a successful venture. Men and women flock to your service. Those who have advertised before will not care you have increased your price."

"I have already raised the price to five pence per issue."

"Appropriate," said Germaine's aunt, followed by the scraping of chair legs on bare wooden floor. "Raise the ad rate, *per word*, my dear. After you do, I shall pay the remainder of your father's bills!"

"Oh, Aunt! Wait! I cannot allow you to… Wait!"

A tall, imposing woman—ship of the line, his father would have said of her formidable build—paused in the doorway to the other room. At her leisure, she examined him…and his trousers. "Good morning, sir."

He inclined his head in a polite bow. "Madam."

She toyed with a grin at him, at the little boy and at the jam they both wore. "Like horses, do you, sir?"

"Indeed, madam."

"Excellent!" She tugged at her gloves as her niece—Germaine, that would be—appeared behind her. "Here is another advertiser for you, dear. Smart, good-looking, too. Also enjoys horses and feisty imps decorated in berry jam." The lady winked at him.

He could not suppress his chuckle.

Germaine—all hustle, bustle, and businesslike embarrassment—hurried around her aunt with apologies and her arms out to Bellamy. "Oh, sir. I will take him. Thank you. Come, Teddy." She clasped her boy to her. "My aunt and I were so engaged. I do hope you were not waiting long."

"Invite him to your office, Germaine. I take my leave. Good day to you, sir."

"Lord Bellamy, at your service, Lady Peregrine." He gave her his name, as he had recognized her. "We met years ago. My father introduced us then. I was quite young, and you were very kind to me."

"Bellamy…" Lady Peregrine pondered his name and his countenance. "I am sorry to say I do not remember you, sir. Not as a younger fellow. But I do recall your father. Charming man. Devilishly good looks, too, which you have generously inherited. I do gather, by your assumption of his title, he is no longer with us?"

"No, ma'am. He passed away four years ago."

"A shame. You've taken up management of his mills, I assume?"

"I have." He did not wish to talk about the textile business. "Forgive me that I do not take your hand—my fingers are sticky with jam."

"Germaine," Lady Peregrine barked, "do get a soapy cloth for his lordship!"

"Of course!" Germaine went beet red. "Please, my lord. Do come with me."

He hesitated. "I am here to speak with the publisher." Was that Germaine or her husband or father?

"Lord Bellamy," said Germaine with authority, "please come into my office. I will happily assist you. Thank you, Aunt, for coming and for the kind offer. We will talk again of it—"

"No, we won't. You will take it, my girl." Juno adjusted the collar of her combed wool Clarence-blue pelisse. The color was one his father had perfected more than eight years ago in the Bramley Mill. "You tell her, my lord, I am right about the pricing."

Germaine blew out a sigh of exasperation. "Good day, Aunt."

"Goodbye, dear." Juno kissed the jammy cheek of Teddy, and sailed away with a ting-a-ling of the bells.

"Please, my lord, come through." Germaine led the way into her office.

Here in the room lined with shelves full of account books and smaller books—poetry and novels, from their size—Germaine indicated a pair of finely carved gothic Windsor armchairs. He ignored the tracks of red jam down his fawn wool-covered thighs and set his hat on a nearby table.

"I do apologize for that." She disappeared into another back room and emerged in a moment with a cloth for his fingers. Then she sat down and bounced Teddy on her lap. "I can get the jam out for you if you… Well, hmm. You can't very well take your trousers off, can you?"

"No. And it's not a challenge, really." He dabbed at his fingers. "My staff are good with working stains out of material. I introduced myself as Lord Bellamy to your aunt, madam. But you know me as 'M. St. John.'"

"Oh, I see. One of our advertisers." Her hazel eyes lit in delight. "Marvelous! Thank you for it, sir. Matrimony is a new service we offer at the *Chronicle*."

"I had my cousin ask about it here in Town. He assured me of your intent," he said, and brushed a hand down his marked trousers. "I was assured that you were discreet."

"We are. Very. I wish to ensure that for future customers."

"A sound idea. I am here today to talk to the publisher."

"I am the publisher."

"Ah. Very good." She was the "G. Hammond" at the bottom of the postings. He hadn't expected a woman. Females who owned businesses were a refreshing change from the grumpy sorts with whom he often met. "I received your note to come today. I was delayed upon the road, and postponing our meeting served me well."

"The lady you are to meet was detained as well. It was she who arrived here yesterday and asked if she might meet you today."

"All acceptable."

"You are early, sir."

"I am. Do allow me to get to my point. I wish to discuss your advertising."

"Oh! Wonderful! I have a rate sheet here." She began to open drawers in her desk, but stopped and stared at him. "You wish to take another Matrimony ad?"

He put up a hand. "No, I am here not to take another ad. I come to terminate the agreement of the one I took."

She deflated. It was as if he had let the air out of a balloon. "Oh. Unfortunate. I… Hmmm. Well, I do not know how we can proceed."

"I am most pleased with your service. My decision has nothing to do with that. The twenty-four responses you sent me were…" Astonishing in their variety. One showed her need for money. Another, quite frankly, needed a husband quickly. "Eye-opening."

"Twenty-four. And one was suitable. We were thrilled with the number of responses. I was so pleased." Yet Mrs. Hammond grew trepidatious. "But now we have failed you…?"

"Not at all. My decision reflects only my change of heart, not your service."

"Oh, good to know, sir. But—" She regarded her mantelpiece clock with wide eyes. "It is nearly two. Your appointment is then, and the lady arrives soon. And now you say you are not inclined to continue?"

How could he? After a search of his soul and the attraction he felt toward Miss Smith, he would not do the applicant the justice she deserved. "No. That's why I've come early to explain to you and to apologize. I will certainly extend my regret to the lady who responded and see to it that she is not—"

The front door bells jingled.

Well. If that person arriving was his intended, he was in the stew now. He sighed. *It is what it is. Make do. Make apologies.*

The bells at the front door rang again, and a brisk wind swept through to the back office. Yips met Bellamy's ears.

So did the entreaties of a lady whose dulcet voice he knew quite well. "Pip! Pip! Come back here!"

Bellamy shot to his feet. *Pip?* Pip was here?

Teddy squealed and jumped from his mother's lap.

Pip and the boy fell upon each other like long-lost lovers, bound together like glue in a joyful hug. Teddy giggled. Pip appreciated the child's strawberry jam.

Germaine rushed to separate boy and dog. To no avail.

Bellamy scooped up Teddy to help separate the two, but as he raised his eyes, he found himself mesmerized by the welcome sight of Miss Smith. Delicate Miss Smith of the mail coach, the snowstorm, and The Angel and Swan.

Miss Smith. Of his much-too-fond memories, one erotic dream. And his regret at her loss.

"My lord?" she addressed him.

He—uncertain if her words were a greeting, a question, or an exclamation—did the courteous gesture to bid her good afternoon. More overjoyed to see her again than was rational, he gave her a broad grin. Was his Miss Smith also…?

"You arrived in London safely, I see," he said like an utter idiot. For impossible as it was, she looked more devastatingly lovely than she had amid snow and wind and flickering candle-light. She radiated good health in a walking dress of pale tangerine Naccarat and an ivory and orange Victoria straw hat. Few women could wear such a color in abundance and not drown in it.

She smiled at him at first. But then, sobering, she winced and shook her head as if she were confused. Even at that, she looked appealing as a peach. "Sir."

She was nervous? Why? He laughed at his good fortune to see her again. "Miss Smith, how good to see you once more."

He meant it, of course, though his attraction to her was the very reason he had decided not to pursue his proposed wedding to an absolute stranger. But, caught off guard, he could only be himself. Delighted to see her. Even if he hoped to be seated soon to cover his embarrassing and evident joy at their meeting.

But why was she here? Looking for a husband? Oh, the irony of that!

Frowning, Germaine stared at her. "Miss…Carr?"

Miss Smith swung about with a strained smile for the publisher. "Yes. Good afternoon, Mrs. Hammond."

Is that so?

Ice settled in Bellamy's veins. He knew not what to think. Or believe.

Miss Carr was the name of the lady who had answered his advertisement and whose letters, two of them, he had appreciated for their earnestness.

Miss Carr was the woman he had come to London to marry. Miss Smith was the woman whose very essence had revived his physical desires for a woman he might grow to respect, even care for.

Which was she?

"PLEASE," GERMAINE HAMMOND said to both, "do sit. I will make tea, shall I?"

"Oh, do not trouble yourself for me, ma'am." Verity flushed with embarrassment.

"Tea would be helpful," Lord Bellamy said, his gaze never straying from her.

Fie! She didn't need tea. Nothing could sweeten this charade. Of all people, to find Lord Bellamy on the day when she was to meet her intended. And for Mrs. Hammond to hear from his lips of her use of a false name. Why, it was most unsettling. Not that the man would have any reason to think ill of her for it. She had her reasons. But she owed him nothing.

Well, that's not true, you twit. You owe him your health after a terrible mishap in the snow.

"Please let me take Teddy, sir." Germaine held out her arms for her son. And once he was tucked under her arm and Pip back up in Verity's, the lady strode toward the back of her office and disappeared.

Verity's attention swung to his lordship.

He blinked, and she understood she was to sit before he would consider it.

She sank to the finely carved chair. "I'm happy to see you, sir."

He examined her with the attention of a man to his ledgers. Her eyes, her lips, her walking dress and cape, her hat and hair, all were his, as if he were the sun absorbing her, melting her down and taking her up into his very self. She was reduced to an amorphous mass, like the jam on the little boy's lips. Lord Bellamy ate her up. "Are you Miss Smith or Miss Carr?"

The simplest explanation would be her best. "I am both. I used the surname Smith for my journey. A thousand Smiths live in the north, and it seemed useful. But I am certainly Miss Carr. Forgive me for that use of it, my lord. I am Verity Carr." She extended her hand. "How do you do, sir?"

His features—so sharp and strong, so unforgettable that she had rendered dozens of depictions of his handsome face to her sketchbook—softened. Then he put his hand to hers. The frisson she had recalled far too often and treasured too much these past few days rippled through her. His touch, days ago, had unnerved her. For never had she felt such a reaction to any man. Save one...and that was not this yearning desire to keep this man's hands on her. Not this magnetism that drifted to her core and lured and stirred and burned. Truly, she wanted him to put his hands all over her.

"You have not traveled alone before, I take it?" He did not let go her hand, though his dark eyes, unfathomable as they were, held traces of forgiveness for her behavior.

"That's true." Verity beamed at his acceptance. She glanced toward the front door. Would her future husband find her amiss that she sat enjoying some strange man's conversation? "Always before, I was with my father or my aunt."

"Aunt Agatha," he added with the twitch of long black brows and a teasing glint to his large, dark eyes.

Was he flirting with her? "Indeed. She of my flask."

"And your whisky."

She nodded with a grin. She should not appear so taken by him. If Mrs. Hammond returned or her prospective husband appeared, she would appear odd.

Then Pip leaned over to lick Lord Bellamy's fingers. The dog was so smart. *Would that I could lick him too.*

She flushed at the absurd idea and pulled her dog away. "My apologies. I have a handkerchief."

"I do too." He used a cloth that sat upon the table beside him. "I trust you have found good accommodations here in town."

"I have." He sought more details of her visit here. That was not anything she should share with him. He did not need to know it, and her future spouse would not approve. She'd turn the subject to him. "Are you in London to visit relatives?"

"No. I have business here."

"I see." She pursed her lips and caught a glimpse of the door to the back room. What kept Mrs. Hammond? The woman was having a heated discussion with a man and another woman, while Verity wished her to return soon. What if Verity's intended groom appeared and found her so deeply engaged with chivalrous Lord Bellamy?

She licked her lips, hot and nervous. "And do you take advertisements in the *Chronicle*, sir?"

"I have in the past, yes. I doubt I will need to in the future."

"Ah. Good." He surely did not advertise for a wife. No toffs did that. They had other means to scout for a proper partner. The *Chronicle* did also post notices for runaway dogs and sale of soap and diuretics. "The adverts worked, then, is that so?"

"I had great ambitions for it, yes." He kept looking at her as if he could not get his fill. "Advertising is such a mysterious means to an end. Many would question the true quality of the goods."

She perspired and quivered beneath his regard, as if she were a flower blooming in a humid glass conservatory. "If we did rely on truth in ads, we would be drinking herbal remedies for many a quid when instead we could make a brew from our gardens for free."

He shook his head, his umber eyes dancing, as if he were at once amused. "Not all have the knowledge or time or inclination to find such a product or make one. We have to believe in something."

"We do. Oh, yes. Perhaps the word of friends?" She tried to lighten the conversation. Afraid her own correspondent and husband-to-be would appear and take unkindly to her sitting here discussing tonics with a stranger, she wished to run away…and take this man with her. "Recommendations from family? All good ways to discover a new product, eh?"

"A declaration of worth works best of all," he declared, and his intonation said there was more here than his words.

What were they really discussing here? Not simply advertising for soap or a new book of poetry.

She tipped her head. "Dare I surmise, sir, that you are in business? Or have an investment in certain products?"

"In business, yes."

Most would be shocked to hear that of an aristocrat. But to Verity, being in business was the norm. "My papa and grandfather were accountants for the Hayward Mills in Eccleshill."

His eyes widened.

Her heart pounded. What was wrong with her? To tell him she was from Bradford was one thing, but to point out her village was idiocy.

His dark eyes turned cold. "You said Bradford."

She froze, hating that he'd think her unprincipled. "For good reason. I did not wish to give my details to a stranger, sir. You can understand that. A woman alone on the road. Odd. At risk. Even with a pistol. But you…you know Eccleshill, sir?" With that, she knew she'd turned the point of the conversation from her fib. But she had to ask if he knew her village. She had to learn.

"I do."

She kneaded her hands. This was disaster.

"I know the village very well."

And others in it? Who live there and close by?

"I own Armstrong Mills."

Armstrong! She swallowed hard against the shock of who he was. Her mind filled with only one certainty. He was one of the richest men in Yorkshire. One of the three who owned the most cotton mills in England. But he was Lord Bellamy, and now he was telling her he was also—

"Verity, I am Miles Armstrong." He took her hand once more and stopped her anxious wringing. "Miles St. John Armstrong."

Lord Bellamy who saw to her rescue. Bellamy who had been her companion in his carriage and so kindly to her at the inn. Bellamy of the compelling, dark good looks and courtly behavior. "And 'M. St. John,' who wrote to me of marriage."

"Yes, I am he."

He. Of good humor. Of generosity and strength.

"Here I am!" Germaine Hammond announced as she rushed back into the room. "My maid will have our tea for us in an instant. I see you are getting on." A quick view of their hands entwined had her smiling. "What do you say? Lord Bellamy? Miss Carr? Might we speak plainly now?"

No! Verity took back her hand, her hope, and seized on logic. She could not marry him. Never. The very purpose of her leaving home—the reason she'd accepted these outlandish means to marry, the reasons she'd concealed her journey to London—was now all such a muddle. She needed a minute to think. What could she tell him? What should she not? "Please, Mrs. Hammond, I must speak with Lord Bellamy in private."

Germaine turned a grim face on his lordship. "You have told her, then?"

"That he is 'M. St. John'?" Verity noted his dismay as he winced. Ready to apologize, then, was he? She had done that at the very start of their meeting. Two birds of a feather, they were. "Yes, he has."

He set his teeth and looked up at Mrs. Hammond. "We need a few more minutes, ma'am."

"Very well. I leave you once again. Please do let's get on with this!" Germaine went in an angry swish of muslin skirts and petticoats.

Chapter Three

VERITY WATCHED THE woman depart, and wrinkled her brow. "Why is she vexed with us?"

Miles sat back, ready to be more honest with this woman who so appealed to him in so many ways. "Me. She's upset with me, Verity. I may call you that, may I not?"

"By our letters we are acquainted beyond such formalities." She drew back. "But friends, sir? I must know more before I venture there. Why is Mrs. Hammond angry with you?"

Honesty was a quality he valued and, in the past decade, had not found in many. But he had resolved to demonstrate it to the woman who'd written to him. The woman he had asked to marry him. "I arrived here early today for our appointment to tell her I was no longer interested in our arrangement."

Her lovely features fell. But her spine stiffened and her jade-green eyes stayed focused on his. "Why not, sir?"

He felt like a schoolboy now. Explaining this would show him for the conflicted man he was. "I had second thoughts about the marriage. The agreement. Strangers who agree to the most intimate vow they can take. I worried that I had no right to ask it of anyone." *Not of correspondent Miss Carr, whom I assumed would hold no candle to beautiful, funny, impassioned Miss Smith.*

She tipped her head to and fro in consideration of his words. "To advertise for a spouse is unusual. To answer such an appeal is rarely done, I would imagine. Yet you sought out a mate, and so did I."

"You made yourself appealing in your letters, Verity." That was an understatement.

"Did I?" She sniffed and scanned the ceiling. In a rush, she got to her feet and took two steps away toward the front printing room. "I did not plan that. Only shared with you a few facts that might show my character."

"And you did do that. Easily. So much so that I was attracted." *Even before today and the revelations of the past few minutes. To say nothing of the time together on the road.*

She whipped around to stare at him. "But not attracted after meeting me."

"No. Before meeting you here."

She shook her head. "I am confused, sir. I must hear your explanation of your lapse of interest."

He was used to negotiations in business dealings. A discussion of numbers and projections between men who knew their products, their workers, their mills' capabilities were matters of fact and logic. He was less skilled at conversations about his emotions. He'd learned early in his marriage to avoid raising the issue of feelings. Yet here with Verity, he owed her that very quality. To do so would require a courage he had buried years ago in the rubble of his boyish heart's expectations. Surely he had not predicted to need it with the applicant to be his second wife. At least, not quite so early in the relationship. Here he could share his true opinion with her, if just a portion, and for the offering, he'd rip away only a piece of his toughened skin.

"I will be frank."

She stood, her head high, her hands clasped before her, her expression guarded as she waited for him to tell her why he denied her. She was the very picture of a woman rejected, vulnerable, torn. That alone was the most extraordinary expression he had ever seen on a woman for whom he cared.

He rose, the realization of what a callow fellow he was washing over him.

"I told Mrs. Hammond I was here to cancel our agreement because the woman I met on a snowy road outside Doncaster was more appealing to me than a woman whom I had met in a few well-written letters."

"*What?*" she breathed.

He strode toward her. He gazed down into eyes swimming in tears, his heart wrenching at how much this meant to her that she could cry. A weeping woman had in the past put him on alert to lies and perversion. Yet not here with her. He'd share the truths he could. "I liked Miss Smith very much. The few hours I spent with her infused me with a joy at her repartee and humor I had not thought to ever gain with a woman. I feared when I met Miss Carr I would do her a disservice by comparing her unfavorably to Miss Smith."

She searched his expression, a piercing examination that blossomed slowly and told him she could be flattered by his admission. When it came to her in full flower, she blinked back her tears and blushed. "I marvel at your words, sir. But what does it say for your expectations of Miss Carr? That she would have no wit? Or brains to hold a decent conversation?"

"It does sound shallow of me, doesn't it?" He dared not tell her more. Not the full of his astonishment at his attraction to Miss Smith. Miss Carr would run from him—his erotic fantasies of her were not appropriate to reveal to her, now or for the foreseeable future. If she even still wanted him. "But it is true."

"You expected a bloodless creature to appear here today to take up her place in your house, at your table, and in your bed." She raised her brows and shook her head. "Perhaps not that last. But how could you marry anyone like that?"

Because I married once before expecting a union of minds and a rhapsody of bodies, and I had none of it! None!

Roiled by memories of betrayal, visions he had long blacked out of his mind, he set his teeth against an outburst. He was tempted to turn his back on her and avoid this discussion at all costs. But the price would be to lose her, and so he held his spot. He'd give her the raw reason for his advertisement. "I wanted a companion."

She said nothing.

He noted her silence as she perused what he was certain looked like anger on his face. He lingered, his gaze on her sad one. He glanced away. To his left stood a bin, a tray of type stood out with ads set for a new issue. All columns began with *Matrimony!* A cursed state. For him, it had been. But he had one superb example, the finest, that a marriage could exist and endure in friendship and bliss.

He fingered the edge of the metal tray. "I wanted a companion. A helpmate. A friend."

"As did I," she said it as if it were a prayer. "I needed one. We all do. Have you no friends at home?"

"I do. One. My cousin. He stays in London more than York. I see him less often than is good for both of us."

"A friend is a living organism, very like a garden. To be nurtured. Fed. Watered. You should visit with him while you are here in Town. More than you planned. With surprises amid the usual thrills."

Her concern for his need for companionship swamped him with refreshment. Who thought of him and what he needed or how he could improve it? *Only Miss Smith* was his first answer. *Only Miss Carr* was the next one.

"Having said all that, I am of a different mind than when I arrived."

Two fat tears escaped her long red-blonde lashes, and anger came with them. "You want me? Or you don't?"

Fraught with dismay that he had so upset her, he dug from his pocket a handkerchief and tucked it in her fingers. "I want you. I do. Please don't cry."

She brushed her tears from her delectable cheeks. "I'm not!"

"You are," he said with a small smile, moved much too close to her, and thumbed her warm, fat tears away. "I wish to discuss our wedding."

She hiccupped, covered her mouth with two fingers, and glared at him. "First you say you will not wed, then you will. I am not used to a man who changes his mind. My father, God rest him, was a resolute soul. I liked that in him. I loved him."

"As you should. Forgive me. I am delighted with who you are." *So much so, my reactions are much too risqué. I draw too near to you, should not, and yet can't seem to stop.* "I would like to discuss wedding plans with the delightful Miss Carr. Might she come out and ignore my hasty decision to abandon wedding a woman I presumed could not be anything like her…but is more than she ever was?"

She gave a laugh and swiped the last of her tears from her plump cheeks. "You do know how to compliment a woman."

"Aye." *I once practiced the art to my own disaster.* "I chose my words carefully. Nor have I used them in years to charm women for my own purposes."

"A good assurance to one who would expect fidelity from you."

"Would you? Expect fidelity of me, Verity?"

"If you were my husband, yes." She swayed a bit closer to him. "You would expect that of your wife, would you not?"

"I do. I certainly do." Full to bursting with the need to shout his agreement, he merely stared into her eyes. "So then," he ventured at last, "tell me why you applied to my advertisement."

"Ah." She dabbed at her cheeks. "Why would I marry a stranger?"

HOW MANY REASONS could she tell him? How many would endear her to him?

"No men of my acquaintance in Eccleshill appealed to me. I am twenty-four and a spinster. More and worse than that, I have a good education and opinions! No female should have either, especially opinions!" She gave a rueful sigh. "My father died in March of this year. He encouraged me to look for a good man to marry, and I did. But I found none." *Only one man whom I would never call good.* "Like you, I want a friend. A companion. Someone to enjoy my days and find pleasure with in my years."

"You have an education. Why not consider employment?"

"As a governess? A companion? No, I would not do either. I...I was raised to think for myself. My brother too."

"You have a brother?"

"I did not write of Jonathan. Not because I wished to ignore his life, but because to talk of him is painful. He was my best friend. Two years older than I, and my protection—and, as brothers often are to little girls, my torment. But he loved me, and I him. He died in Spain, last year at Nivelle. He was with the Fifty-First Light Infantry. Gone, compelled, he said, to do his king and country proud. His death was a great loss to my father and me. To my Aunt Agatha, too. She is my mother's maternal aunt and a great boon to us all."

"Did she encourage you to leave and find a husband?"

"She did. She even approved of my answering your advertisement."

"Courageous lady." His smile was consolation. "A good example for you."

"Indeed. She met her own husband in a unique way." She licked her lips and couldn't help laughing. "She attended an autumn harvest festival, and Uncle George was swimming in the nearby river. Naked."

"Ah. So Agatha fell in love with her husband at first sight."

That had her chuckling. "Nothing concealed there!"

His lips spread in the most delicious smile. And his eyes heated to a dark enchantment. "I wish to see you laugh more like that. Unbound."

She blushed. His admiration of her set her blood afire. No man had ever done that to her. Though one man had gazed at her with lascivious intent, this by Miles St. John Armstrong was the opposite. Kind. Complimentary. Endearing. That which she had hoped for from a husband but had not dared to dream she might have. "Thank you. Would that I could help you do it as well?"

"I welcome your efforts," he said with a severity that told her he dared her to try.

She ignored that. "I think you need a hearty measure of laughter."

Pip came running toward her, and she scooped her up, eager for the diversion that might give them time and space to re-establish propriety between them.

"Shall we advise Mrs. Hammond that we have resolved our initial challenges?" he asked.

"We do have a few more." *My need to pursue my art foremost among them.* "Like the use of the money you requested in the ad. A dowry, I suppose?"

"I asked for that, not because I wanted it. I assure you, whatever funds you have will remain your own."

"Then why make it a stipulation?"

"I wanted in some way to ensure that the persons answering would have some means, some education, some refinement."

"Ah. No ladies of flash, eh?" she teased him.

"None. I knew not how else to assure myself of an applicant with whom I might have an intelligent conversation over tea." He gave a small laugh. "I'm eager to know more of you."

"We need more time to decide." *And I must take this appointment with the solicitor.*

"We do, and to that end, I can arrange that you stay at my home this evening. I will take a room at my club, if you wish. Under the circumstances, you should not feel burdened by my presence."

"There is no need for that, as I have rooms elsewhere. I left my valise and trunk this morning on the off chance that you and I might not find each other to our liking."

He nodded and smiled. "I find you much to my liking."

She was pleased he said that with a pleasant tone that held nothing of the fires she previously saw burning in his eyes. She'd seen lust from one man and welcomed it not at all.

He added, "I can send my coachman to fetch it all, if you like."

She hesitated at that. "I have an appointment I must keep this afternoon."

He tilted his head in question. "Wherever it is, I can take you there."

She had only propriety as the reason to refuse him. And one to accept him. That odd feeling she'd had this morning as she left her lodgings at the carriage inn. The hair at the back of her neck standing on end. That had happened to her twice before. She had fled her home because of it, and prayed to God the cause had not followed her here.

Chapter Four

MILES TORE HIS gaze from the front door of Dunlap and Finster, Solicitors, and regarded his new little friend Pip. She sat like a prim lady on his knees. "Been in there a long time, hasn't she?"

The spaniel tipped her head this way and that.

"Right. You wonder about this meeting, too, I see. Tell me, my lady, does your mistress know these men?"

Pip gave him more of the curious looks.

"Hmmm. That's what I thought. New solicitors. Fellows in that profession are usually quick to the point. Unless they are new to you." He stroked the dog's sleek fur, but his focus returned to the front door to the red brick building. Miss Carr had been in there for almost an hour. Jessup had taken them round the streets twice since Verity had gone in. "Then they take their sweet time warming up to an issue. Don't want to lose a new client before the ink is dry."

One hand on Pip, Miles rapped his fingers on his leather armrest. He'd offered to go in with Verity, but understood her desire to go in alone.

"Whatever Papa did with them," she'd told Miles as they rode from Fleet Street to the offices, "is something he told me about as he lay dying. But he had not the breath to give me details. Only that I was to write to them after his passing and come to London to meet with them. I thought it odd because I'd never heard him speak of them. Only of his regular solicitor, Green and Sons in Shoe Lane. They are the ones whom my father dealt with for all his other matters, including the sale of our house in Eccleshill. I saw the Greens yesterday. Odd, though. They knew nothing of Dunlap and Finster, or this matter. But I promised to see them, and so I will."

"That's unusual that you have no idea what they wish to speak about. But the ways of the law can be ponderous and slow."

"Agreed."

"We can go afterward to your lodgings to acquire your belongings," he'd assured her.

She'd given him a warm and grateful smile, then stepped out. "I doubt I will be long."

BUT THE LONGER she remained in there, the more anxious Miles became. He knew men who controlled finances and legal matters could be intimidating. Verity Carr was no shy miss, but he didn't want anyone taking advantage of her in any way.

Besides, after the anxiety of their first meeting, he grew eager to decide this issue of their marriage. Whatever went on in that solicitors' office might add new dimensions to that…or not.

Bollocks. He was nervous as any bridegroom. Not only was he now convinced he had chosen well among the applicants to his ad, he had greater conviction that she would be precisely the kind of wife he needed. She might even become the wife he always hoped for. One he never thought to gain. More than that, he wanted her. Wanted her freshness, her laughter, her quick thinking with a pistol and her love of good whisky. To his surprise, he wanted her physically too. *Hell.* He chucked Pip under her little chin. He even wanted her dog!

"You want I should walk the 'orses again, milord?" Jessup called down to him.

Miles would not disturb her in conference with the solicitors. "No, I—"

"Sir?" Jessup alerted him. "Sir, look!"

Miles peered out the window.

She stood in front of the red brick offices, a statue, gaping like a madwoman, mouth open, at two ancient hackneys across the street.

"What's she doing?" Jessup asked.

Thinking of hailing one of those old hacks? Why was she focused on them?

She got the most appalling, frightened expression on her face. And he feared at once she was either in trouble or about to run from him.

He could not imagine why that would be, and so he did not wait longer. He put Pip to the squabs, jerked open the carriage door, and went to her.

"What's wrong?" he asked.

She stared at him as if she'd never seen him before, her lovely lips moving and no words coming out.

"My dear," he soothed her as he put his hands to her silken cheeks, "you're quivering. What's happened?"

But she had no response. Only the vacuous gaze that told him she was in shock.

He did as he had days ago in the snowstorm—he bent to catch her in his arms and carried her like a glorious prize to the comfort of his carriage. Jessup was there, door held wide, to help him put her inside on the seat. Miles climbed in beside her and, without thought or delay, took her in his embrace. She was not shivering, but shaking—and alarm rang through him like shot from cannon.

"Verity," he called to her. One arm around her shoulders, he pressed a kiss to her forehead. He tipped up her face. "My dear, look at me. What is wrong? You tremble. Tell me what I might do to help you."

She bit her lip. "Oh, Miles."

He curled her close, tucking her face into the crook of his neck and stroking her back. "Talk to me, please."

She curled one hand around the collar of his coat. Her fingertips grazed his throat, and he grew suddenly harder than he had ever been in his life. This was too wild an affair to be attracted to her in such a short time. To want to save her from anything that might harm her. His protective instincts, so long dormant, emerged like the roar of a lion. He was shocked, pleased, undone, and alert to her every mood. She needed him. As no woman ever had. She nestled closer into his embrace, her nose snuggling into the folds of his cravat. She sought succor. *His.* Christ, he'd give her that and more.

"Walk on, Jessup," he told his man, who waited, door open, for instructions. "Take us down to the river and around the tower. Keep going. I'll tell you when to stop."

She pulled away to look up at him. Dazed, she said, "My trunk…"

"We can get your things now, if you like. Is that what you want?"

"No. No," she said, and sank back into his embrace. This time, she wound her arm around him as if he were a lifeline on a sinking vessel.

For long minutes, he sat like that with her. The only sound was the clomping of his grays as Jessup took them through the City. She remained silent, her chest so close to his that he could feel the pulsing of her heart. In the rush to get her into his chaise, he'd dislodged her Leghorn straw bonnet, and the small feathers at the brim tickled his nose. Gently, he removed her hat, set it opposite, and curled her back into his arms. She came, pliant and solemn. He did not disturb her reverie. Whatever her matter was, she must have all the time she needed to sort it. He had that. Time. Care. Desire.

They'd circled the tower once and were about to start round

again when she pulled away. Embarrassment colored her cheeks as she began, "I apologize. This is unseemly."

"Don't even think about drawing away," he warned as he shook his head. "I am here. You needed someone. I wish to be that person. And, it seems, you instinctively agree."

She looked out the window as if she sought some sight to bring her to reality. Then she smiled up at him and took in his rumpled hair over his brow as her lips trembled with quaking emotions. "I've mussed your perfection."

"Perfect, my dear, I never was. Muss me, please, again if you wish."

She gave him a look he'd not seen on a woman's face in years. Her exquisite jade eyes spoke of utter appreciation for him.

He opened his arms.

On a moan, she sank back into his embrace. Her entire body snuggled against his own without reservation.

They'd traveled once more around the tower, and the sun was setting in a haze of bright yellow and red as they turned west and she finally stirred.

Her head against his shoulder, she gazed up into his eyes. "Tell me something?"

He pushed tendrils of her sun-kissed hair from her cheek. "Anything."

"When you wrote your advertisement, you requested that a lady who applied have at least three hundred pounds." She spoke with more authority, recovered somewhat from her shock to be logical and ask a pertinent question.

"That I did," he confirmed. The stunning woman he held in his embrace was one he wished to aid and comfort all his life. Money be damned.

"I have three hundred."

He gazed down at her. "Keep it. I told you I've no need. It is yours. Only yours."

She gave him a sweet smile of gratitude. "I have use for it."

"Marry me. I'll give you all the pin money you'll ever want."

"You are a dear man, Miles St. John. But no. I don't want endless drafts of money from you. I wanted to continue to support a charity in Bradford. I send them ten pounds a month for food and clothing for their residents."

"Inmates?"

"Women and children fleeing the abuse of husbands, fathers, and brothers."

It fit her. That she would want to aid those less loved, less fortunate than she, was no surprise to him. "And so, you should continue to do so."

"But now, I may change that."

He stroked her cheek—he could not help himself. The applicant to his advertisement was a caring woman. "Do as you want, always."

She licked her lips, perplexed. "But now, you see, I have a challenge."

"What is that?" He'd almost called her his darling.

"Mr. Dunlap and Mr. Finster told me about a document they received when I was three months old. I never knew of it. Not until now. Dunlap and Finster say that was the plan. For it to come to me at my father's death, my twenty-fifth birthday, or my marriage. Papa knew I had replied to your advert, and he wrote to them in March as he lay dying. He told me to consult them after he died. This is my first journey to London, and…and so I am here. I am here to tell you that…"

Fear stabbed through him. The woman in his arms was going to disappear. Like a figment of his imagination made flesh and blood, humor and beauty, was about to leave him. "Tell me what, Verity?"

"I have more than three hundred."

He was delighted for her. "Is that it? You have *more* money? That's wonderful." She could keep her money, spend it, give it all to her abused women and children—he could not care a whit. "And it is all yours."

"But…but you don't understand."

He adored her eyes, the fierce confusion in them. "What, then? Tell me."

"I have ten thousand pounds, nine shillings, and sixpence."

Joy for her burst though him. "*What?*"

"I am an heir to a ridiculous amount of money. Invested, it was. That's why the odd amount."

The bubbling enthusiasm that he'd experienced at her announcement was not one she shared. In fact, she wrinkled her brow, apprehensive, torn.

"I am shocked at the amount of money, yes, I am," she said with distaste. "But more than that, I am utterly astonished at its mysterious source. How could it be so large? Was it an investment in sugar plantations? Or slavers? If it was, I don't want it." That, she said with disgust.

They were only two ugly ventures. There were so many more. Sale of church treasures. Forging of old art. Pillaging of French chateaux.

"And there is more!" She pushed away, and he felt her loss, his arms empty. "The ridiculous thing is…it is anonymous."

That confounded him. "There is no reference to the benefactor?"

"They say none. And even if they knew, they are bound by the terms of the grant to never tell me."

He thought for a moment. "Where is the money deposited?"

"Child's Bank."

"We'll go tomorrow."

She grabbed his hand and clasped it tightly. "Do you think they will tell me the source?"

He doubted it. "We can only go and ask."

"You will come with me?" Hope sparkled in her gorgeous green eyes.

"If you want me."

"*Absolutely.*"

He beamed at her. "And do you come home with me?"

"I do, sir."

"And the name of your carriage inn is what?"

"The Yorkshire Grey in Hampstead."

"Jessup." He rapped upon the roof and gave him the location of Hampstead. "We go to fetch Miss Carr's belongings. Then home."

Chapter Five

No. 18 Upper Brook Street
Mayfair, London

MILES INTRODUCED HER to his butler at the front door. Saying she was his friend, Miles said naught to the kindly fellow about the fact that she might soon become the lady of the house.

Withers, a reedlike man with a wide smile, accepted the simple explanation without the batting of any eye. "Would you and Miss Carr wish tea, my lord?"

Verity didn't know whether to be pleased or anxious about the fact Miles had said nothing about their wedding. For herself, she wanted that discussion soon. She could not dawdle here in London if they were not to be married. If he had second thoughts, she must open that subject and settle it quickly.

But for the past hour, her search of the courtyard of the Yorkshire Grey had consumed her. When she'd alighted with Miles to enter the inn and collect her baggage, she'd eyed the fullness of the courtyard. Coming out, she'd done it again. But her concentrated perusals of the carriages coming and going to the old inn brought her little comfort. She searched for the suspicious black hack that had loitered outside the offices of Dunlap and Finster when she emerged from her meeting. Oh, yes, it was similar to others of its ilk. Even the fact that the aged gray mare who pulled the hackney in London did not look like any in the Hampstead yard gave her little peace. True, to make that trek, her stalker would have had to change horses or hacks. And she knew he was resourceful enough to do it. But she was wary. Always on guard.

She forced herself to focus on the fact that Miles had brought her to his home. A safe haven, she presumed. If no one had followed her, and she prayed it was so.

Miles, thank heaven, seemed unaware of her unease.

"A light refreshment," he said to his butler, "would be good, Withers. Do tell Mrs. Dunwoody that Miss Carr will be with us this evening for supper and for the night. Perhaps for the foreseeable future. I ordered the footmen to bring in her trunk, and this is Pip." Miles deposited her dog in the servant's arms. "Pip needs a walk in the back garden."

"Very good, sir. And Miss Carr is to be in the third-floor guest bedroom?"

"Exactly." Ever congenial and responsive, the butler showed no sign he thought it unusual for a lady to visit a gentleman's abode alone. "Would you care to follow me upstairs, Miss Carr, and take a moment to refresh? I can show you to your rooms."

She accepted and went off. Delighting in the cheerful yellow and green sitting room, bedroom, and boudoir, she did her ablutions and combed her hair, then made her way downstairs.

Walking into a serene Wedgwood-blue room with soft pink and alabaster appointments, Miles awaited her and indicated a chair for her. "I gather everything meets with your approval?"

"It does. Everything is lovely. Thank you," she said as she perched on a silk blush Chippendale chair. "Do your staff know of my coming? The possible marriage?"

"I had alerted Withers and my housekeeper to the need for preparation of the third-floor front bedroom. They know no particulars of how you and I met, rest assured. In addition, I did not say when or why the bedroom might be in use. After we dine tonight, I will retire to my club. You can rest easily."

"Don't go." Her words were part plea, part order.

He examined her for a moment. "If you are certain."

"I am."

"Your room is far enough away from my own suite on the second floor that all propriety is served by accommodating you there."

"Good. Do stay. I do not wish to be a burden."

"You are not." Miles clasped his hands behind his back and paced to the front windows. "Withers and Mrs. Dunwoody, my housekeeper, are relatively new to me and eager to please me."

He seemed uncomfortable discussing his staff. Still, Verity sought to learn more about the house. "Withers seems agreeable, even if he is a recent hire." She surveyed the double cube of the lovely room and debated if she should ask her next question. "Why is he recently hired? Did your previous staff age and need to be pensioned off?"

"They were pensioned, yes," he said.

Which answered only part of her question. So then, it was a subject to be explored later. But she cast it aside far too quickly as she wrung her hands and told herself to stop fretting about the old hack. She could be worrying unduly. From across the street, she had not seen the passenger's face clearly. Her glimpse of him had been brief. A thin man with sharp, angular features that reminded her of a starved fox. Enough to alarm her. Enough to…

Stop! Stop this!

She must change the subject, and to Miles, she said, "The house is lovely."

"My mother is responsible for all you see here, and in the dining room—the breakfast room, too, downstairs. We also keep up her small but robust kitchen garden at the back, which I am told by my housekeeper and cook is the envy of those on the street."

"I like to work in a vegetable garden," she said as she ran her fingertips over the pale silk damask. "Digging in the earth keeps one…"

"Grounded?"

She grinned. "Touché."

"I did not ask you if you would prefer something stronger than tea." His brows knitted, as if he were worried about her.

He'd been solicitous. And she'd been so undone that she'd accepted his embrace. A man she barely knew. And yet his kindness felt so sincere. What need had she of such? Oh, greatly had she needed his succor. *As warm as spirits. As warm as…*

"Would you prefer a brandy, Verity?" He held a decanter aloft.

She'd been gathering wool. "No. Later. Thank you. I am…I am taken by the house." With one sweep of her hand, she brushed away any drift of the conversation toward more severe topics. "Your mother had a fine eye for color."

"Indeed, she did. My father often consulted her on dyes for the cottons in our mills. Her loss was a cruel one."

"Is that her?" She pointed toward the portrait of the dark-haired woman hanging to one side of the fireplace. The lady sat upon a white garden chair amid a green field of wild pansies.

"Flowers, my father said, would raise their faces to her as she passed."

"How wonderful." She admired the fineness of the artwork, the skill of the portraitist. "Did you have her with you long?"

"Until I was twelve. I remember her laughing. Always laughing." He stood at one end near the Adam fireplace, watching her take the measure of the room and him in it. "And you? You have fond memories of your mother, I would imagine."

"I do." She gazed at this extraordinary man with a curious regard. She'd not met many men who displayed such kindness toward women. "Why would you say that of me?"

"How could I predict it?" He paused to think. "I suppose I see in you a young woman gentled by a feminine nurturing."

"My mother was a joyful creature. Finding fun in daily life. She used to make up poetry. Ridiculous rhymes. 'There once was a girl from Calais, who carried a wedding bouquet—of daisies at best, but her frequent request, was that gents pay her court every day!' That is one of her most frequently recited works and makes very little sense. But there you have how her attempts made my father and me laugh. Even if we did so ruefully."

"I see," he said with feigned horror. "And in the doing, taught you how to appreciate good writing."

"Precisely!" She gazed about the room. "As yours taught you to see the world in complementary colors."

"She did. She often went with my father to the mills. Concerned with color and fine texture, she took good care of our workers. No children younger than eighteen could work for us. A small pension for those who had to end their working days because of aches or pains. A fund to pay for funerals for our longtime workers."

"I have heard of how well those at Armstrong mills are treated. By such actions, you, sir, do more to challenge other owners, and, I daresay, you make no friends among them."

"Good of you to recognize the problems I face with competitors."

She smiled but did not feel much joy. The events of the past few days had unraveled her ordinary composure. To meet a man on a snowy road, find him sweet and kind and very appealing, but to come to London to meet a different man, a possible husband, and now to find the first man and the second were the same, was all too roiling. But the inheritance topped it all.

"I'm sorry. I am quite beyond talk. Do forgive me." She shot to her feet. "I cannot sit."

"Pace if you wish." He had taken the matching chair opposite. "I would if I were you."

She took the length of the room. "You think me possessed."

"No. It's been quite a day."

She stopped before the window to the street. She searched—in vain, thank God—for a rickety black hackney with an old gray mare.

"Would you like to walk, Verity?" He was beside her, one

warm hand to her wrist, his words a caress to her ear. "Outside? Shall we?" Toward Hyde Park?"

"Would you come with me?"

He turned, headed for the bellpull. "We'll get our coats. Come."

THEY WALKED DOWN Upper Brook Street to the park. At this hour with the sun set, two lamp men ran down Park Lane with their long brass poles, lighting all the flames in the street lights. Three town carriages passed them. Few residents walked about. Most were inside, enjoying late tea or dressing for dinner or social engagements. Miles and she strolled in peace.

Yet he saw in her stance that she was disturbed. She took note of the conveyances on the street and those who strolled past them. The news of her inheritance, he surmised, had shocked her. It was a large sum, and he was happy for her, yet alarmed at her own dismay of it. That the source was unknown to her was odd. That she had no one to whom she could talk about its source was also an issue. What she had said sounded as if her father might have known of the source. But he had never told her of the sum. Odd, that was, too.

This business with her inheritance or gift or whatever it was presented numerous questions. Verity and he had not yet settled the issue of their marriage, and he did not wish to create gossip or turmoil among his staff. He'd had enough of that before, changing servants often because of it. He would not countenance it now. He had to know, and soon, if she would take her money and leave or still considered marriage to him.

He had not known her for more than a few hours, but he'd noticed her shock over the bequest. Certainly, he could revel in the good fortune of anyone. If she had suspicions about who had given her such a large inheritance and did not wish to discuss it with him, he could understand that, too. But her newfound gain, enough to support her at current standards in meager means for her lifetime, could lead her to break their agreement to marry. The possibility of losing her created an ache in his heart. A place he'd never expected to feel anything at all ever again.

As they entered the Grosvenor Gate and passed the park wall, she strode more slowly and breathed more deeply. They took a turn on the path south, and one glance at her told him she was more at ease.

"I hate to spoil your enjoyment," he said, "but I think we should not walk here much longer. The shadows grow deeper."

"You are right, of course." She had her hands in her coat pockets as she stopped and spun toward him. "You have been very good to me today."

He raised a hand, his smile wry. "No more gratitude, please. I am quite thanked."

She stopped, faced him, and tipped her head, suddenly the coquette, though to him, she did not seem to have planned the spontaneity of such an attitude. She was without guile—and he valued that unexpected characteristic more than he could ever have told her.

"You are a darling man," she said with an honesty that emphasized her simplicity and lack of artifice.

"You are kind to think so." He remembered a few instances when the moniker he deserved was the opposite. *Savage. Insane. Gullible.* All came to mind in a rush of bile.

She put her hands to his and held tightly. "Do you still want to marry a woman you barely know?"

"I'd like to marry you, if you'll have me."

She shook her head as if the whole idea were impossible. "Why? Why?"

"I want a wife. A friend. I am lonely. You seem a gentle soul. I think we would do well together."

"I cannot imagine that you have not met a thousand young ladies you know better than I who would not make you a friend and wife because they do know you better."

But they knew his past, too. His wife. "I would never find happiness with any I've met. They see me as the mill owner, a *cit* with a new title, an upstart viscount, too rich for his station. They also see me as a widower." *Not knowing I am more aggrieved than grieving.*

She stood immobile, only her large, beautiful eyes searching his for what he would not reveal. "Did you love her?"

He ignored the lurch of his heart at her question, and gave her one truth. "When I married her, yes."

"And do you miss her?"

And so, one more truth. "No."

She nodded. "I see. Then your loneliness comes not from her lack."

"No. It does not."

She bit her lip, then shook back her hair. "Do you want children?"

He blinked and peered up at the deep blue clouds scudding across a darker moonlit sky. "I have not wished for that in many years. But now," he said as he met her frank gaze, "I believe I would."

She smiled as if he'd just given her the keys to the kingdom. "I would, too."

He stepped closer to her, dropped her hands, and cupped her shoulders. Her luscious curves fit into the planes of his suddenly very needy self. "Might we proceed to getting them?"

She let her eyes dance into his. "First we must be wed."

"Will day after tomorrow do?"

"Quite well," she said on a delighted laugh. "And then we must become better friends."

He sent his fingers up into the heavy coil of hair at her nape. Her skin was as soft as charmeuse, and her hair smelled of lavender. She'd been in his arms again today as she had been the very first they met. He'd wanted her there then. She'd come both times. Once for expediency. Once for comfort. Now, he would test to see if she might come for a new and startling reason. Might she come because she could want him? Want him as a man? As her lover?

She pulled back a little, a serious matter widening her eyes. "Friends kiss."

"They do," he said with a smile that grew from a friend's to a ravenous man's. "Shall we?"

She studied his mouth and swallowed hard. "Oh, yes. From the first moment I heard your voice on the Great North Road, I have wanted to know how you taste."

"Well, then…" His mind filled with the wonder of her as he loomed over her lips. "We must not delay."

She wrapped her arms around his shoulders and pushed up on her toes. "Please don't."

The temptation to take her with all the ardor he bore her raged through him. He could not devour her like a satyr. He was a man who had foresworn passion and love. A man of reason and temperance. But then…

She put her lips to his, a brush of warm temptation. The sensation of her desire met the one of his quest, as if two stars collided in the dark of night. Blinded by it, he groaned and caught her up. Her mouth was lush, and as his tongue invaded, he knew how succulent her body was. How sweet. He swept the inside of her mouth and felt her complete surrender. This was what he'd craved. A woman who might want him. Love him.

He pulled away, breathless, cupping her cheek. "Darling, we must stop."

In the shadows of the soft spring evening, she tipped her head and smiled at him. "You'll kiss me again?"

"As often as you wish."

There again was that sweet woman who drew him to her with the artless look of enchantment. "Must I ask you each time?"

"No," he said on a laugh, and hugged her close, then set her from him. "Only look at me like that, my darling, and I am yours."

"As I am forever yours," she said, and put her arm in his to turn and walk home.

Chapter Six

SHE AWOKE THE next morning as Pip gave a yelp when the maid assigned to Verity entered her rooms. The servant cooed to the dog, then drew back the drapes to let the sunshine stream inside her bedroom. The maid—Mary was her name— introduced herself last night when first Verity had slipped upstairs to visit her boudoir and comb her hair. Mary was young, twenty if a day, with an accent that declared she came from the northern climes.

"York, miss," the girl had told her when Verity asked where home had been.

"Have you been in London long?"

"No'm. Only after Christmas I come. My mother died last harvest, she did, and she gave me ten shillings to come to London to make my way."

"Was there no work in York you wished to take?"

"Oh, no'm. I wanted a city life. Always did. My ma knew it and bade me leave our village."

"And this is your first position?"

"Aye, miss. A good one, too. All of us are new here but Bertha, the scullery maid."

"Is that so?"

"Aye. Bertha's a good girl, a bit slow, you ken w'a I mean? 'Is lordship did not let her go."

"Good of him," Verity had replied.

"Mr. Withers and Mrs. Dunwoody were new last June, and the rest of us come on gradual, like. But Bertha, she's been here."

The maid had given Verity a toothy grin.

Just as she did now. "I can take the little dog outside, if you wish, miss. And would you be wanting a breakfast tray?"

"Yes please, do take Pip out and give her a bit of leftovers from the kitchen. But do not trouble yourself to bring up a tray to me. I will go down." She was not yet lady of the house to ask such favors. Besides, she was eager to see Miles again. Over the breakfast table, too.

She gave a laugh.

"What do you do for your morn? Would you like a bath too, miss?"

"In truth, I would." She'd been traveling for days, followed by more days running to and fro to the solicitors' and the *Chronicle*. "Will it be a while?"

"Oh, no, miss. The water's ready, and I can have the footmen fill the tub in a wink."

"Good. Please do."

"I'll just go and tell them to fetch it, then I'll be back to help you dress."

Verity sat up, pushing back upon the giant pillows. She thought to refuse the offer of assistance, but she would not refuse the girl, especially if she'd been told to aid her. "Very good. I'd like that."

Off Mary went as Verity took hold of her long nighttime braid and brought it over her shoulder. The blonde skein hung to her waist, and for the first time, she wondered if she were fashionable enough for the man, the mill owner, the noted viscount whom she was to marry.

She'd lain awake for hours thinking of him, how he had been her help and her succor for the past few days. An assault of fear struck her about this venture to marry a stranger—and she pushed it away.

But she was assailed by that other fright. The man who followed her. She cupped her forehead. It could not be *him*. Why? How could it be? She'd covered her tracks south.

She squeezed her eyes shut and put starch in her spine. What she had seen had not been *him*. No, just a man who looked like him. Thin and hawklike, evil.

She threw back the covers and put her feet to the thick pile of the rug. Comfort, once more, drove out fear.

She would forget him.

Forget him!

She cupped her elbows and walked to the window to overlook the street. So early in the morning, only one barouche passed, a glossy brown conveyance, drawn by two matching chocolate horses. No worn black hackneys. That was logical. After all, few of the *ton* would be up. Only a young boy with a broom walked the cobbles. He was, she supposed, a sweeper who worked the corners clearing horse dung from the path of the gentry and their fancy carriages.

"You will soon become one in those carriages," she said to herself in awe. That had her shaking her head. Such status had not been her goal. Oh, she was educated, and now—much to her shock—she had money of her own. But she had not expected a house like this. A home in the city. *A man like Miles.*

He was kind and gentle. *And he cares for me. Me!*

She'd hoped for a man who would treat her well and one who might grow to love her.

"Did you love her?" Her own question to him yesterday came back to her now.

"When I married her, yes." His response had confused her. Though he could love, had loved, he had grown out of love, away from it. Why, was the question that she had asked herself in the wee hours of the morning. *Why?*

What happened? Was it the tale of a love affair stale with age? A nobleman's arranged marriage gone to dust?

What right had she to ask?

She rubbed her arms. Only one reason. Only insofar as he might lose interest in her. Turn aside and welcome a woman to his bed who was his to treasure, never to wed.

She would leave him. If she wed him and he took a mistress, she would never abide it. That, she should tell him. And she would.

But oh, she could hope he would love her and keep only unto her for the rest of their days. She was that plebeian. That proud of her own worth. If she would never take a lover, she would make it clear she would require him to do the same. No one would dishonor her so. Not that way, not others, either. For she knew, sadly, there were far too many ways men and women could ruin each other with excesses.

The memory brought up her scare of yesterday. She spun away from the window and sought out the dressing room and her clothes. She had a day dress of good muslin with a ruffle of peach ribbon round the hem. She preferred it for today. She'd get it. Shake it out. Have Mary press it, if need be. She would do Miles proud here in Town. She would!

He wished a wife as companion. A friend. A confidante.

And to be his lover, as well. A lover who might show him affection so often that they would have children.

"All that I can give him," she told herself, and felt the lingering embers of their kisses burst upon her in a new fire.

SHE APPEARED IN the archway and found Miles still at breakfast, his coffee cup to his left hand, newspapers to his right. He lifted his gaze, and his eyes locked on hers. At the desire she saw there, she clamped her hands to her quivering belly.

"Good morning." He got to his feet.

She waved a hand and told him he must not. "Dear sir, if you do that each morning for fifty years, you will have back pains."

Withers, good man that he was, suppressed his grin and pulled out a chair at the opposite end of the square table. She pointed toward the one next to Miles, and the butler hurried to accommodate her.

"I will see to Miss Carr, Withers." Miles pulled out the chair she'd chosen. "I gave orders to have a tray sent up to you."

"I prefer to dine with you, sir." She'd keep to proper address while servants were around.

"Marvelous. I applaud it." He regained his seat and ran his gaze over her, this time with more scrutiny than desire. "Did you sleep well?"

"Passably." She settled beside him, and the butler placed her serviette across her lap.

"Hmm. As did I. Much to do today." Miles paused while Withers poured tea, then offered her a serving platter of sausages and bacon.

"Indeed." She took a few of this and that, as well as a fried egg from the other plate he presented.

He watched as the butler ambled to the sideboard. "Since you are up so early, we can go first thing to your appointment."

The bank, he meant. She nodded and took a sip of the strong tea. "That was my hope too."

"So shall it be," he said with a grin.

She was hungry and attacked her meal with diligence while Miles turned to his newspapers.

When she finished and found her tea tasted best while she sat and admired the handsomeness of her future husband, Miles glanced up, surprised and pleased.

He arched a brow at her.

And she looked away, laughing.

"Withers," he said to his servant, "will you please call Mrs. Dunwoody to us now?"

The man bowed his way toward the kitchen door. "Of course, my lord."

"I will introduce you to my housekeeper and tell them both

you are to be my wife."

"This will shake their world," Verity replied.

"I doubt much. I think you will be a good woman to serve."

"I will endeavor to be that. I've only organized my father's house. A cook, two maids." She ran her gaze over the rich appointments of the cheery pink and lavender breakfast room. "I will allow them their head."

"Do as you see fit."

At length, the two appeared. Standing opposite her, the butler smiled, and the housekeeper kept a straight face as Miles introduced Verity as his fiancée. "We marry in a small ceremony here tomorrow morning at ten. We will have four guests. And I look for a modest celebration afterward. White wine. Simple fare, but a wedding cake. Pastries. Do buy from the shop you like on Piccadilly, Mrs. Dunwoody."

That offer made the housekeeper happier. "I will, my lord. And may I offer my congratulations, sir. Miss Carr, I am pleased to meet you, and I welcome your advice on the management of the house."

"Thank you, Mrs. Dunwoody," Verity replied. "You will find I take your lead in many things, especially in these first months."

That pleased the lady immensely. "I will be your help, ma'am."

"We have appointments this morning," Miles told them. "We return later. Do expect us for tea. For dinner, my cousin, Lord Edwards, joins us with his fiancée, Lady Lianna Collier."

The two discussed dinner times with Miles and menu with Verity. The housekeeper then excused herself.

"May we inform staff, sir and miss, of your impending nuptials?" Withers asked as he refilled Verity's teacup.

"Please do," he said with smile at Verity.

She reached for his hand. One formality of their wedding done. A few more to come. But for now, in this moment, she welcomed the heat of Miles's caress.

"I will do so, sir." The butler cleared his throat as he stood watching Miles entwine his long fingers in hers.

"That will be all, Withers," Miles said, his hot umber gaze melting her. "I will pull the bell when we are ready to leave."

She caught her breath, rejoicing in his order to the butler. How could she want Miles so badly? At such an ungodly early hour of the morning? Her body gushed with need of his hands on her. So novel was desire, she blushed.

As Withers closed the door down to the kitchen and she noted the click of the latch, Miles lifted her hand and drew it to him. He bent, turned her hand palm up, and pressed his lips to the center. His kiss scorched her. His tender regard dizzied her. "I thought of you," he murmured, "all through the night."

His admission burst through her like fireworks. "I tossed and turned with thoughts of our wedding."

His smile spoke of slow, sensual abandon. "It's good we marry tomorrow."

She sought to quell the revelry in her heart. "It cannot come soon enough."

He urged her from her chair to his lap. "Come sit with me, my darling."

She chuckled as she went. She'd been in his arms so often since they met, any place other than there seemed far too distant, far too cold. Once in his lap, she wiggled about in search of some comfort that did not put her near his straining cock. He arched a long, knowing brow and tutted at her. Then he slid his arm under her knees and lifted them over the arm of his chair. She stared at him wide-eyed, glowing with delight at his *savoir faire*. One arm around his broad shoulders, she hesitated and toyed with the simple tie of his morning cravat. "This is not usual behavior for the morning in a breakfast room."

"Never. Know, however, that I want you here, but if you wish to leave—"

"No!" She grinned at him. "No. I like it here."

"Then you should stay." He took hold of one of her curls at her ear and pulled it long and let it bounce. "I like *you* here. With me." He shifted, and she knew by the growing length of his cock that he did like her immensely.

Desire pooled in her mouth. "Wise of you to tell Withers to leave us."

"I shall make it a rule to serve on the sideboard and leave us alone. Never to return until one of us pulls the bell."

She considered his mouth and how she hungered to taste him once more. Dare she say how much? "At the moment, I've no wish for food."

"Nor I." He put his hand to her throat and wrapped his fingers around her in tenderness.

"I prefer you," she managed on a breathless note. In the intimate room filled with the aromas of coffee and bacon, to possess him was all she sought in this world. "Might you be on offer?"

"To you, I always am."

She clutched him close. She inhaled his breath, full of the flavors of jam and toast and coffee. "I've never known desire. Never knew it could be so…so…"

One side of his luscious mouth tipped up. "Overwhelming?"

"Yes," she whispered. "You'll think I'm forward. I'm not."

"Only with me?" he asked as if it were whimsy.

"Just you."

"Well then," he crooned, "come kiss me, my darling, and take your fill."

She quivered. "I'm not good at this. I've not kissed any man before you."

He gave a little laugh. "One learns by doing. And perfection only comes with repetition."

Her heart picked up in tempo, and desire burned in her belly. Then she put her lips atop his. He took her at once, his lips hot and hard. His hand to her throat became a gentle vise. His other trailed down her shoulder to urge her closer to him. He kissed her with tender exploration, and she moaned her approval. And like last night on their walk, he opened his mouth and sent his tongue inside her to taste everything she was.

She clamped her thighs together, wanting his touch. His hands. His caress.

As if he knew her body cried for him, he sent his hand down her legs and drew up her skirts. He stroked her ankle and her calf, leaving her writhing for more. He wrapped his hand around her thigh and squeezed, then found the center of her being with his palm. There he cupped her bare flesh, his fingertips splayed into her nether hair. And in response, she felt her body pulse in wild appreciation. She moaned, not knowing if she should be pleased or embarrassed. But he groaned and broke away.

"I will stop," he said, his lips to her forehead. "This must be done in privacy and comfort."

He was right, though she objected and clamped her thighs together to ease the throb.

"I know, my darling." He crushed her close to him. "Tomorrow."

She pulled at his cravat, then gazed up at him. He was as dazed as she. "All our tomorrows."

"Every one." He shifted in his chair. "I promise."

She grinned, reaching for a levity she should grasp. "Even in the breakfast room?"

His features fell to drastic depths. "In every room we own."

She toyed with the length of his undone cravat. "Do you believe in luck?"

He shifted once more, his attempt to find a position that did not poke her with his intentions failing again. "No. Do you?"

"I am feeling very lucky to have found you. And to marry you."

He grew somber. "There is no such thing as luck. Good or bad."

"To what, then, do you attribute how well we"—she bit her lip and rolled her eyes—"get on?"

He burst into laughter and hugged her madly. "There is no such thing as bad luck. Only people making bad choices."

She regarded him with bright circumspection. But he had

turned away and retreated into some grim reflection on a past she knew nothing of.

She caught his jaw and turned him toward her. "We've made a good choice."

He examined her so closely, his perusal was as if he'd never seen her before this moment. "Yes, my darling. The very best."

Chapter Seven

THE DAY HAD fled quickly. The wall sconces burned brightly in his dressing room that night as he allowed his valet to brush the sleeves of his dinner coat. Miles shot his cuffs and considered the figure he cut in his mirror. The man reflected there was the picture of a fellow he knew well. Businessman, thirty-eight years old, viscount. That man was one he was proud of. This other fellow—sanguine, cheerful—was an intriguing fellow. A stranger. A bridegroom, eager as a boy to be wed on the morrow.

If he had told himself four days ago that tonight he would be as happy as a callow youth, he would have laughed off the very hint of it. Yet here he stood, less than an hour from the smiling presence of his betrothed, and he could not wait to have her beside him again.

She fed his need for so much he had not known he lacked. Solace. Gaiety. Humor. Sexual congress. Passion.

A young man's fantasy of true love.

That last tore him asunder. Conflicted as he was about his magnetic attraction to his bride, he yearned to put Verity in his bed and show her the joys of sexual fulfillment. Astonishing to him it was that he might want that again after enduring for so very long the lack.

His gaze slid to the far door connecting to the rooms he had not entered in more than a decade. He scowled. How could he have forgotten them? Their hideous condition merited some discussion because tomorrow night his bride should expect to have use of them. And could not.

"Will that be all, my lord?" Taylor, his valet, paused to gaze at Miles in the mirror.

"Yes, thank you. Do go enjoy your supper."

The man took to his heel to leave.

"And Taylor?"

"Sir?"

"No need to see to me after dinner. Take the evening to yourself. We will be up early on the morrow."

"I can, sir. Thank you. I will awaken you at seven?"

"Six tomorrow. And I've a mind to take my wife to Brighton for a few days' honeymoon. We will go alone."

The young man blinked in surprise. "Wonderful, sir, but won't you need a man there?"

"We will stay at one of their hotels on the shore. It's possible to hire servants by the day. You may enjoy a holiday, Taylor."

"Sir. I've had one for six months while you were in York. I am happy to go to Brighton."

"You are most kind, Taylor," Miles said to the man whom he'd hired last December when he first applied to the *Chronicle* to find a wife. "But the trip is my honeymoon, and I do wish the privacy."

The young man, formerly a wounded sergeant in His Majesty's Fifty-Second Regiment of Foot, reddened.

Was he all of twenty-two? How marvelous to be that young and view the world as opportunity and adventure. Miles could do with a bit of that.

His man inclined his head. "Yes, sir. Of course, sir. I understand. Good evening."

Miles watched him go, and the wariness that had grown within him throughout the day blossomed.

He spun to the mirror once more and fingered the button on

his formal navy frockcoat. The gold silk waistcoat and bright white stock only heightened his impression of an older man embarking on a young man's escapade. What was he doing marrying a woman fourteen years his junior? A beauty. Fresh, vibrant, innocent, untouched…yet eager to be touched by him.

He scoffed at himself. "Are you fair to her?"

Are you wise to marry her, sullied as you are by what you endured?

At the very least, he had to explain the condition of those rooms!

"Stop!" His father's stentorian voice rang through him in his oft-repeated warning. The man had not wanted Miles to endure any more pain than he already had. He had urged Miles repeatedly to end his misery. "Stop torturing yourself, my son! Send her away. If you will not divorce her, send her away!"

His father's deathbed advice came to him often. Now he promised his sire what he had really wanted. "After I marry tomorrow, I will be quit of her." *She will be my past. Irrelevant.*

He'd found happiness and was determined to embrace it.

He went to his dressing table and picked up the small royal-blue velvet box. This was the beginning of many things he would give his bride for the treasure of happiness she bestowed upon him.

"ANY WAIT IN the Doctors' Commons to get the special license?" His cousin, Walter Higham, Lord Edwards, sat at Miles's left at the dining table.

"None," Miles replied, and smiled to Verity far down the long expanse of the dining room table. "I've arranged for the vicar, too. Ten promptly, he told me. He has another wedding to perform at eleven."

"Not surprised," proclaimed Walter. "It is wedding season here in the great city of London."

"We're delighted to attend and very honored to be your

witnesses," said his fiancée, Lianna, Lady Collier. She was a widow with twin sons. Her husband had died two years ago June in a hunting accident. Lianna had been the love of Walter's life since they were youngsters who lived near each other along the Thames in Richmond, but she had been forced by her father to marry Collier, a wealthy baron. Walter and Leanna's happiness had been thwarted by the age-old practice of marrying between families to gain land and money.

Verity smiled at Miles, a vision in cerulean blue, soon to be his bride who came to him of her own accord. And by heaven's grace, now by her own desire. They'd gone to the bank, and she had argued her own case well. Surprised at a lady's insistence, still the bankers had not budged. They were uncooperative as to the source of her inheritance. Citing legalities and precedent, they refused to dig into the twenty-four-year-old documents. They could do nothing for her by way of unsealing the records of the anonymous gift she'd been granted. They only repeated the terms and expressed their inability to accommodate her wishes.

Miles had accompanied her home and, soon after, departed to Doctors' Commons and the family jewelers in Hanover Square. Though she'd been put out at the bank, she seemed to have accepted the result. When he had returned home and they called for a small tea, she put aside her dismay over the bankers' decisions and looked forward to meeting his cousin and his future wife.

Indeed, as Miles admired Verity from the far end of the table now, he was proud that here was the lady who would grace his table until the end of their days.

"We are happy to have you with us," she told their guests, and took a sip of her wine.

Miles cocked a brow at his cousin. "Perhaps attending Verity's and my wedding might give you the impetus to hasten yours, eh?" They had postponed their wedding twice since Christmas.

Lianna shook her head. "My boys are ten and have suffered greatly from the shock of their father's death. Walter has been kind to allow them more time to accept that I will marry again."

"Lord Collier," Walter confided, "was well loved. I do not wish to change their world too drastically."

"I would marry sooner," Lianna told them, "if only Walter would agree."

"I don't want problems, Lianna. No more than we have."

She tried to smile and failed. Directing her attention to Verity, she brightened. "Have you known each other long? Walter told me Miles thought of marriage last year, but this sudden announcement was a surprise."

"Yes," Verity managed with a glance at Miles. He had told her that Walter knew everything about the *Chronicle* advertisement, but neither he nor she knew how much Walter had shared with Lianna. Obviously at sea about what to say, Verity offered, "We, too, are shocked at the suddenness of our intentions."

"Have you plans to return north?" Walter asked of Miles. "I understand London is to have a few celebrations, since Bonaparte has finally been chased down to Elba. Lianna and I would have you to dinner with us."

"We'd like that," Miles said with Verity's nod of agreement. "Perhaps in a few weeks. Springtime in London can be enjoyable."

"Well!" said Walter with a flourish. "There is the new bridegroom, waxing jubilant over springtime in the city."

"Do stop!" Miles said with a chuckle. "Shall we have a brandy and leave the ladies to dessert?"

"Indeed."

The men rose.

In the small parlor, silent communion reigned between them. Miles was distressed that his cousin who sought happiness with the woman he adored had continuing challenges with her offspring. He and Walter had discussed this often and found no solution. Much as once they had discussed Miles's dilemma.

Miles sought a subtle way to open the subject but found often that directness worked best. He poured draughts of brandy into two snifters and handed one to his cousin. "Do I detect your hesitancy to wed is because you continue to have problems with the Collier boys?"

Walter sat back, downed a healthy swallow, and crossed one leg over the other. "You could tell, eh?" He took another drink and winced. "Hell yes."

"The male tutor has been no help?" Walter had found an emigre, a Dutchman with excellent credentials from Heidelberg who was well versed in dealing with unruly boys. The man had taken up his duties last October.

"Herr Gunderson resigned last month. He was, as he said, 'at a loss' as to how to contain the boys. The oldest ran away from home in February. The youngest refused to eat for days until he was found and brought back. Lianna is more overwrought than ever."

"I can see why. Did Gunderson help with their attitudes?"

"Ha! Do you mean have they become less rude? Irreverent?" Walter growled and took another drink. "No."

"What of your suggestion last year to Lianna to enroll them in that special school for unruly boys in Aberdeen?"

"Lianna is reluctant to send them so far."

Miles took a long drink of his own brandy. "Sometimes, the best way to live your own life is to show those who would destroy it that you will have no part of their mayhem."

Walter stared at him for a long minute. "That worked for you. I am ready to try it. The school tolerates no chaos, and those two children make her life bedlam every day."

"I sympathize with you both."

Walter lifted his glass in homage. "I am happy for you that you are well out of your own chaos. Verity is a lovely young woman. A rare find."

"Rare, indeed," Miles said with a nod. *And so fortunate a find.*

Withers appeared at the open door. "My lord, sir, Lady Collier readies to leave."

Both men finished their brandies and stood.

Miles started for the hall, but Walter hung back. "What have you told Verity of the past?"

"Nothing."

"Is that wise?"

Miles did not appreciate being needled about this. Yet…he owed his fiancée explanations, all words he did not wish to utter. All he had not had time to plan out carefully as he should. Thus he said to his cousin and friend the only thing he knew to be true. "Verity is nothing like her."

Walter balked. "Does that matter?"

"With Verity, I have no cause to remember. Nor to act as I did." *That is apparent to me.*

"Yet the reason you chose this means to find a wife was so that you would not care too much for anyone. Yet any blind man could see how you care for her. And justifiably so."

Miles contained his anger. But it was not at his cousin, who meant well. But at himself.

Walter stepped near him. "Are we not shaped by our pasts? Good and bad?"

"Irrevocably?" Miles scowled, his old bitterness at the one who had caused it in him rising like gorge. "I hope not." *Yet I feel the rage I once did simply by recalling the old torment.*

"And I hope you are right," Walter told him. "I wish you well."

Miles gave him a smile. "That, I do know."

⋙⋘

"I LIKED THEM both very much," Verity told him as they climbed the stairs, arm in arm.

"So I saw! You have two new supporters in this venture you begin tomorrow, Miss Carr."

"*New friends*, Lord Bellamy, sir." She took a step to continue on.

But Miles stopped at the second-floor landing. "I wish to talk to you. Will you come with me?"

"Of course," she said, trusting that he meant no anticipation of their vows by taking her to his suite.

He opened his door. "My bedroom suite."

She entered a truly masculine abode. The walls, Wedgwood blue, cast a mellow light upon the sweeping lines of gilt Rococo mahogany furniture. Bold and polished to a high gleam, the armoire, wardrobe, and sideboards declared that the master of the house relaxed and slept here. The fireplace of veined blue and white marble sat at one end, with two massive gilt wing chairs to either side of a sofa. Those were upholstered in bold blue and white Ming damask silks.

"The bedroom, my dressing room, and bathing room are beyond," he said as he went toward one chair and extended a hand to invite her to take the other.

She readily took it.

"I brought you here because I wish to tell you more of who I am. I've been remiss and must be fair to you." He inhaled and smoothed a hand down his trousers. "You know I was married before and am a widower."

She nodded, and he went on, his face turned toward the small fire his servants had lit.

"My wife has been dead for three years. I have not sought to find another until I posted in the *Chronicle*. For most of those three years, I did not think I would ever wish to marry again."

He got to his feet, as if he could not contain his thoughts. Then he went to the fireplace and put his hands to the mantel, facing away from her.

Between his hands, he lowered his head for a moment, then came up and said, "My first marriage was not happy, Verity."

She waited as she realized with a jolt that he sounded agonized, so torn, in fact, that he was about to tell her things that most likely he had never shared with another.

He swung about to face her. Crossing his arms before him, he grew stern. So grave, he appeared to be stepping carved in relief from marble. "I made many mistakes marrying. I take what blame is mine, and there is a lot of it to carry. I do not excuse myself from responsibility. But I wish to be fair to you and tell you what I experienced and what I learned from my marriage's utter failure.

"I learned to listen. To accept differences of opinion. I tried to learn to be more patient. I did not do well at that. When we wed, I was twenty-five, far too young, green. My wife was nineteen. From a prominent family, well received, and very socially adroit.

"My family was different. Mill owners, business owners, traders. New to our titles, the *ton* and its…peculiarities." He frowned. "The truth is, Verity, I married for all the wrong reasons. She was…beautiful. Stunning, actually. Acclaimed as the Diamond of the Season. Vivacious and lauded. Good with the toffs at Almacks. Crafty at cards and dice. Poetry itself in a ballroom. She was…sought after. I was…" He inhaled and stared straight through Verity. "I was enchanted."

Verity clasped her hands. She did not know how to absorb that. Was she jealous? Afraid? Threatened?

"We married after only three months' engagement. Both families applauded. A good arrangement. She brought connections to her family's ancient barony plus a healthy dowry and valuable acreage in the town of York. I gave her the financial security at which it was known her father had failed. She was an only child, and the title and headache of improving the estate went to a distant relation. She came to me, happy.

"Or so I thought. I believed." He strode away to a French bombe sideboard upon which stood an array of brandy and wine decanters. He took the stopper from one and poured two hefty portions into crystal snifters. When he came to hand her one, she took it but put it to the deal table next to her.

"We married, and I took her to my home in York. She began to spend money, using my name as credit. I did not mind. My mother had been dead many years, and our home needed improvement. I did not limit her spending, nor did I need to for over a year. Soon she decided she disliked York and wanted the Society of London. We'd owned this house here since my grandfather had it built in the mid-fifties. But my father and I had spent little time here, and it was not, as she put it, up to snuff. Though she complained of the amount of money I gave her for refurbishing, she made it into the house she wished for entertaining."

He took a drink of his brandy and paced. "More often than not, she lived here." He waved a dismissive hand and stood, stiff with anger. "At first, during the June Season, then during Parliament, later months on end. By that time, she and I were…estranged. Strangers. No longer intimate. No longer—if we ever were—friends.

"I took solace in work. Improving the quality of our cloth and buying up more buildings to convert to mills or building new. Always expanding and improving what we had. We were well off. I found pleasure in success in business. But it was not…enough. I knew a lack. I was not happy.

"But she was. In her element, in Society, she cut a grand figure. She lived here as she wished, and I lived in York. She did not want to come north. I had no great interest in coming south. And so we grew apart."

He emptied his glass and plunked it on the mahogany sideboard. He went back toward the mantel, one arm along the white plaster. "Four years ago, she became ill. She informed me of it and told me she wished to remain in London. Better doctors here, she explained. I offered her to come to York. She refused. I did not argue with her. Almost a year later, she died. Alone. It was what she wished."

He ran his hand over his mouth. "I mourned what we might have had together. I did not mourn her."

Verity mourned for him. She shifted and, after long minutes, said, "I am honored you have shared that with me."

He examined her, his eyes narrowing as if he did not recognize her. Then he shook his head. "You look lost, my darling. Did

I spoil your view of me?"

"No."

"I've fought with myself to tell you all of that. I worried. But I knew I should not allow you to think me more than I am."

Her heart ached for him. "I want to know who you are, Miles. Who you were. How we are here." She must share more of herself. Her past. Her efforts with painting. Her life had no such challenges as he had faced, save the recent one of her nemesis at home. Now, however, was not the time or place to speak of herself.

He walked to her, grim still, and offered his hand. "There is more. Come."

She took his hand and let him lead her to the far door. He opened it to a stark and empty room. The drapes, either a dark blue or black, were drawn across the far window. They were devoid of curtains. Three walls were a covered in a disquieting Chinese paper. With little light coming from his suite, they shone in a ruby, ebony, and gold Chinese silk pattern that made the room fit for an Oriental emperor's harem. Upon the remaining wall, what once had been plaster bouquets of climbing roses and twining vines were broken, cracked. As if someone had hit them with a blacksmith's hammer, bits of plaster dotted the bare parquet wood floor. The room, devoid of candles, lay in shades of gray and smelled of dust and decay. Smaller rooms led off, probably the dressing room and boudoir. They most likely were dreary as the rest. Not a stick of furniture stood anywhere.

"This is the matching suite for the lady of the house," Miles told her.

Oh, no. No. This would become hers? The looks, the smell, the atmosphere of it repelled her. All of it was an ill omen. Something warned her from it, and she took a quick step backward.

"It can be yours," he said with clipped tones full of old regret. "Or not. That is your choice. But it is yours to gut. Yours to make your own."

Of course, she could redo it. Remove the ugly wallpaper.

Restore the broken plaster sculptures along the walls. Paint it in restful shades of green and blue, design *trompe-l'œil* flowers in a garden of respite. Hire cabinetmakers to craft furniture to fit her desires for a dressing table and clothespress, a wardrobe, and a canopied bed wide enough to hold the mistress of the house and her loving husband.

"And if I do not wish to make it my bedroom?" She fixed him with her purpose. "If I wish to transform it into something more useful? Would you object?"

For the first time since they'd come upstairs, he smiled. She saw his shoulders relax.

"Never," he said. "What did you have in mind?"

"Oh," she said in gay contemplation to have such a glorious space remodeled, and tossed her head. "A nursery? A studio for my art?"

"I see. Then where would you sleep?" It was a question that elicited as much humor and hope as fear from his dark and questioning eyes.

"I thought I might sleep with you, sir."

"In my room?"

She swallowed hard. "Yes, yours."

"You would like that?"

She considered what pain it had cost him to tell her about the conflicts he'd had with his first wife. He was dear to do it, proper to share it. "Indeed, sir, I would. You see, I have great aspirations for this marriage."

In one bold step, he had her crushed against him. One hand to her nape, he kissed her with a ferocity that she felt in her very blood. His lips held the joy of her acceptance, and his kiss told her tales his words could not convey. This was the man she would treasure. This was the man who had survived hardship and wished to live again.

Too soon, he broke away. "We will do more of that tomorrow," he said with a grin. "Time for me to escort you upstairs."

*

He led her up. "A bride needs her rest, you see. And I've a gift for her."

"Do you, indeed? What fun!" At her door, she spun into his embrace and shook her head. "I regret to say I do not have one for the groom. I wish I had thought of that, but in the rush, I was remiss."

"No need." He held her loosely, lest he succumb to all manner of temptation to kiss her lips, march her backward into her bedroom—and take from her her innocence before she allowed him his rights to take it from her. "What you give me in the favor of your person as my wife is all I wish for."

She gave him that effervescent look that warmed him through and through. "One day soon I will find a perfect bridegroom's present. After all, have you not heard these days that I am a lady of means?"

"Hmmm. Yes, considerable it is, I do understand, my dear Miss Carr."

He took from his waistcoat pocket the velvet box that had been warming next to his heart all evening.

She licked her lips, her eyes dancing. "Jewelry? Ohh, I am covetous."

He barked in laughter. "If ever a woman was the opposite of covetous, it is you!"

"Do open it. Let me be the judge, sir!"

He flipped up the top.

For decades, till the end of his days, he vowed to remember the look on her face and her quick, silent tears.

"Oh," she said, and touched a fingertip to the drop pearl earrings. "How wonderful. And they're mine!"

"For you on your wedding day. No match to the splendor of your complexion, but these poor things will try."

She hugged him. Then kissed his cheek. "Thank you."

Feeling suddenly like a stodgy old uncle, he knew he must go, but still hated to. "Sleep well, my darling."

"Until tomorrow…" she said on a winsome note, clutching the little box to her bosom. Then she winked. "I've decided I will take my breakfast in my rooms. Just for tomorrow."

"A wise plan." He laughed at how silly he'd been to think he could cancel his marriage to this irrepressibly charming woman. "Only for tomorrow."

"Just tomorrow," she agreed, and whirled away from him.

"Tomorrow." He resolved it would be a bright day. *When you are mine.*

Chapter Eight

MARY BENT TO the mirror, and her happy brown gaze met Verity's. "I hope I've done ye proud, miss."

The girl had woven Verity's long curls into a heavy coil at the nape of her neck, her forehead clear and her cheeks framed by ringlets. Miles had sent up a catch of white roses and white sea campion with a few sprigs of rosemary and thyme. Mary had wound a white ribbon with one of the flowers into her hair over her right ear.

Pip barked at Verity, then ran in frantic circles.

"Oh, she has to go out," she told the maid.

"Not to fear, miss. I'll take her."

"Oh, that's kind, Mary. You have indeed done well by me." She rose. "I'm ready."

Verity brushed a hand down the skirts of the gown she'd chosen for today. The sea-green crape dress was the only one she'd not yet worn from those she'd brought with her in her trunk. With elbow-length fitted sleeves, the gown was simple. Modest, too, with a high neck without collar, and the gown fitted her bosom, caught beneath by a wide satin ribbon of ivory. With a Van Dyke trim at the hem, the gown suited her intention to appear unpretentious.

All her life, she'd understood the use of fabric and color to enhance a woman's appearance. Years going with her father to the mills had taught her much as he introduced her to dyers and pressers. Today, Verity wished to appear a credit to herself and to the man she was about to marry. A woman of taste and discretion with an eye and appreciation for the impactful moment of her marriage. She was also very aware of what Miles had told her about his first wife, and her intention was to be herself. If, thereby, she formed a natural contrast to the woman who sounded so very different from her, that was good.

Verity came out of her reverie as she saw the maid reach for the small jewelry box atop the dresser. Verity stopped her. "I'll add Lord Bellamy's earrings," and she clipped them on.

Nervous, she went for the door to the hall, but spun. "Will you take Pip down with you and keep her until tomorrow morning, please? There is so much to do, and I…" *Don't know how to proceed here, embarrassed as I am!*

"I will, miss." Mary picked up the wiggling dog and scratched under her little muzzle. "I never had a pup, and she's a sweet one."

"Thank you for everything, Mary."

She curtsied. "Ye are most welcome, miss."

Verity smiled, noting how the maid had been growing more respectful with every hour.

"I'm to transfer your clothes to the master's suite so yer ready for tonight."

Tonight. Butterflies danced in Verity's stomach. The very thought of this evening with Miles alone was one that had kept her awake at her little escritoire drawing him last night. She had done that for the past few days, ever since the North Road, and now she had dozens of renderings. She had sorted them all into batches last night. Those she thought preliminary. Those more true. Others disturbing to her because, in them, she had caught his expression, and it was one in which he agonized over an issue.

There were a few that she liked, but knew them not quite the fullness of his personality. She promised herself that over the years, she would perfect him. Happy. Happier. Accomplished. All of her illustrations, she had stuffed into her reticule. As she grew to know him better, so too would she grow in the ability to reflect his goodness to the world. What he had told her last night about his first marriage explained much about the lines at his temples. More, it revealed why when they first met, he was slow to smile. She vowed to help him erase any lines, bear any burdens, and find ways and means to help him smile.

"Miss? Is there something else?"

She caught her breath. "No, Mary. I am daydreaming. Do go to your work. But do make time to come to the wedding. Lord Bellamy and I want all of you to attend."

"I will be, miss. I'm to get your clothes during the wedding breakfast." Mary nodded as if to shoo her onward to her wedding. "Yer lovely, ma'am. A credit to us all."

IN THE MAIN salon, Verity rounded the open double doors to halt in her tracks at the sight of Miles. In formal morning attire and gleaming white satin waistcoat and ivory stock, he turned toward her with a heartfelt smile of welcome. His handsomeness stole her breath, his shock of black hair dipped over his brow, his umber eyes were agleam. She stood still, imprinting on her mind his dashing perfection. One day she would capture him not just in ink but in oils.

"Good morning," he said as he took up her hand and kissed the back. "You are beautiful, as ever."

"Your pearls help immensely," she said.

"Humility," he said with a laugh, "adds to your charm. But truth is truth."

She blushed and was surprised to feel it so forcefully at the age of twenty-four. Miles's gallantry and his praise made her proud and keen to have this ceremony over and done.

He took her arm. "Last night you met Walter, Lord Edwards,

my cousin on my mother's side. Today I wish you to meet two of my father's family." He led her to two men who sat on a settee and promptly stood to greet her. "Allow me to introduce to you my great-uncle, Mr. Willard Simpson, and his grandson, my second cousin, Mr. Dominic Frasier. Gentlemen, my bride-to-be, Miss Verity Carr."

The family resemblance among the three men was astonishing. The older man was once as tall as Miles, but was now bent with age. His hair, a silver crown, was thick and wavy like Miles's and clearly an inherited family trait. Mr. Frasier resembled Miles even more closely. Verity was astonished. Only the man's blue eyes denoted his difference. Both were jovial.

Mr. Simpson welcomed her to the family with the offer of his hand. The poor man shook with palsy. "My son and I are happy to see that Miles will ensure good looks come once more to the family."

His grandson, Dominic Frasier, offered her a wider smile. "Grandpapa and I do hope you will visit us in Norfolk."

"Uncle Willard and Cousin Dominic like good company," Miles added with merry eyes.

"What Miles means to say," said Dominic, "is that he knows we like the company of lovely ladies who might brighten our dull old halls."

"I will certainly consider the trip whenever Miles would like," she told them.

"Good," said the older man. "We have no ladies to enrich our conversation. Dominic does not yet find a lady he adores, and the search, I must say, Miss Carr, is getting tiresome. We need you in our family!"

"We've not had the company of Miles with us in far too many years," added the uncle with shrewd eyes and a hard press of her hand. "You look like a fine young woman. We hope with you Miles can forget and live again."

Dominic shot a hard look at Miles.

Verity did not move, but felt the flare of tension between the two younger men.

"Yes, well." Miles cleared his throat. "Ah, my darling, Lady Collier and Lord Edwards arrive."

"Come sit down, Grandpapa." Dominic led the older man toward the settee.

Miles took her hand. "And here is Withers with the vicar. Please come with me and meet him."

SHE TOOK HER vows with an impatience she knew was rare for a woman who had just met her groom only days before. Even though at first she had not known Lord Bellamy to be Miles St. John, she was the better for having met him as the stout-hearted man who had seen to her welfare so graciously. The wedding service, short and simple, suited her frame of mind. She was happy to be done with the formalities and indulge in the companionship of Miles's family, Lady Collier, and the vicar. The household staff had assembled at the back of the salon for the ceremony and afterward quietly left for their duties.

"Shall we go in to the dining room for breakfast?" Miles asked her. She agreed, and he offered his arm for him to lead the way down the hall.

"How did you get my wedding ring correctly sized?" she asked him as he pushed in her chair at the head table. He'd said not a word about buying the wide golden band.

"I've held your hand so often these past days I hoped this would fit."

"It's—?"

"My Grandmother Armstrong's."

The plain gold band became more precious to her knowing Miles had bestowed on her a family heirloom.

He watched while a footman filled his crystal with white wine. "A toast to you, my darling wife."

He waited while a hush fell upon those in the room.

"I wish us to drink a toast to Verity, my bride, Mrs. St. John Armstrong. Lady Bellamy. May I prove as gracious and loving a husband as you have proven to me you will be as my wife. To the bride!"

"The bride!"

"Huzzah!"

"The bride!"

They proclaimed her, and she took it with good humor. But she hoped she might merit such regard in a year, or two, or ten.

An hour later as Miles and she bade good afternoon to their guests in the foyer, she breathed in relief.

"You're tired," he said as they waved *adieu* to his uncle and cousin, who climbed into their carriage.

"I am."

"Would you like to rest? You can go up. I can retire to my study."

"No. I am not one for naps. May I see your study or have a tour of the house?" she asked, not willing to part so much as sit with him in peace.

"Of course. You haven't seen the house really. Forgive me. An oversight."

"None at all. You've had a few other things to do beside show me around."

They took the staircase to the next floor, and he led her toward the back of the house to a room off to the left.

She breathed in the air of his office. A library and also a storage room for account books, the walnut-paneled room was small, cozy even. With a large desk with gilt-edged trim, it looked more of the period of Charles II than late Georgian. But the leather wing chair and its matching settee of deep jungle brown suited the masculine tenor of the room.

"It looks out over the kitchen garden and the mews," she said in wonder as she stood at the panes and gazed below. "This is the exposure that lets in the most light." The same as that of the mistress's suite upstairs. "Might part of the bedroom suite upstairs be suitable for conversion to an artist's *atelier*?"

He came to stand behind her. He did not touch her, but she knew his nearness by the fragrance of his subtle citrusy and woodsy cologne. "Indeed, I think it might be a perfect exposure. Would you like that?"

She turned into his arms. He was so sweet, so warm and virile. She splayed her fingers and put them to his chest, but they did not span the breadth. What would it be like to know this man was hers? To have him care for her as the loving wife she intended to be? "I would like to do it, if it would make you happy too."

"I applaud the idea. The rooms are yours. Call for a mason and carpenters, painters, whomever you need. Make the change."

"I have charcoal and pencils, inks and easels and paints. They are numerous. And messy. I can often wear more paint than I put on the canvas."

"One learns by doing. Create what you must. Whatever you wear, you look wonderful to me."

She toyed with the lapel of his waistcoat. "I ran my father's house, and I am ready to make our home a haven. But I must tell you, I can become preoccupied with my art...and forget the time."

He ran a fingertip along the arch of her cheek and down along her chin. "It's good, then, that we have servants to help you keep time."

"And you won't mind that I take part of that space when it could all be a nursery?"

"You need a studio, a place of your own, a place in your home. Our home. Besides, those rooms are spacious. Use them as you will. We have time to think on where a nursery might best be."

She brightened at the idea of babies of her own. "My Aunt Agatha will be happy to hear it."

He barked in laughter. "Of that, I am most curious! Will she be happiest that you have a studio or that you contemplate a nursery?"

"Both!"

"Marvelous," he said. "Will she drink to it?"

"I do hope so."

"Why not have her come to visit us?" He lifted her chin and brushed the pad of his thumb along the outline of her lower lip.

"She would welcome the invitation."

"Have her, then. Here and in York."

"York will suit her, especially if we send her your very comfortable traveling coach."

"She could not come to London?" he asked, his attention not on her aunt, but on her mouth.

"No. Too far. And she is too frail. Seventy-eight. Very bright, but often, brittle."

"I like a woman with mettle," he said with humor, but came closer to breathe the next words to her lips. "She is like you."

Verity wrapped her arms around his back and curled against him. "She will like you."

"Thank God," he whispered, and took her mouth. His kiss was hot, but brief.

"Kiss me again," she urged, her eyes closed, her heart lost to the euphoria he created inside her.

Her request was barely said when he cupped her nape and claimed her mouth with a new boldness she attributed to his being her husband. His kiss was all persuasion, soft and gentle. His passion quick and then gone, he pulled away. "It is the afternoon, and we should be conversing."

"Is not kissing conversation?" she asked with a hoyden's tease.

He hugged her, then paused to pin her with a fierce gaze. "It is. Tell me what my kisses have told you."

"That you like me."

He put his lips on hers and said, "True."

"And that you want me," she said, and tipped her head, her heart alight with laughter.

"From the moment I first saw you on the road," he confessed, then sank his hands into her coiffure and took away her flowers and pins. Her hair fell over her shoulders, curling over her breast to her waist and down her back.

He caught up handfuls of it and smoothed the tresses over her shoulders, a man captured.

"I could not see you at first in the snowstorm," she told him. "Not really. Only your silhouette. I thought, my heavens," she said, running her hands over the magnificent length of his arms and up over his shoulders to cup his throat, "such a stern and beautiful creature."

"I frightened you?" He paused, and looked aghast that he'd hurt her.

She shook her head and ran her fingertips up his corded throat to tangle in the satin strands of his midnight hair, behind his ears. "You were come to me as black on white. A dashing rescuer in the snow. I discover more of you each day, each hour, each minute with you. I cannot keep up with this new man who appears to me and whom I must sketch with haste and color with new hues. The blues of your generosity. The purples of your ambition. The reds of your passion."

He put one hand beneath her chin and held her there, his eyes ablaze. "I rein in that passion."

"Must you?" she asked with hope and a roaring desire that buzzed in her head.

"Ah, my wife." He molded her to his large and stalwart frame. "I do not wish to send you fleeing from me."

"You won't."

He brought her even closer, his long legs against hers. "I have ambitions to delight you."

"As do I for you. For how could I want you so badly, if I did not feel in my heart that I could trust you with my life?"

Tears sprang to his eyes. "How can that be? We met only days ago."

"Is time the measure of a person's sympathy with another?"

She shook her head. "I think not."

With a look of wonder, he gazed down into her eyes. "Your faith in me is…unparalleled. You are far more than I ever expected. More than I thought myself worth. I am, my darling, awed."

"Oh," she said. "I am the one who is in awe. I want you to be mine. My equal. My friend. My lover."

He ran a hand through the curls at her ear. "I wish that, too."

Wistful, mad with hope, and not a little curious about the act of becoming his wife, she said, "How soon do you wish it?"

He groaned and put his lips to her forehead. "Yesterday."

She laughed.

Then he said, "We must wait until your maid is done."

She rolled her eyes. "How long do you think that takes?"

He went quite still, save for the mighty evidence against her stomach that he hoped it might be soon. "Days. Weeks. Months!"

She rose on her toes and kissed him, deeply. And just as she claimed him, he took her to him with a mighty embrace, then broke it off, gasping.

"That's it!" he said. His hand to hers, he marched her out the door and up the stairs. "She's done."

Chuckling, she hurried to keep pace. "Or she will be."

Chapter Nine

ONCE VERITY WAS in his suite, nerves hit her and she hung back.

He turned. The look on his face spoke of desire suddenly dwarfed by empathy and another emotion that stunned her. Pride. "I understand," he said, and in those two words, she sagged in relief.

She went to him, her arms around his sturdy shoulders, and pressed her cheek to his chest.

He stroked a hand down her spine. "We are in no rush."

"But if we hesitate, when will we know the time is right?"

He nestled his lips into her hair. "We have all our lives to figure that out."

She pulled back and grimaced at him. "If we wait until we're old and gray and cannot walk, then—"

"Good God. I hope not that long!"

"Nor I!"

He led her toward the settee not far from the small fire behind the grate. They sat side by side, and he kept her hand in his. "We speak of other things. What would you think if we went to Brighton on a few days' honeymoon?"

"Oh, yes! I've never been to the sea."

"We could walk the beach. Eat ices. Stroll around the Regent's Pavilion."

"And where would we stay?"

"A hotel in the center of town on the coast." He toyed with her wedding ring.

She worried that privacy might be lacking. "Would we take servants?"

"No. One hires as one needs from the hotel," he told her.

"So you have been to Brighton before?"

He nodded, appearing at once brimming with remembered joy. "Twice. First when I was a boy. My parents took me for a holiday. We rented a house for a week. It was glorious, sunny, with the air smelling of salt. Then later, when I was twenty, my father took me in the heat of August. He had meetings with other men who owned mills like ours. I learned how to swim."

"I would like to swim."

He looked surprised. "The sea is cold."

"But it's supposed to be invigorating. Good for your health."

"Still, it's a challenge. We'll rent a bathing machine."

"I like that idea. What are those machines like? Do they move?"

He described how they appeared to be boxes on wheels, towed into the surf by horses and left there. "You emerge from a door into the water and splash about. It's fun if you don't freeze to death first. But no matter. We can do so much more. At night, we'll go to the local subscription balls and dance. Do you like to dance?"

"I do. Do you?"

"I have not in many years."

"Why is that?" she asked, but then she thought herself callous to ask because he'd told her his marriage had not been happy. "I apologize. I should have—"

"No need to do that. I always did like to dance, and now have good reason to again."

She beamed at him. "I am so glad you do these things again. Things you like."

"I do them because you will be with me." He lifted her hand

and placed a kiss there. But then he rose. "I need a glass of brandy. Will you join me?"

She understood that he was confounded how to proceed with their afternoon. She had few ideas herself and followed him to the sideboard. "Yes, I would. Please."

As he handed her a glass, he said, "Tell me other things you love."

PAINFULLY AWARE THEY had known each other only days, he did not wish to rush her into bed. She was a virgin, young and new to passion, as once he too had been. He would not ravage her. They needed more familiarity to come to a marriage bed. Though he did not wish to wait forever, nor return to the celibacy he'd declared for himself, he would not charge the gates, either. No matter how willing she was, she was a woman who had come to this union with reason and clarity of mind. Far better that than a mind filled with lust and the expectations of a marriage built on sexuality alone. He had had that kind of marriage, and look what hell that had brought him.

She took her glass and raised it to him. "To my husband who understands me already."

"You are kind, madam. Tell me what you love."

"The fragrance of flowers. Roses, best, I think. I'd like to grow them. Have you any at your home in York?"

"Difficult to grow, but we could hire a gardener to aid you."

"I do not wish to run up costs. But I like that idea. And now, I have those funds…" She trailed off, as if she considered them and rued their existence. "I have money to pay for such things."

"I did not wed you to have you pay for the betterment of our lives with your own money. A gardener we shall have." He took a sip of his drink and considered how sweet she looked in her sea green with her hair all around her shoulders. Would it not be grand to find that wealth of hair around her naked and bare to him? He inhaled. "What else?"

"I like books. Histories. Fiction."

"And you will have at your disposal all we have here and in York."

She sipped her brandy and, upon reflection, asked, "Do you like the theater?"

He fought the old hatred rising in him like gorge. To give in to it would not be fair to her. What betrayal had once happened in a theater's box had soured him for plays. That was not rational. But he could change. He could! She was a different woman who liked theater for its intrinsic values. Not for the privacy it afforded for adultery.

"I see you don't." She looked stricken. "I'm sorry."

"Don't be. I do like good acting." *Only on stage.* "Tell me, do you like to go?"

"I've been only to village plays and a few in Bradford. But I had hoped we might go in London."

"And we shall. In Brighton, too."

"Oh, that would be delightful." A smile of expectation wreathed her lovely features. "What do you like best? What kinds of plays, I mean."

"Comedies." He was truthful, remembering what pleased him most. "Shakespeare's histories."

She shook back her flowing hair. "I once saw a production of *Othello*. It was…heartbreaking."

He winced. She'd hit on the very play he despised. The memories, the similarities, gutted him.

She put a hand to his arm. "You've gone cold."

Perceptive of her.

"Will you tell me why?"

He had buried that part of his life. Hadn't he? "The betrayal of a trusted retainer leaves me…bereft."

"I see," she said as if she backed off the edge of a cliff. "I know it happens all too often. You think you are safe with someone.

You trust them, but then you learn to your shock you are quite alone."

She strode away from him and put down her glass on a table. "I had a friend who spurned me. It was a shock. She…she tried to get me to do something for her, and I feared it was not she who asked but her husband."

He felt a black abyss appear before him. What he had seen before with her mention of *Othello* brought back one disaster, but here she had her own. He went to her and put his arms around her and drew her near. "She failed you."

"Yes. Yes, she did. But for a long time, months, even, after her untimely death, I thought it was I who had failed her. I learned…later that was not so. I also learned…"

What?

"That she was entirely different from the person I thought her to be. I was shocked. Heartbroken for her. For myself, too."

"I understand that. I had a similar experience." What irony that the very part of his past he wished to eradicate had returned to him in the midst of refreshing his life with a new wife who was so much more honorable than the first?

"I tell myself," she said with sorrow lining her brow, "that what I saw in my friend, her face, how her features changed over the years, are visions I will never forget. Not because I do not wish to. I do. But because those images reveal to me the subtle changes in a human's expressions are the very essences of what I wish to capture in my drawings. Ultimately, too, in portraits of others."

"That's why I see you drawing so many versions of the same subject."

She cocked her head, pleased he noticed so much about her. "Yes! Mostly of myself. I tire of drawing me!"

"But you've drawn others. Withers, was it not, yesterday?"

"I wanted a new subject."

"You were drawing me that first day on the road in the coach."

"I was taken by you, even then. Yes, I have drawn you. Repeatedly!"

"Will you show them to me?"

She considered it with a whimsical roll of her eyes. "I am not expert. Not yet."

He went to her and traced the elegant arc of her cheek with one finger. "I would never disparage what you do."

"That I know." She caught his hand and held it to her face. "But in all things, I wish to do you justice, sir."

A truth flooded through him and, without censure, he told her, "You graced me with more than that this morning. A stranger to you, I asked your name to be mine and your faith that I care for you until your last breath also be in me. Even though you have that newfound wealth, we both know that law and custom in this country mean that your desires, even your health, especially should you become pregnant, are in my keeping. Your aspirations in art are your own. Your success will be too. In that as in all you wish, I support you and encourage you."

"I do not ask for more," she whispered, putting both hands to his chest.

He caught her up against him, his arms binding her to him so dearly that he felt each heart beat strong and true. Here he found more than the woman he had met on the road. "And I ask for few other things greater than that."

She hooked her arm around his shoulders then and kissed him. Kissed him as he'd never been so before. Eager and unsophisticated, she placed her lips on his in a rushed embrace. He was hard put to breathe, but in all else he was as if laid open. Wanting her, craving her as he had for days, he found himself suffused with the need to take her lips and show her all. His tongue swept in to claim her, and she took it. His hands ran over her, and she gave herself up to him.

She whirled, presenting her back. "Undo this, all of it."

Nimble and quick, he released the buttons of her gown, the laces of her corset, and pushed the fabrics across her shoulders and down. Her skin was flawless. Her arms, bare and free of garments, held up the cloth as he caressed her nape. At once, she let them go, and they dropped to the carpet. Now only in her shift, she twirled to face him, her eyes limpid in the lamplight. With a tug, she lifted the last garment away and stood naked to him as the cotton whooshed to the floor.

His breath came in hard, hot beats. If he dared to be so bold as to look at all she offered him, he believed he'd diminish the purity of her offering, and send her running from so ribald a creature as he. Fixed on her luminous eyes, he sensed lovely, pointed breasts and ripe pink nipples. The rest of her, coolly elegant and full of expectation, belonged to him. He trembled, honored at what she gave, determined that all he had he would give.

He lifted her chin, catching up long, loose, fragrant tresses about her throat. "You are beyond beautiful, my dear wife."

She took his hand and led him, like an obedient man, toward his bedroom.

Following behind, he wanted to memorize the beauty of her heart-shaped bottom. Her trim thighs. Her long feet, soft and certain, trod upon the rugs. She went to his own bed, where she sat upon the edge and lay down, a pagan offering to his tortured soul. She drew him slowly by the hand to sit beside her.

He hovered there, taking in long views of her naked skin. From her pointed toes and little ankles up to her cute knees and thighs, she was a graceful line. At the flare of her hips and the pale curls that covered her feminine center, she was a temptress. To her curved waist to the bounty of her heavy breasts, she was more than the lush beauty he had once envisioned. She was incomparable.

"Come here," she said as she attacked his buttons and cravat. "You've far too many clothes, sir. I need you to blush as I am."

"Blushing, my dear, is not what I'm doing." He rose to the occasion, more furiously than before.

"Well then, prove it to me. I am cold and one big goosebump

of anxiety."

He stood, whipped off his coat and waistcoat, then stripped off his shirt, naked to her from waist up.

She waggled a finger at him. "More, more."

In a rush, he pulled off his shoes and socks, and finally his breeches too. There before her he was bare of all pretense. His cock, long and painfully erect, told her all she might need to know about his desire for her.

She studied it and licked her lips. "My goodness," she murmured with a little squeak. "Now I understand how farmers talk of plowing fields."

He sputtered at her reference.

"Will it fit?" she asked in wide-eyed sincerity.

"Indeed," he blurted.

"Oh!" Her cheeks burned with embarrassment. "I won't ask how."

"Carefully," he said as he came to her and took her hand, then wrapped her fingers around his aching length. *My God, she feels good.* "This is what I am. Learn me as I will you. I will not hurt you or harm you."

She squeezed him and learned his length while he took measured breaths and sorted his intentions. He would fit. He'd had years of practice ensuring that his penis fit into women of all sizes. Before he married, he'd thought he knew all there was to learn about putting his cock into any willing and eager lady. He had not forgotten the finer points, but had long ago discarded the practice. He'd cast aside any memories of seduction to develop the finer abilities of enchantment.

He bent over her and took her lips in a light press of his intentions. "You'll tell me if anything disturbs you. Like this." He swept one hand down her throat to completely cover one large, warm breast. In his palm her nipple grew hot and hard.

She wiggled.

"What do you think?" he asked.

"Lovely."

He crawled onto the bed beside her and bent to kiss the silken nipple and make it blossom in his mouth. He laved her, and she moaned. "Shall we see if the other is as eager?"

She made some small mewling sound in her throat that he took for agreement, then he took her up into his mouth with the longing he could not contain. Against his tongue, her areola was gossamer soft, the flesh beneath it torrid with desire.

He could not get enough of her quickly enough. His palm overflowing with her full breast, he licked her, and laved her to a daring point. She panted, her nails digging into his arms.

Her legs, restless, sought purchase on the bed.

And he sank between them, lifting her thigh and hooking it over his hip. There, so close to her center, he knew her heat and his cock nudged her wet flesh. Too soon, he told himself, but she wriggled beneath him, spreading wide her other leg and letting him oh so near her center.

Alarms rang in his head that he'd rushed her. Could hurt her. He longed to sink into her but would not take her so soon. She had to come with him.

Years of hungering for a woman in his bed had him rejoicing that at last he was here with her. He reached for her lips, eager, needy. She clung to him, arching up at his kiss, clutching him closer with her legs up around his back. He could easily sink inside her and take all of her. Yet he worried.

He pushed her down and sent little kisses down her stomach and across her hips. Starving for years for a willing woman in his bed was nothing to starving for days for this darling woman in his arms. Now the feel of her silken belly and the fragrance of her musky desire lured him beyond his fears he'd rush her or offend her. With two bold hands to her inner thighs, he opened her wide.

She gasped and rolled up to watch what he did.

With his thumbs, he spread out her frilly, glistening folds and put his tongue to the succulent length of her. She tasted of salt and sweet surrender as she fell back to the mattress. She was his now, open, trusting, wet and eager. Clutching the counterpane with anguished hands, she groaned as he tasted her and teased her, laved her and pleased her. And as long as she loved it, he went on.

Slick and saucy, she writhed as he ate her. When he found her little mound, he licked that and sent her keening. But he slowed and sucked her until she crooned a low, long note that told him his time had come.

Two hands to her open thighs, he rose and took her to him, inch by inch. Her surprise was nothing to her rippling delight, and his surging satisfaction was nothing to his triumph when he drove deep and shuddered to make her his own. All his own. Never anyone's but his.

SHE GATHERED HIM close, her breath hard and deep, his body still inside her. What heaven he had shown her was lusty and vigorous. The pulsing sensations still breaking inside her had her curling to him, wanting his succor, and craving the clutch of his body. She had not known coupling could be so enthralling. So rapturous. Her mind was gone, her heart racing, her loins needing him inside her, there, just there. How could she let him go?

He rose on one elbow and brushed her hair from her cheeks. His smile was beneficent, as if they had merely told each other little stories instead of shared their wildest secret selves in intimate communion. Laying a finger across her lips, he urged her to silence and lethargy. In a few minutes, he was back with warm cloths to her private places.

And she wanted none of his ministrations.

"Not that," she told him, and pushed away his hand with the cloth. "This," she said as she brought his hand back to her breast and its hardening flesh. "This is what I want."

And in sweet response, he was sucking her aching nipples into his mouth again, using his tongue and fingers to repeat the pleasure she thought must be her bride's madness. This time, as he massaged her to a maddening throb, he slid inside her and joined her in the journey. He groaned, long and loud, when he was done, and they rolled together, flowing one against the other, no beginning and no end.

She marveled that they clung, arcs to planes and curving muscle to bone. She sighed. He took her lips in a drugging kiss, his hands binding her to him as he wound her long hair around and around his fists.

And then they slept.

HOURS HAD GONE when he woke. Startled at the night sky spread beyond his bedroom window, he wished to know the hour. He strolled into his sitting room to see the clock, but did not recall shutting the connecting door. At once he understood when he saw a large tray upon the sideboard. Withers had come at some point with the tray of sandwiches, sweet tarts, and a large pot of tea. Miles put a hand to the belly of the pot and found it still warm. He poured a cup and returned to his wife.

She lay, languid as he had left her, but now her eyes were open, drowsy with sleep and passion. "Hello, husband—what have you got?"

"Tea to warm you." He leaned over her and offered the cup.

She rose, her breasts bare and bouncing, the sheets falling from her like she were a statue of some goddess unveiled. And then she bypassed the cup of tea and drank from him a lurid kiss. "Mmm," she said, and licked her lower lip. "I like that much better than whatever's in that cup."

"I agree, but you need your strength." He put the cup into her hand.

"Because we will do that again?" She was a winsome girl.

And he, poor fellow, could not refuse the tease. He took the cup, put it down on the bedside table, and gathered her up against him. His hands were full of graceful spine and lush buttock, and his heart was full of something he had once called love. Something he knew enough now to never name.

He cupped her behind her head and kissed her swollen lips thoroughly. "Yes, Mrs. Armstrong. We do that again. Now. Because you are generous and delicious, my darling. And I am quite smitten."

Chapter Ten

MILES OPENED TODAY'S *Sussex Advertiser* in search of the description he'd scanned yesterday of bathing machines for rent. He and Verity had come to Brighton six days ago. They'd come sans servants, leaving even Pip in London in care of Verity's maid Mary. Today, the weather was much warmer than previously. Not that they'd thought of doing much else but strolling the walk along the rocky beach, eating fresh seafood in the local cafes—and returning to the privacy of their suite to make love.

Every afternoon after their stroll, they would climb the stairs to their rooms. He would lock the doors against all interruptions and carefully undo each button of her gown, reveal her shoulders and her pointed breasts, and take her unabashed and naked in his arms. There, with a surprising hunger, he enjoyed a rapture he had feared was never to be his to have or hold. She came to him with sighing ardor and became to him his true mate. In those blinding erotic moments, he feared the hour when she learned he could never return the gift of love she so reverently bestowed on him.

His gaze strayed to her. His wife, his partner of merely days, had slowly transformed into the friend of his sunlit hours and the siren of his sexually abandoned nights. She sat in their chaise longue, her morning gown of embroidered muslin complementing the natural glow of her cheeks. She nibbled at her lower lip, her long, wavy red-gold hair unbound over the natural line of her shoulders and full breasts, her head tilted as she ran her pencil across her sketchbook to draw him.

She did this each morning they'd been here. Her practice, she'd told him, was to draw early each day when her mind was clear and her ideas fresh, unfiltered. As of yet, she'd not allowed him to study her work.

He did not push her. He could wait. After all, he understood that the best things developed with time. Dyes for new colors, flowers, art—and his good fortune to have found such a treasure as she. His new wife.

He shook out his paper and read about increase of the packet business between Brighton and Dieppe, owing to the end of hostilities. Refugees and former prisoners of war flooded the little town. Verity and he had commented to each other about the crowded streets. A new wool bill was before Parliament. He'd ask for further information on it from his cloth agent when they returned to London. The war's end would open up new markets. He made a mental note to have his agent examine new shipping rates and any new ship-building companies that might offer better fees for service. He did not think he'd dabble in wool, but one never knew where business might lead.

Society notes included the statement that a cousin of the regent was to arrive in Brighton today—and that the Earl of Albermarle was still in town. Miles found both irrelevant, as he had never met either man.

News too was that Lady Harley was to give a ball tomorrow night at her home on the Steine, the main thoroughfare through town. Two mornings ago, Verity and he had received an invitation to the lady's event. Verity had been eager to go. He could deny her nothing and, in fact, had insisted she seek out a modiste here in town to see if she might sew quickly a new ball gown. He'd gone with Verity to her shop and liked the Italian jade silk she'd chosen. The seamstress would have the gown ready tomorrow afternoon. As for Lady Harley, Miles had met her once years ago, when very young. In fact, he met her on the same occasion he'd met Lady Peregrine, the aunt of Germaine Hammond, the publisher of the *Fleet Chronicle*, where he'd placed his ad for a wife.

He skimmed the next few sentences, then paused to reread the last.

Among the few arrivals of the past week we have to notice Sir H. Parnell, bart; Hon. Mrs. Dawson; and Lord and Lady Bellamy, newly married last week by special license in London.

How had the newspaper learned details of his marriage? He understood that Verity and he had been seen here in town. Day before yesterday, he'd greeted in the lanes two of his associates in the cloth business and introduced Verity as his wife. The men—here with their spouses to take the air and celebrate the end of the wars—told him they were eager to meet with him to coordinate expanding their sales to foreign markets. He'd put them off until he returned to York next month, explaining he and Verity were on their honeymoon. But he'd said nothing about a small ceremony, nor that it was by special license.

He ought to chase away his worry about gossip. What did he expect, anyway? All would learn of his second marriage eventually. They would comment or not, approve or not. Sooner or later, they would see that he was happily married, too. A good thing.

He glanced at Verity. She sat, not drawing now, but the stub of her pencil rested against her lovely cheek.

"What troubles you?" she asked him in that pleasure-soaked voice that roused his senses.

"It seems," he said with a light shake of his head as he put his paper to the dining table, "we are famous."

"How so?" she asked, her pencil now in her lap.

"Our marriage is announced in the local newspaper."

Concern chased away the nonchalance on her face. "How do they know that?"

She disliked the news released more than he. He frowned.

"My associates, Mr. Carton and Mr. Fuller, and their wives must have spread the word about."

"May I see that?" She was up, her hand out for the paper.

He gave it over, his dismay over hers growing. "What do you think?" he asked, trying to be lighthearted about it as she read it and cringed.

"They don't list my maiden name."

No.

"Nor where I come from." She dropped the paper to her side and strode to the window that overlooked the Marine Parade.

"Is that an issue?" Alert to her stiff demeanor, he recalled how she'd seemed troubled in London the day she learned from her solicitors of her inheritance.

SHE SET HER teeth. This was silly of her. Disclosure of their marriage was a small matter, since it had not come with her maiden name or home village. It should not create panic in a bride whose wedding announcement appeared in the newspaper. Any paper. Heavens, there were so many! Often papers reprinted what had been reported in others. She should have expected a report of her marriage. She was not noteworthy. But Miles was a prominent man, a viscount, a businessman, a well-known mill owner. Two of his friends had hailed him the other day in the little alley where he and she had bought pastries in the bakery shop. This announcement should not be as disturbing as she made it out to be.

Yet she scrutinized the pedestrians in the street below. Their carriages, too. No one looked remotely familiar. Not like that other day in the City when she'd thought she glimpsed Thomas Frobisher. They all appeared so far away, three stories beneath her, and whom could she really recognize? No one. Truly, no one down in those streets resembled his slim, sharp form. No one.

"Verity?"

She owed her husband answers for her behavior. She spun to face him. "I'm being too sensitive."

"You are. Why?" He narrowed his gaze on her. "If they *had* listed your maiden name and home, would that have bothered you?"

She had not fully answered his question. She needed to try to lead him to the matter without appalling him. "Many will eventually know. I am proud to have married you. I just wanted it to be our secret for a while."

He did not take his eyes off her.

Oh, yes. His stern façade told her much about how he processed her explanation. She understood his point of view—and what he lacked. She owed him more. "There is someone I do not wish to learn of my whereabouts or my marriage. Not soon. Not ever, if that is even possible."

He waited.

She swallowed her reluctance. "He is the husband of the friend of mine who…turned from me. He is mean, vindictive. I wish never to see him again."

Miles folded his hands in his lap. "Does he wish to see you?"

A note in Miles's voice sent shivers through her. "I doubt it. When last I saw him, I was outraged, furious. I insulted him." *Cursed him.* "He deserved it."

"So you can be dangerous when you are angry?" At a question of her character, his was cool, almost impersonal.

She shrugged. "Cannot we all be when provoked?" she asked like it was her bane to be so incensed by that man. "He was ugly to my friend, my cousin. And when I learned of it, I wanted her to leave him. I urged her to do so." She turned to watch the street again but saw only Amanda, her bruised face and hands, and her sorrow that her marriage had become a nightmare. "She refused."

"I see," Miles said in such a way that she heard he'd accepted her explanation and his anger had gone. "Then, my dear, on the off chance that this man ever appears, I demand that you alert me."

She pressed her lips together. "I would."

The street below had cleared. As if her worries should too.

Miles came to her and put his arms around her. He was gentle, his lips warm beneath her ear. The natural exuberance she felt emerging from him more each day cancelled the bitter taste of her revelation to him. "Now then, for our afternoon," he said as he hugged her back against him, "shall we rent that bathing machine?"

Chapter Eleven

TWO NIGHTS LATER, Lady Harley took Verity arm in arm toward the supper laid out beyond the ballroom in the seaside Old Ship Hotel. "Lord Bellamy tells me you are in Brighton for the first time."

"That is true," Verity told their hostess. The ball was given by Lady Harley and her husband in the assembly room of the grand hotel fronting on the beach. More than one hundred guests had come to dance and dine to celebrate the ascension of Louis XVIII to the throne of his ancestors. The ballroom, for brilliance and fashion, was decorated with wreaths of laurel and white flags embroidered with crowns and fleur-de-lis. The band that played was from the First Surrey Militia. "The musicians are excellent, ma'am. I've never been to so elegant an affair as this."

Lady Harley patted her hand. "Bellamy looks very proud of you, my dear. As he should be. I predict he will bring you out to us all with regularity."

"I do hope so." Verity leaned closer so that her husband might not hear her. "He dances so well, and I think I must show him off."

The older lady chuckled. Her precarious green silk turban wobbling on her head, she winked at Verity. "The poor boy did not have a chance to show his skills before. I am delighted he enjoys himself. Tell me, has he badgered you to go swimming yet?"

"Indeed, ma'am. We did that day before yesterday." Verity felt herself blushing. The adventure of disrobing in the tiny bathing machine and swimming in the nude had been exhilarating. Miles and she had made love in the tiny wooden structure with a speed that warmed them both. "We asked the owner of the machines to take us up to a secluded place near Hove."

"Ha! To the west. Private there, true. And will you go again?"

"I will."

"Good for you." Lady Harley led Verity to her and her husband's head table and awaited both men, who were detained by greeting another gentleman. Another fellow approached Lady Harley. "Ah, here is Lord Croyden."

"Good evening, my dear Lady Harley." A tall blond fellow with a craggy, ready smile made a bow to them both. "Forgive my tardiness to arrive so late, madam."

"A matter of cards, Croyden?" Lady Harley regarded him with a jovial but critical eye.

"Very bad ones, I'm afraid. I left as quickly as I could. And I am happy to be here now. Especially because I see you have very fine company with you. Do make me acquainted, would you?"

Lady Harley paused, the moment pregnant with a reluctance not lost on Verity. "I can. You will be proper, Croyden."

"Always, ma'am." He grinned at Verity. "How could one be other, with such a beauty?"

Verity stiffened her spine. Was he a rogue? She'd take odds.

Certainly, Lord Croyden fit Verity's image of a polished man of the town. Ladies—she had the most dangerous feeling tingling up her spine—must dangle after him. With a debonair superiority about him, he lifted her hand and kissed her glove in homage. Saying the right words, he meant to compliment her. But his merry blue gaze did not warm her as he stopped to devour her lips and twice over savor the measure of her breasts. No. He chilled her to the bone.

And when Miles appeared at her side to wrap her arm in his,

she pressed back into his possession. She glanced up and stilled at the unique emotion in her husband's eyes. Contempt.

"Lord Bellamy." The man inclined his head. His blue eyes grew narrow, the mien of a thief about him. "I have had the honor of meeting your new wife."

"You will leave us now, Croyden." Miles gave him no quarter.

"So unkind, Bellamy. Do regard that all can see."

"Let them."

Lady Harley said not a word to alleviate the tension.

Verity felt the security of her husband's tightening embrace.

The two men did not move an inch, but stood, glaring at each other.

But it was Croyden who blinked, tipped his head, and left the field.

Verity wished only to go home and find forgetfulness in her husband's arms. Why that should be with Croyden exchanging only a few words with them both, she could put to one feeling. The man seemed…salacious.

Miles watched him go, his umber gaze aflame with hate, his mouth in a severe line of distaste.

"Are you well?" Miles bent to asked her minutes later when the Harleys were in conversation together and the other guests were devoted to dining. He'd been silent, almost brooding, as they chose their supper dishes from the serving tables. She wanted to know why, but she was too off balance from the interchange with Croyden to ask.

"I am, thank you." She picked though her roast beef and potatoes, suddenly nauseated with her realization that Croyden reminded her of the very man she'd come south to escape. Another type, a different set of goals, but nonetheless a creature who defined a woman by her vulnerable sexuality.

"You are not eating. Yet you said you were hungry."

She inhaled. "I did not like him." She dared not name the man, lest others overhear. *Yet I wish to clean my palate of him.*

"Your instincts are correct, my darling. I'm shocked he's here. But then, he is always where he is not wanted. But not near me or you."

"Is he a business colleague of yours?"

"No." Miles stared at her. "He's a rotter of the lowest order."

The man had something to do with Miles's first wife, then. Croyden had hurt her, or…?

Verity wished to know. Ask. Understand. But she shouldn't be intrusive.

With a clatter, she dropped her fork. Her hands shook.

Miles caught both and stilled the chaos rampant in her blood. "Forget him. You never have to speak to him again."

"I don't wish to." The panic in her soul told her that she might never escape men like Croyden. They would be forever in her path. "It appears the Harleys prepare to go. How long must we stay here?"

"Not a minute more. I'll take you up." He brushed a hand along her cheek.

True to his word, as the Harleys stood to return to the ballroom, Miles led her away. She picked up her skirts, and the two of them raced along the hall, hand in hand, up the back stairs. At the landing, Verity pushed back the urge to weep, she was so thankful that Miles had whisked her away. She caught him back and hugged him. "Oh, Miles, I am so glad to have found you. Never leave me, will you?"

"Never. You belong to me, my sweet. I to you. Come upstairs. We will celebrate that once again."

HE RELEASED THE covered buttons of her new ball gown one at a time. The emerald-green gros de naples silk was the finest, and he'd picked it out the other day at the modiste's for Verity to wear tonight. His beauty, his wife, he wished to show off to society. She was his delight, and Brighton society, including many of his business associates, found her as charming as he had from the very start. He loved the gown, and she'd wear it again. But at this moment, he wanted her out of it. Naked to him, for him to love.

With a kiss to her nape and her shoulder for each button he took away, he sought to fix in her mind that she would always want him, prefer him, need him. And no other.

God knew, Verity was the one he needed, and he would never want for any other. She'd stood like the strong and sensitive woman she was tonight as that mongrel inserted himself into Lady Harley's presence when Miles was otherwise engaged. How astute of the fiend to take advantage of her split second alone to try to mark her.

The cur. Scouting, tracking a female like a beast in rut, dedicated to carving her out when her mate was occupied. It was what he'd done with so many women. Arriving late. Seeking privileges from hosts and hostesses. Swooping in to compliment, enthrall, and seduce.

Francesca had regarded the creature as a master of the hunt. Finding willing girls to train to abandon themselves to all manner of wanton appetites. Keeping them anxious and needy. Plied by liquor and Chinese tinctures of opium. After such induction, many led lives in the *ton* known for their questionable appetites. But a few proved incapable of maintaining the distance between the demands of their unconventional desires and those of society's barriers. Those they had ruined whispered of their indoctrination. Few left their ways to journey back to normality.

Miles would forget him. He would. As he had before tonight's reminder. Here, where he had found the way to live a life filled with beauty and light. Here, with his new wife.

He smoothed the silk from his wife's shoulders and let it fall to the floor. To take her like a gentleman who revered her, he worked silently and diligently on her half-corset and rid her of her shift. Then he slowly turned her.

Dazed and eager for him, she met his gaze in their moonlit room with the desire and enchantment for which he praised her. She was his everything. Smart, sensitive, insightful. And oh, yes. He drifted his open palms over the ripe mounds of her breasts and her hard, rosy nipples. To brush them was all he needed to spike his cock higher. He'd not thrilled to a woman so much in years. Nor with such honest devotion. He licked the tip of one round breast, and she mewled. He smiled. He was becoming a randy bugger, but he loved her.

He froze.

He was about to suck her sweet nipple into his mouth, but he told himself *no*. He must discipline himself. Yet his cock jumped, strained, demanding to be buried inside her. But *no*, he chastised himself again. That desire was not because he loved her. He did not. He admired her. Desired her. Could not stop himself from taking her at every hour of the day or night. But what he felt for her was not love.

Never love.

That was dangerous. Destructive.

His wariness died in the wake of a frenzy to lave her, take her, put her to the bed and offer her the homage he could give her. His hands, his tongue, his teeth and cock.

He set his teeth. In control again, he licked her large, lovely nipple. Then bent her over his arm and took her other breast. She sighed and dug her nails into the wool of his frockcoat.

As so often before, he swept her up into his embrace. All his, his alone—he could possess her as if he strode the world with her, the one man she should ever need. He put her to the mattress, and he'd gone to rise to disrobe when she caught him.

One hand to his cheek, she fixed him there. "You still think of him. Why?"

"He is a letch."

"But he is not here. Not important. Not to me. Never was or can be."

He nodded. *Yes.* He saw her. Heard her. Verity. Who spoke truth.

"I don't want him or any other man. Somehow I fear you think I would."

He dropped a hot kiss into her palm. It was so unfair of him to think she was anything like his first wife. "I want to brand you as mine. So that no one will ever take you."

"No one ever will." She led him down and kissed him with all the passion she'd ever poured into him. "I swear it. How can you assure yourself that's so?"

He took her invitation. A man of need and wild desire, he would be the one to have her as he wished. So he took her to him in the caring ways a man coupled with a woman. He had her on her back, her strong thighs spread wide as he plunged into her, and she rose, urging him onward. He gave as he had not before.

If he thought of why that was, the reason flashed past his brain. Tomorrow, he promised himself he'd explore that.

For that moment, he drowned in the symphony of her skin sliding over his, her kisses wet and lingering. He took her to the height of need; her thighs clamped his hips as he plunged into her, and she cried in unison with their thrusts. Yet he did not want this done, and withdrew to prolong the ecstasy. She objected and thumped his shoulder with her fist. He kissed her fingers and sank his own inside her wet folds to lead her to arch up, reaching for her climax. Then he came back inside her, his cock buried so deep, he could not say how they blended, nor if his cries were hers. This time, they both claimed the bliss they sought.

After it all, she slept. For minutes, he gazed at her, her glorious hair a riot upon their linens, her breathing deep. Exhaustion claiming him at last, he kissed her swollen lips and promised never to doubt she belonged to only him.

They did not rise until after noon the next day.

Then he called for a bath, where he crawled in first, took her to him, and bathed every inch of her hair and gossamer skin.

All his.

Only his.

His wife.

Chapter Twelve

**No. 18 Upper Brook Street
Mayfair, London**

Two days later, Miles and Verity returned to London. He had scheduled meetings with owners of a new shipping company bound regularly for British settlements along the Gaspe Peninsula and into Quebec. He planned to increase his exports of cotton cloth to compete with those produced in the new United States. But his specialty—muslin dyed Prussian blue—was also being produced more cheaply in the former colonies. Planters in South Carolina grew the indigo plant quickly and cheaply. Miles had to find a new dye or a new market in order to make any profit. He did not elaborate on his problems to Verity, wanting to concentrate on other issues with her.

"I also want us to see the celebrations in Hyde Park for the peace of Europe," Miles told her the fourth morning they were home. He put his newspaper to the breakfast table and finished his coffee. "The Russian tsar will attend, and many German princes."

"That should be a grand affair," she said, then told Pip to seek her bed in the downstairs kitchen. "I'd like to go. There will not be anything like it ever again."

"There will be fireworks and pantomimes for four days in

mid-June. After that, I wish to go north to York. Will you be finished with the refurbishment of the bedroom suite by then?"

"I think so," she told him. She'd ordered a division of the rooms into a small art studio for her near the windows and, nearer the master suite, a nursery with an adjacent room for a nurse. A mason and carpenter had begun work last week. "I will check with the carpenter, who was sectioning off the back room for my studio, and ask if he'll be finished. Even so, he should have most of his work completed. The painter can do his work even if you and I are gone north. But I have a few other matters to take care of before we leave."

"Such as?"

"I must go talk with my banker at Child's to discuss access to funds. Once in York, I want to be able to continue my work with the women's charity in Bradford, and I plan to increase my contributions to the house. Living farther away from them now in York, I won't go to Bradford as often, and I don't want them to think I've abandoned them."

"A good idea. Also, before we go, do find a modiste you like here in town. Order a heavy coat for the winter. New hats, too, if you like. A few gowns." He grinned and reached to cover her hand with his. "It's colder near the sea, and you need to be warm."

"I feel odd spending your money."

"You're my wife. Do please get used to that, darling."

She hesitated. "I'm new to it. Plus, the renovations of the bedroom suite are expensive."

"You will spare no expense to have the rooms as you see fit. I will not have you cutting costs and being unhappy. Buy the finest. Enjoy the best." He drew her hand up and pulled her to his lap.

"I feel as though I should be paying for what I want, especially now that I have all that money."

"No. I won't allow it." He sank his fingers into her loose chignon and drew her lips to his. "Keep it. Save it for yourself."

"Save it for a dowry for our daughter?" She watched as he

imbibed that idea with a smile of joy.

He kissed her quickly on that. "A fine idea."

She settled closer to him, her arms around his shoulders. She adored his amorous endeavors at the breakfast table. She'd grown these past few weeks to know the signs of how she desired him. The heat in her blood, the rush in her pulse, the madness to be caressed by him. This morning her breasts, scandalously unbound beneath her day gown, blossomed against the muscles of his chest. "I want to please you."

"Oh, my darling. If you please me any more, we'll never get out of bed!"

Smiling wickedly, she brushed her mouth on his. How he could inflame her at a moment's ease. "I need to write to my Aunt Agatha. She's been a faithful correspondent, and I have lagged."

He took her mouth, his tongue claiming all of her. "A fine idea. What else?"

She was besotted by him. "I'd like to buy more pencils and watercolor cakes before we go north. I'll also begin to experiment with oil paints. I understand that Ackermann's Repository in the Strand is the very best place to buy all that, as well as easels and paper, too."

"Such sensuous talk, my wife." He shifted a bit, his interest in her a heavy protrusion against her hip. He slid his hand to her nape, a move she anticipated whenever he was ready to kiss her into distraction. "Buy up all the paints in London."

She combed her fingers through his thick satin hair and caressed his strong jaw. He was so handsome, and she was so very fortunate to have him as her own. "I have a very good subject."

"Do you, my dear?" he teased her.

"You."

"Ah. Not good enough." He nibbled his way up her throat to nip her ear. "I should paint *you*."

She arched her neck to give him greater access. "Have you talent, sir?"

"Not to paint you, my pet. But to love you? Aye. Of that I am quite capable."

Are you? She yearned to hear from his lips his ultimate declaration that he cared for her. She understood how his affections for his first wife had changed and died. But Verity hoped she could represent change for him. She kissed his jaw. My heavens, she loved him. Had for so long, since the day they met. Could he not care for her as well in return?

She wiggled against him to imply her need of him. It was also to cover her growing dismay that he did not declare he loved her. Did he need her? Yes. Want her? Oh, most definitely, he did. But was he capable of loving her?

He gave her much so generously. Largesse to redo his house. Buy new furniture, draperies, and appointments. Even to buy new clothes. To use her money as she saw fit. And take nothing from her. Not even to ask for any of her inheritance. He was well-to-do. Rich enough to not need her money. Mindful of what those funds meant to her and how she could, if she wished, save them for a daughter or two or three.

She grinned at him and kissed him soundly. "Withers, poor man, thinks we are heathens."

"To cuddle and kiss like newlyweds? No. Besides, he'd never say a word."

"A wise man."

"All butlers are men of discretion."

She gathered in a large breath, sighed, and pecked him on the cheek. "We'll do the same. You are off to your appointment, my darling. And I—"

He pulled her back, his face stark with a fire in his eyes. "What did you just say?"

"Hmmm." She knew. But she was surprised at herself, and she was sheepish, embarrassed at having been so vocal in her affection for him. "You're off to your appointment?"

He narrowed his dark, sweet gaze on her. "And you called me…?"

On her feet now, she widened her eyes like a coy numbskull. "My darling? Yes, that was it. Well. You are, husband. My darling man." She bent and dropped a nonchalant kiss to his laughing lips. "Tonight, I'll prove it!"

"No." He hooted in laughter. "This afternoon."

Hands on her hips, she challenged him. "Oh, I doubt it. You see, I have to—"

He was up out of his chair and lunging for her.

With a yelp, she eluded him and sprinted for the stairs.

He caught her at the first landing and lowered her ever so gently to the carpeted floor.

"They'll hear us in the servants' quarters," she whispered as he licked his way down to her cleavage and pulled the muslin bodice of her morning gown from her breasts.

"Not if you promise to be quiet." He cupped one breast and circled her nipple with his tongue.

She wanted to scream. "Come inside me, and I promise I will be good."

He rucked up her skirts, pressed her thighs wide, and sent two fingers sliding inside her hungry body. "How's that?"

She grunted and beat a fist on his shoulder. "Terrible. I need *more!*"

"Here?"

"Now," she demanded.

And when he slid inside her and she groaned, he had them both pulsing in torrid minutes.

"You were quiet," he said as he helped her stand on shaking legs.

"But you, my darling man"—she tsked—"roared." Then she gave him a shoulder and a wink before she waltzed away.

THE HIRED HACK stopped in front of the shipping company's offices. Yet Miles had no mind for business.

Only her.

My darling, she'd called him. Miles was undone, even now.

Hours later, ready to meet men to discuss shipments, all he wished to do was rush home to laugh with her.

He was becoming devoted to her. Her humor and her frivolity. He'd never had so much fun in his life. Sparring with her, matching wits, simply sharing the day's events with her. He might not even have to make love to her to crave her with him. But that act alone, having her luscious body meeting his, sinking inside her, yes, that was enough to make him marvel at his good fortune.

To find himself in a daily paradise that he'd never imagined was far beyond what he'd expected or planned for himself. And to hear her claim him with an endearment so heartfelt filled him with more contentment than he'd ever known.

"I shouldn't be long," he told the driver. He was not used to riding in hired carriages, but his wife had had many errands lately, and he preferred she be accompanied by Jessup and one of his footman. This hack was a personable fellow, and Miles would ask him to serve him tomorrow as well as now. "Return at two."

The man tipped his hat and clicked the reins on his obliging horse.

"Lord Bellamy!" one of the two owners of Frobisher and Sons Shipping hailed. Phillip Frobisher had written to Miles two weeks ago to open negotiations with him to transport his cloth. "Good to see you this morning. Lovely day."

"It is indeed." Miles knew Frobisher socially. Had met the man and his older brother, Thomas, many years ago when in London. They had often been in each other's company in York, but this was the first time they'd discussed doing business with each other. Miles opened the door to Jameson and Company, one of two other shipping companies he began inquiries with this morning. "After you, sir."

They were greeted by a clerk and ushered into a larger room. "Please have a seat, sirs. Mr. Gaylord Jameson joins you in a minute. He apologizes for his delay."

Frobisher took one of the four chairs situated around a large walnut desk. He was a snappy dresser, all crisp linen cravat and nut-brown frockcoat and gold brocade waistcoat. With curly, dark brown hair and brown eyes, he had the pointed look of a falcon. Yet his smile was ready and eager. "I saw your wedding announcement in the papers, Bellamy. Congratulations are in order, sir."

Miles had become used to the many who commended him on his marriage. He smiled and thanked Frobisher.

"I apologize for my brother's inability to meet here today. He was suddenly taken ill."

"Nothing serious, I do hope," Miles said, but did not regret the failure of the man's older brother to appear. Phillip was a more pleasant bird of prey than his brother Thomas, the Earl of Marlton. The older man, always smooth with the ladies, had lost his wife last year, and Miles had seen him in public enjoying his new freedoms.

"No. A mild congestion. It will pass soon. I am to negotiate for us both."

Within the hour, Miles had the draft terms of each company's offerings. The men rose and shook hands.

Jameson addressed him with an affable smile. "My wife gives a dinner party next week and sends out invitations—I do hope you and your wife, Lord Bellamy, and you, Mr. Frobisher, and your brother, Thomas, will accept her invitation."

"We are delighted," Miles said with a nod.

"Thank you, sir," Frobisher added. "I regret that my brother, the earl, and I are slated to return to Yorkshire day after tomorrow. However, I do hope we might return the favor and have you to our soiree during the harvest festivities in mid-September."

All agreed, and Miles and Frobisher took their leave.

Miles sank into the seat of the hackney, pleased with himself. He'd been able to begin his research to open a new market and gain more profit.

So much was going right for him since he'd placed the advertisement in the *Chronicle* and found a new wife, a new life.

And true love.

Chapter Thirteen

"Tonight, we must rest," Miles said as he opened the door to their suite. "Tomorrow the celebrations in Hyde Park will test our endurance."

The past three days in London had seen a feast of spectacles. Royalty from the Continent had arrived in London last week, and each day since last Thursday, there was a momentous dinner or parade. The prince regent was in his glory, leading his royal guests in state coaches to the London Guildhall, Burlington House, dinner parties, and the theater. Tomorrow were the promised Hyde Park festivities. Traffic was at a standstill to let all royalty pass. To go anywhere in town by carriage was nigh unto impossible. Miles had given up and declared if anyone in the house wished to attend any appointment, they should keep only those they could reach by foot. Verity had decided to go nowhere. Home was safest. Lord Croyden's approach had upset her. Her lingering memory of seeing someone who resembled Thomas Frobisher compounded her desire to go north soon. When Miles assured her they would leave in a week, she looked forward to the Hyde Park celebrations.

"We will never see the Russian tsar and the Prussian princes again in our lives," he said with a boyish anticipation. "Plus, I understand that our cavalry and infantry march and that we shall have twenty-one-gun salutes by the artillery. Even East India

Company soldiers will march, and I wish to see them."

She had to smile at his pride of country. "You like all this drama."

"I do. If I'd not been so involved in business, I would have liked to make my mark in the army. Do my duty, and such. I like to applaud those who have risked their all for us."

She kissed his cheek. "I shall be proud to go with you, too."

The next day, Verity strode beside him, her arm in his, with all their house staff welcomed to walk down to the park with them. The day was bright and crisp for June. The attendance was quite a crush. They thrilled to the pomp of the bands and the drums, the artillery barrages and all-too-brief glimpses of the prince regent, the tsar, and his sister.

Miles caught one man attempting to lift a few coins from his pocket. He grabbed the fellow's hand and twisted it. The scoundrel yelped but slithered away. Pickpockets, Miles told her as they walked home, always saw full employment on such public occasions.

"Cannot the Bow Street Runners do more to deter such thieves?" she asked him, as irritated as he.

"They are a small number of men. And they are more interested in capturing those who commit more horrendous crimes."

At home that night, Miles and she and their staff dined on cold sandwiches and beer and went to bed early.

"My lord! My lord!" Miles's valet called to him hours later.

Miles caught up his banyan as the valet knocked repeatedly on the bedroom door and left their bed.

She rose, but he waylaid her. "Stay where you are, my dear. I'll see to it. What is it?" he asked Taylor at the door. "Withers, too? What's wrong?"

"A fire, sir. The shed in the kitchen garden's gone up." Withers, whom Verity could see in the dim light of a flickering candle, looked weary and sore afraid.

"I went to investigate with Withers, sir," said Taylor. "Whoever set the fire tore up the plants too."

Verity winced. Such devilry roused a memory of similar mischief by a band of young men years ago in Eccleshill.

"Vandals?" Miles shook his head. "On the night of the celebrations? Any sign of them?"

"No, sir." Taylor frowned, angry. "I thought we should alert the night watch. I went in search just now, but I haven't caught up with them yet. I will, though."

"Good man," said Miles. "Nothing else? No other damage?"

"No, my lord," said Withers. "We thought the roughing of the garden was done most likely while we all were at the park. The fire later."

"You didn't hear anything?" Miles asked.

"No, sir," Withers replied. "I heard two tomcats fighting. They woke me up with their bellowing, and I went out with my broom to chase 'em away. That's when I saw the earth dug up."

"Terrible mess, sir," said Taylor. "I was alerted by the cats, too, and went out with Withers."

"All our vegetables and herbs are torn up, sir. Gone."

Verity grabbed her robe, slipped it on, and went to the door. Withers would be devastated. He loved working in that garden. So did she. Both of them tended it as if they were children talking to the lettuces and parsleys. "We shall assess the damage in the morning, Withers. I shall help you replant."

"Kind of you, ma'am. But you need not."

"I will, Withers. We all benefit from it."

"Go to bed, both of you," Miles bade the two men. "We will fix it up in the morning."

He shut the door behind him and put an arm around her waist. "People get into such mischief during a holiday. They were probably in their cups."

"I wonder if other kitchen gardens were vandalized."

"Could be. Not to worry, sweetheart. We'll learn more tomorrow."

The next morning, Withers reported that he and Taylor and one of the footmen had gone along the alley to see if other gardens had been attacked. They hadn't. Their garden was the only one destroyed.

TWO DAYS LATER, Jessup slowed the town coach to an idle before Marks and Dingall in Wigmore Street. Miles had shown Verity a newspaper advertisement for the dress shop in Cavendish Square, which boasted that some of its wares were readymade clothes. Verity took the suggestion because she had not been pleased with two other seamstresses she'd visited in Half Moon Street lately, and she refrained from asking Miles where his first wife had shopped. Such a place would be one she would avoid.

She took Jessup's hand to alight and surveyed the storefront, petting Pip in her arms as Mary climbed down. The windows were beautifully decorated with a day gown of yellow corded muslin plus matching hat and gloves. A small, discreet sign boasted of *An elegant assortment of Cottage Twills, Stuffs, Bombazines, Sarsnet, Satins Millinery, Pelisses and Dresses*. She confessed to herself that she was as excited as any woman at the prospect of new clothes.

"We'll see what they have, eh, Pip?"

The dog wagged her tail, always happy to go shopping and inhale the fragrances of new people.

A salesperson opened the door for her and Mary, and Verity indicated she was interested in seeing a selection of wools for a new pelisse.

"Yes, ma'am. If you will come this way, we have a new shipment. New styles, too." The young woman led her to a wide display table. Upon it she laid out a bolt of green and orange plaid wool. "This would look lovely on you, and it would go well in a three-quarter cape."

"Thank you. The colors are lively, but I'd like subtler colors. I need a full-length coat. We go north, and I need the warmth."

"May I be of assistance?" An older lady with silver hair and round, pleasant features approached Verity. "You are new to our establishment. I am one of the owners, Mrs. Dingall, and I would be happy to help you."

Verity introduced herself.

"Lady Bellamy! An honor to welcome you here."

Announcements of her wedding to Miles had been in quite a few newspapers. Verity had become used to people congratulating her. Earlier in a milliner's, the owner wished her great happiness. She'd purchased a smart little hat for dinner parties and left, realizing everyone in the world must have read of her marriage. In her recent letter to Verity, Aunt Agatha had written how many had commented to her on Verity's good fortune to marry so well.

Into a title, as well, her aunt had written about one person's awe of it. *She did herself proud. And went far away too.*

Verity pressed the smooth wool between her fingers and wondered if she had gone far enough from home to escape notice by one particular person. Yet soon she would return to the north. Thereafter, she would travel west to visit her aunt just outside Bradford. Would she not invite questions by her very presence?

As long as those announcements of her wedding kept the worst person away, she would be happy.

Yet, here in London once more, she found herself wary—and for no apparent reason. In Brighton, as she and Miles went about their days and nights, she'd felt free. Her hair had not stood on end. Not as it had those first few days she'd come to London. Her honeymoon had been a blissful holiday during which she'd forgotten the reason she had wished to escape her home. The ugly reason she wished to change her name, her life, and escape into a new one.

Chasing her fears away on such a bright day, she threw herself into examining other bolts of cloth. Muslin she could judge easily. She'd grown up watching it made and listening to her father discuss production of cloth. Thus she could tell by looking at a length its thickness, quality, and appropriate price. But she needed only two new nightrails of muslin. Aside from a serviceable full-length winter coat, she wished to order one promenade dress, two carriage dresses, three dinner gowns, and another ball gown. Miles had requested she order that last for the September Harvest Ball in York, of which he was a patron. They would attend, and he wanted to present her to his associates. He also hoped to host dinner parties at home, and she had agreed she would do so, happily. He wished her well prepared for the events with a wardrobe she liked.

She embraced the prospect of being in the society of her husband's friends and colleagues in York. She was not shy but enjoyed good company. She gave as she got, too. She'd had a very good education. In history and art, she was well versed. The fine skill of conversation had been one her mother, her father, and Aunt Agatha had instilled in her as a necessity of life. At math, Verity was proficient, though one did not speak of numbers at table. To hostess dinner parties and attend balls did not frighten her. But the possibility that one man whom she never wished to meet again might be invited to any engagement shook her. Surely, if Miles knew that man, his name would have come up in conversation. She prayed that Miles never met him.

"My lady?" The owner called Verity from her reverie. "If you do not like this Pomona green, I have others."

"Pardon me, Mrs. Dingall." Verity came back to herself. Mary was across the room gazing at model Leghorn hats propped on head racks. "I am woolgathering—and not paying proper attention to your wares."

Pip made a terrible commotion, barking and wriggling. She darted from Verity's arms and ran to the door that had just closed.

Outside, a lady and gentleman whom Verity had not noticed in the shop strolled away. Their backs to her, they talked to each other as they made their way across the crowded street.

For some reason, Pip had disliked them awfully much.

"Forgive me," Verity said to Mrs. Dingall, and went to scoop up her dog. "She is usually very respectful. I promise to better control her."

Mrs. Dingall was accommodating and said nothing of the commotion. Instead, for an hour afterward, she continued her display of the most luscious materials.

Verity was thrilled to select quite a few for her new wardrobe for the north.

Only afterward, as Mary helped her change for dinner, did she reflect on Pip's behavior. The dog had disliked only two people in the world. Two men. One most terribly. And justly so.

Verity recalled her view of the shop floor that morning. She found no trace of either man. And so she dismissed Pip's outburst as an aberration.

"Dogs," her father had often said, "can take a dislike to any-one whose nature they perceive as evil."

Verity suspected there were more than two in the entire world who fit that description.

Meanwhile, in London, as in Brighton, she'd seen no one and encountered no one she remembered—and hated.

Chapter Fourteen

MILES CRUSHED A letter Withers had just delivered during breakfast. His scowl was the first Verity had seen since he had resumed his business meetings after their return to London.

"What bad news do you have?" she asked him.

"Business." He waved it off.

"You can tell me. I know a setback can spoil your day. Anyone's." She reached across the table to stroke his long, lax fingers. With a simple touch, she had seen how she could help to brighten his countenance and his concerns.

"One of the shipping companies I investigate," he told her. "I thought their fares the best offered to date. But they cannot continue the negotiations."

"What is the name of the firm?" She'd heard him speak of a few with whom he hoped to work.

"Jameson and Sons."

"Ah." The name, like so many, meant nothing to her. "And does your contact say anything in particular about the reason he has withdrawn from talks?"

"He says he has doubts about the quality of our cloth."

She left aside the matter that quality of a product rarely concerned any shipping company. "Does he say from whom he got this idea of lack of quality?" she asked.

"No."

She took a sip of her tea, the sweet beverage she favored lately. That suited her, as she had no appetite this morning for anything served on the sideboard. Her tea and a crispy biscuit were just the right things. "Ask him."

Miles stared at her. "Usually not done. But you are right. I will."

She loved it when she pleased him. And so she asked, "Are there others who can be as advantageous as Jameson to work with?"

He nodded. "Two more."

"Well then," she said, "let's pursue those. We need not go north until you have a finer idea of your options, isn't that so?"

"I like the way you think, Mrs. Armstrong." He lifted her hand and kissed her fingertips, then pulled her to his lap. "My company is yours. And *we* are certainly one."

JULY CAME TO London hot and humid.

Miles and she were settling into their married life with a routine marked by good conversation, laughter, and reading new issues of Germaine Hammond's newspaper, recently renamed the *Fleet-of-Heart Chronicle*.

Miles attended to business in the City with negotiations for new shipments of materials. Verity devoted herself to the finer details of the renovations to the townhouse, especially the mistress's suite upstairs. She returned to Marks and Dingall for fittings for her gowns—and to none of those appointments did she take Pip.

Miles had asked her to invite to dinner Walter Higham, Lord Edwards, and his fiancée Lady Collier. When the couple came, they said gleefully that they planned their wedding for next June. The lady's two sons had gone off to school, and reports said they did well.

Two evenings later, Miles and Verity welcomed another

couple for dinner, Mr. and Mrs. Roger Newhouse. The gentleman had been referred to Miles by Gaylord Jameson, the elder of two brothers who owned Jameson and Company, the shipping firm. Gaylord had been the one who had cast aspersions on the quality of Armstrong cloth. Both Miles and she considered the referral odd, given Jameson's criticism. Nonetheless, the referral was one Miles pursued because the Newhouses owned a small mill in Durham that they wished to sell. Miles considered buying it. The men had met once and discussed preliminaries. During dinner, Miles had discouraged much talk of the sale, but asked to meet Roger Newhouse on the morrow for more discussion.

"I enjoyed their company very much," she told Miles as they climbed the stairs together after the Newhouses departed. "I invited Mrs. Newhouse to tea with me next week."

"Good. A new friend for you."

Verity and Charlotte Newhouse had much in common. Charlotte was the daughter of a mill owner and understood the business well. Verity had liked the lady instantly and sympathized with her and her husband over their struggles to make their mill profitable. Her husband had been honest in his statements at dinner that he had not the expertise to grow his business and wished to search for a position as mill clerk.

"Do you really consider buying his property?" she asked Miles. "The addition would expand your line of products."

"I'd have to see their facilities first, of course. Are they in good working order or require improvements? Is transportation out of Durham a challenge? My issue is that, at the moment, I should not devote funds to a new endeavor. Once I have secured new transport, I may reconsider expanding my output. One new project at a time is best."

She tucked that away for another day. For she had wealth now, and if her husband needed means to expand his business, she could help him.

⫸⫷

CHARLOTTE NEWHOUSE SIPPED her tea and set it aside. "I am so pleased you invited me. I enjoyed our dinner last week, and I would so like to be friends."

"Thank you. I feel the same." Verity and her guest sat in the renovated beauty of the main salon that Verity thought so refreshing now that it was redone. "Since I married and moved to London, I have felt that lack of companionship."

"You seem very happily wed."

Verity beamed at her. "We are. A month and a half married, and we are very comfortable together." *Delighted with each other so much, so often, the two of us act like silly youths.*

"Roger and I are married a year in October. I hope you don't mind I refer to him by his first name. We are not titled, and I am not used to such formalities. I hope you will call me Charlotte."

"I am happy to do that, and I hope you will address me as Verity."

"I am delighted. I need a friend. Roger and I both do. We are so lost in this city. We have only Roger's uncle and aunt here, and we make our way slowly." She stirred her tea and seemed to be embarrassed to continue. "Forgive me. I rattle on. You said the other night that you are new to London, too. Where was your home?"

"A village in Bradford."

"I've never been there. My family come from Doncaster, and of course, you know that Roger is from Durham."

"Have you been in London long?"

"We were invited to come for the celebrations by Roger's uncle and aunt. They know Roger seeks to sell his mill and thought coming here would increase his opportunity to meet those who might be interested in purchasing it."

"I hope it has," Verity said as she offered a selection of cakes.

"Yes, thank you, I will have a slice of the lemon cake. I own a portion, as my father gave it to me at my marriage. That's how I can help Roger decide on business matters. We have met quite a few gentlemen who inquire about buying the mill. But I cannot say Roger has been impressed with many he's met."

"I think it takes a few meetings to understand the true nature of most people. Especially when one is involved in business dealings, one must be careful."

Charlotte frowned. "Many of the businessmen Roger meets are devoted to seeking out profits in whatever way possible. I understand that the profits in cloth production are slim. We have lost money. Oh," she said, and put a hand to her brow. "I am sorry. I talk too much business. Roger says I display my background too often and that many do not wish to hear the problems associated with milling cloth."

"I do," Verity said, and put down her cup and saucer. "I grew up learning about the challenges of owning a mill. Trying to find good weavers and dyers. Trying to avoid overworking them and yet estimating correctly for your own profit."

"There! You agree. I knew you would. Roger hates that he's had to employ women and children to work twelve and fifteen hours. Many of them get so sick. Men, too. But the children, my heavens. They look so terrible. Pale and bent. They should be out in the sun, playing and having their lessons. But to have a mill in a town and turn away any able-bodied worker seems a sin, too. They are so poor. So hungry. So many need work. The whole enterprise has killed Roger's spirit. He cannot go on."

"I understand. My father had similar challenges and cried over those he could not persuade his employer to change. The mills can be crucibles of torment."

"But there must be a way to make cloth, sell it for a reasonable price, and not cripple or kill those who make it?"

"A question I have asked myself over and over. Yes."

"That's why Roger must sell."

Verity sat straighter in her chair and seized upon the opportunity to ask Charlotte about the referral of Miles by Gaylord

Jameson. "It was good of Mr. Gaylord Jameson to recommend Miles as a potential buyer of your mill."

"I thought so, too. Roger needs a quick sale, you see. Mr. Jameson said you recently had come into an inheritance."

Verity blinked. How would Jameson know about her windfall? "I did not know so many had learned of it."

"I speak out of turn. Oh, I make a horrid impression on you."

The woman certainly spoke more freely than most would. Honesty was useful, but in this case, Charlotte's alarmed Verity.

Her mind raced. Who else knew of the inheritance? Who had gossiped of it in society, and to a man she did not know? Why would they?

"Please don't fret, Charlotte," Verity assured her, although she felt uneasy herself." This is not your fault. I find the information disturbing, it's true, because I thought the news of it private. Perhaps the bankers at Child's spread it abroad." She arched her brows at her guest in question.

Charlotte nodded, understanding what Verity sought. "Mr. Jameson says he learned it from friends of yours in the north."

Aunt Agatha? No, impossible. Her aunt did not gossip. And if others had mentioned it to her aunt, the lady would have written to Verity about it. But who else might know?

Verity clutched the armrest of her chair. *Surely not...him.* Why would he know anything about such a large sum of money granted to her at birth?

"Roger and I go north to York in two weeks. Roger has heard of two prospective buyers for the mill who live there."

"We go to York as well, and soon." Verity was happy to change the subject. "I hope you and your husband will come to visit us while you are there."

"We'd be delighted."

THEY LEFT LONDON in the traveling coach on a sunny day in mid-July. Jessup was at the reins, a stable boy at the rear perch. Pip rode in the cabin with Miles and Verity. Taylor, Miles's valet, and Verity's maid Mary were behind them in a smaller chaise with much of the luggage. The journey north in pleasant summer weather was a trip done in leisure, and in contrast to the one they'd both experienced in May. Now they enjoyed quiet companionship.

Miles sat back in the squabs and grinned at her. "This journey along the Great North Road is different from that we did in May."

Full of delight that they were on their way out of London, she tossed him a flirtatious look. "I have my flask of whisky."

"And your pistol?"

"Always be prepared," she said, patting the new, fashionable reticule she'd purchased for everyday use from Mrs. Dingall.

"I never asked you if you have been trained to use that thing." Miles was full of humor and practicality.

"I am a good shot. Or was. In truth, it's been a while since I've fired the thing."

"We should set up a target for you in the back garden."

"Do you practice as well, sir?" she teased him.

"Indeed, my lady." He gave her a little bow. "We shall improve together."

"Superb," she said, and relaxed back into the comfortable squabs.

SETTLING INTO MILES's home north of the town of York was a process that alternately gratified Verity and confounded her. Suddenly, she was mistress of a house with eighteen rooms, servants' quarters fit for a maximum of twelve, and grounds that needed to be tended. Miles had kept only a small staff of underlings for himself after his first wife died.

This meant that Verity was at once in the process of hiring a housekeeper, a butler, and a kitchen maid, using the references of a service in the town of York. Their two footmen, one housemaid, a head cook, and a scullery maid, Miles had retained. The groomsmen, two stable boys, and Jessup, Miles's coachman, lived in the stables in the yard near the edge of the wide, imposing ha-ha.

The house of dressed white stone with eight bays of tall gothic windows marching along the front elevation had at first been a smaller house in the vein of William and Mary architecture. Miles's grandfather had renovated it by expanding both wings and putting in larger windows. Serviceable, with the dining room and breakfast room accessing a long hallway to the huge kitchen, many of the rooms were large and unused.

In the month Miles and she had been in the house, Verity had managed to find linens in the closet for one of the bedrooms. From a draper in town, she had ordered a matching counterpane and draperies, then asked him to reupholster an old Chippendale settee and chair she'd found covered in white cloths in storage in one of the vacant rooms.

An atelier, the grand likes of which she'd never expected to have, she created in a corner of the orangery. A large room that was an extension of the main house with tall paned windows facing southeast, the orangery benefitted from the sun. With only a few ferns and herbs in old, tiny clay pots, the plants struggled to survive. Verity had ordered the house painters to scrub the room top to bottom, then had them put a fresh coat of whitewash on the walls. She moved in two overstuffed chairs that might have been stylish in old George II's time and set up her new easel, a worktable, all her pens and pencils, watercolor boxes, and brushes. She'd added a small bookcase she found in another empty room, and there she stored the art instruction books she'd purchased from Ackermann's. Following the books' directions, over the past month, she'd improved her techniques and even admired her results.

Miles remained her favorite subject. Sitting in the orangery each morning as the end of August saw the light fade and the sun travel low in the horizon, she began to experiment with use of her selection of watercolors. She'd told the clerk at Ackermann's that her ultimate objective was to paint portraits. For that, he had sold her a selection of oil paints to choose from.

For Miles, she needed oranges and browns, a bit of black for his hair, glossy and dense. A robust stain for his cheeks. A mix of brown and black for his intense eyes. More umber for his long lashes and the bit of stubble that appeared each evening on his jaw. Experimenting with blending crimson lake and whites with walnut oil, she found a proper combination to make Miles's exact flesh tones. Then, using a smooth brush and thinning her paint, she'd accomplished a series of portraits of him that showed him in different poses at different times of day.

But capturing his character was her greatest goal. She believed that a portrait must illustrate a person's constitution and individuality. If she could perfect her artistic skills, she might show the world her husband's superb sense of ethics, control, and intellect. That man was whom she'd first met on the Great North Road. He had quickly become the one who had shown her humor and determination. In the offices of the *Chronicle*, he had turned into an even more thoughtful and caring fellow. Days later, after their marriage, he had become her lover. A charming man with a hunger for her bound in respect. All of that she valued more than she could say. To do him justice in all aspects of his persona was what she wished to express in color and texture—to summon in paint the aura that was uniquely his would be her challenge and her unique privilege.

As yet, she had not shown him her efforts. She waited. For there was an aspect of him she did not know. Either he had not shown her that piece of his character or she had missed it. Whatever it was, she looked and waited patiently to see it. The question whether what she sought was the part of him that declared he loved her was one she ignored. Whatever the aspect, it would appear. At some point in the decades ahead, she would discover more of his character. She hoped it would not take years. But then, she had her own challenges to reveal to him, didn't she? And they would show him her own diverse characteristics, minor or major as they truly were.

Meanwhile, she was happy to show him one aspect of her own skills—the improvements she'd made to the house. Color, texture, and symmetry were elements she understood, but they were also aspects of his profession. He had certainly paid attention to how hue and tone complemented her own complexion, and applauded certain colors on her. By listening to him speak of his work with cloth and by consulting him on the house renovations she did, she'd perceived that. He enjoyed those in his private life—and she had worked diligently to provide it for him.

On her own projects, she worked last.

"Here are our suites," Miles had told her the day they arrived and he took her up to the master bedrooms. "As in London, your rooms lie empty. Do with them as you wish."

She always slept with him and would not consider leaving him for the mistress's adjoining suite. She did not brood over the emptiness of the lady's chamber. "And for all the other unused bedrooms, may I furnish them as I will?"

"For guests, for family, anything you want."

She'd gotten to work, and within a few weeks, she thought she had the beginnings of a comfortable home. She had asked the draper to begin her next project immediately. With the main salon and dining room given a fresh coat of paint by Yorkish colormen who specialized in house painting, she had ordered upholstery brocades in complementary shell pinks and apple greens for the furniture. She wanted the public rooms to be cheerful places of comfort where many could enjoy each other in peaceful surroundings. The wooden pieces, all of styles of the past century, were of cherry or walnut in graceful arcs that connoted fluidity and elegance. They were in excellent condition and needed no refinishing by a cabinetmaker.

As she finished the major renovations, she thought that Aunt Agatha would enjoy the results and might consider coming for a visit. Verity missed her and wished to have her near. The lady was spry and good company. Miles would enjoy her many *bons mots*. But Verity had another hope, and that was to confide in her about the inheritance that still piqued Verity's curiosity. Her aunt was the only member of her family still living, and Verity wished to probe her knowledge more deeply. If anyone might shed light on the source of the money, it was Agatha.

By the end of August, Verity wrote to her aunt and invited her to join them in York for a few weeks to celebrate the autumn harvest. The lady agreed. It was then one morning that Verity requested a favor of Miles.

"Next week, if you do not have a use for the traveling coach, I thought Jessup might take it to Bradford to get Aunt Agatha."

"A fine idea. Your aunt will definitely be more comfortable in that than in a mail coach."

When she first suggested the trip, he had welcomed her aunt, saying he knew so little about Verity's family. She'd realized with a start that was true. She had shared little about herself. Having considered her youth happy, she also considered it rather unremarkable. To have her aunt here would verify that she had enjoyed a normal past. With only one outrageous incident that had sent her flying from home, leaving all she'd been behind, she'd led a largely uneventful existence.

"I thought I might go along and fetch her home," she said. "Do you mind?"

"Only that I do not know if I can do without you."

Oh, he was too dear. "Nor I so far from you."

They were at breakfast, so he smiled as he usually did and lifted her hand, then drew her to his lap. The new butler whom she'd hired had been given the same instructions as Withers had once received. He disappeared from the breakfast room immediately after she appeared each morning.

"I thought I would look in on those at Goodwood House and

explain my new circumstances." The charity house for women maltreated by their husbands or fathers was always in dire need of those to help them.

"And their new windfall?"

"Not in detail, no," she told him. "But I do want to talk with the director, who is the local vicar. Charles Whitley is his name. He'll be surprised and pleased at the larger donation. You would like him. He is, like you, a fine man."

"I should like to meet him."

"He once might have been my husband."

"Is that so? Did you refuse him?" Miles traced the outline of her lower lip with two fingers.

"I did."

"Hmmm." He kissed the hollow behind her ear. "Should I come with you and show him how well wed you are?"

She tingled to the touch of his lips to her skin. "No need. He is engaged himself, so writes my aunt."

"Ah, good. Then I have no need to fear that he might run away with you."

She cupped his cheek. "You have nothing to fear from any man."

"Good to know." He gave her a quick kiss.

"When I return, we can begin those dinner parties you wish to schedule."

"You think the public rooms are ready for company?"

"I do."

"Then I'll write up a list of those whom I'd like to ask you to invite. Let's start after your aunt settles in."

"Wonderful. Say, a week afterward?"

"A good idea. That gives us a few weeks to become acquainted before the Harvest Ball September twenty-first."

"I will be ready. I expect my newest ball gown to be finished before long. Mrs. Dingall wrote me last week that she would send it soon."

→»»——«««←

THE AFTERNOON BEFORE she was to leave for Bradford, Verity stood in the empty mistress's bedroom suite upstairs checking for last-minute items to be finished. With her notes for her renovations in her hand, she recalled how Miles had smiled in approval of her work. He encouraged her in all she did. The renovations in the house. Her art. Her support of Goodwood House in Bradford. Additions to her wardrobe.

She grinned, anticipating how he'd approve of her new ball gown for the harvest event. She'd chosen a spectacular French dark apricot velvet with silver trimming at the bodice and over the puffed short sleeves. Narrow at the waist, gradually wider at the ankle, the gown was cut extremely low at the bodice.

Mrs. Dingall had encouraged her to do it.

"You have a flawless décolleté, madam. One should use such lovely assets, always."

Verity had felt adventurous.

And I hope the gown still fits me.

Suddenly she swayed with fatigue. A hand to her forehead, she prayed that expense of the gown would show her to best advantage. But she had grown more robust lately. She knew why, too. She'd not had her courses since days before Miles and she were married. She'd never missed her monthly cycle, and she longed to tell Miles the news. But she hesitated until she could count three months of her term. Her mother had experienced many miscarriages, and Verity feared she'd be like her.

"Ma'am?" Mary was at her side. "Are you well? May I help you to sit?"

Verity allowed the girl to take her arm and lead her to an old chair in the far corner. A footman had brought it up the stairs the other day when she needed a place to rest. "I'm well, Mary. Tired."

The maid, who became more protective of her each day,

frowned. "You work hard, ma'am, to make this whole. At least we have some furniture to use. Not like in London. Thankful we must be that his lordship did not burn all this, too!"

Shock at the maid's words rippled through her. She stared at the vacant room. "He…he burned the furniture?"

Such ferocity was not like Miles. *Was it? Who burned furniture?* Good wooden pieces were costly and took cabinetmakers weeks and months to finish.

"Aye, ma'am. All of it."

Verity caught her breath. Was such anger what she had missed in Miles's character? "How do you know that? Who…who told you such a thing?"

"The scullery maid at home in London? She said so. Bertha. Aye, ma'am. Not just the bed, but the dressing table and all! After his first wife died, he ordered all the furniture in those rooms burned. Behind the kitchen yard, it was, aye." Mary paused, her eyes wary as she contemplated Verity. "Ye did not know?"

"No. I didn't." What more could she say? *It's not important?*

But—in reality—it was vital. A facet of her husband's character she had not seen.

Chapter Fifteen

M ILES AWOKE THE next morning earlier than Verity, and, instead of rising, he propped his head on his hand and watched his sleeping wife.

She whistled, her lush lips pursed and blowing air like a bird. He gave a silent chuckle. The lovely rest of her lay abandoned on their bed. Her right arm thrown above her head, the other to her side, she faced him. As every other night, she wore nothing to their bed. Neither did he. A practical measure to be nude—they abandoned the artifice of clothing nights after they'd first loved each other. He kept her warm and, he dared to say, happy. She more than made him satisfied. He had grown to crave her. Her artless surrender, her sighs, her cries, her luscious body—all his. Every inch.

Was it his imagination, or had she grown more beautiful since first he'd seen her on the Great North Road? To him, she grew more vibrant, more essential each day.

She ordered his houses, his meals, his staff. She chose the colors of his life and painted his existence in a happy rainbow of her laughter and fond regard.

She offered him her perspective, full of her own positive outlook and her generosity. He'd forgotten how to perceive the world through such prisms, and he believed that, within a few brief months, she had revived much of his enthusiasm for the delights of daily life.

Her golden-red lashes fluttered, and she sighed, curling into him. Languidly, she opened her green eyes and gave him a drowsy smile. Luring him like a magnet, she draped her arm around his waist and snuggled against him.

"A superb way to wake up," she told him, her voice a lower, sleep-drugged version of her usual seductive contralto.

"I agree," he said, sliding against her warm body and hooking one leg over hers to bring her closer to him. Entwined with him was how he preferred her. A part of her was how he always wished to be. Living celibate for years, parted from his wife as he had been, he was amused at himself now that, married to Verity, he craved her with a regularity that shocked but pleased him. He wondered how he had lived without her sweetness in his arms—and his life. Once a bedeviled man, he had lived in a nightmare of blacks and reds, angry oranges and outraged purples. As his anger of his past marriage had worn away, he existed in grays and browns. Drab. Lifeless. Defining himself only by his work. But for what and whom?

Then he advertised, and the shades of his existence lifted. And when he met her, shadows parted—when he saw he could live with her in some shred of happiness and order, the colors in his world brightened like dawn burst upon him. Days after meeting her, he saw rainbows in prisms of light that he'd not glimpsed in years.

She nestled her face into the crook of his shoulder and kissed his throat. "I will miss you these next few days."

Her admission thrilled him, and he scooped her tightly against him. His cock rose to proclaim how dearly he would miss her. Still he told her more. "I won't know how to get through my days without you near."

He felt her lips curve in a smile against his skin before she pushed away, examined him with fires of invitation in her eyes, and sank her long fingers into his hair. "Nor I. I am so partial to you."

"Partial?" he teased her, for he had learned by her looks and sighs and words the depths of her regard for him. How she enjoyed his conversation and his teasing, his recommendations and his humor. "Have a fondness for me, do you?"

She put her lips to his and kissed him deeply. Then she pulled away, panting. "I adore the way you taste."

Hungry himself, he could be inside her with one slight move. But he held back, not wishing to be a bore and take her within minutes of her awakening. "'Tis good, then," he breathed, "we like to dine on each other."

She narrowed her eyes, a wickedness there. "Morning is as excellent a time as any."

"Not so, I think," he said with a seriousness that intoned his desire to not make love to her.

Her look was a pout, though she was not a manipulating woman. "No? Have you an early appointment?"

"My darling." He caught her cheek and said, "You are not your best recently in the mornings."

She pressed her lips together.

"You come to breakfast late."

She shook her head.

"I do see you here in bed. Sweetheart, you change. Your pretty breasts are larger than when I first saw you as my bride."

"Oh, Miles," she whispered, and hugged him, her lips against his cheek.

He drew back and looked into her tearful eyes. "Sweetheart, I caress you and I hear how you suck in your breath when I kiss your nipples. You do not set me away, so I do take it that you still want me. I know you do. And I've learned to be more gentle. Verity, darling, you enjoy breakfast with me and come down as soon as you can. But you drink weak tea and eat a slice of toast. You look ill. I take your hand and pull you into my lap, but you are not jovial, darling, until hours later. Then there is the fact that you and I have had the pleasure of each other at whim through each night and day since first we wed. So I am well aware, my lovely wife, that you have not had your monthly courses in the past three."

She clutched him close. "Oh. Miles. I want you as much, as often as you want me. More! But—"

He smiled at her sweetness. "Yes?"

She ran her fingers through the shock of his hair at his brow and down his cheek to cup his jaw. "I am with child. I waited to tell you until the Harvest Ball. I wanted to be certain that I…that I would not lose him."

"Verity, my darling—" He tried to take her against him.

But she pressed the flat of her hand to his chest. "My mother spoke often of how she lost all her babies. How she mourned. How she wished for a child, and she and my father kept trying to conceive. After eight losses, I was the only one who survived to birth."

He paused. "I understand now. I'm glad you've told me. I want to be happy with you, make you happy. But, my sweet wife, you must always tell me your fears."

She knitted her brows. "I want to…"

He pulled away, surprised at her sudden turn of emotion. "But are reluctant to."

She glanced away, then returned to meet his gaze. "Yes."

He withheld a part of himself. He was guilty of that. How could he question her if he had not come forth with his own problems? It rankled him each day. Had done since they had grown closer with each kiss, each sigh, each night with her in his embrace. He wished to be himself, at ease with her totally, and yet…yet… What stood in the way was his own reluctance to reveal the part of him that he dared not share with anyone.

She rolled away.

But he caught her back to him. "Don't go. This is my fault. I feel it. I know it."

"We have much to tell each other," she said, as she reached an arm around to sink her hand into his hair and draw his head down so that she turned and gave him a ravishing kiss.

He wrapped his arms around her, cupping her heavy breasts. *I love you,* he longed to say…and yet did not. He did not deserve to claim her in that way. It might not be logical of him to conclude that—after all, his first marriage had no similarities to this one. But he needed to reveal the past, unburden himself of it to her. Show her all of him, his past, his failures, his desire for a happy future with her. Then he could tell her how he cared for her. Then he'd be whole and…

She spun in his arms. Naked, her long curls swirling around her like a halo, she confronted him. Her eyes were clear and stark with bold intention. "Did you burn the furniture from the mistress's suite in the backyard of the London townhouse?"

How she knew, when or from whom, was not important. That she had learned the worst of him and did not understand the reasons for his actions was the barrier to ultimate trust between them. He'd long known it. To refuse to grant her that would condemn them both to waning intimacy. Failings unshared, secrets denied, tragedies untold. They poisoned a marriage.

He wanted perfection with her. Wished to work for it, too.

She waited for his answer.

And so, at last, he said, "Yes."

"Will you tell me why?"

"Yes."

The air rushed out of her lungs. At last, he'd share another vital part of himself.

But he rose to his knees and made to leave the bed.

"No," she cried, and caught his arm. "Don't go. Tell me here. Now. Naked as we are. We don't need distance." She ran a hand down his chest from clavicle to ribs and rose on her knees to put her skin on his. "But this."

"You," he managed with a growl, "can tempt me to follow

you from here to eternity."

"Will you share with me what moved you to burn those pieces of your past, or will I wait until we both are in eternity?" With those words, she knew she pushed him to the brink of breaking some promise he had made to himself. She had her own problem to share, and she would too. But this time, coming so spontaneously as it did upon them both, was for his.

He sank to sitting on the bed, then let her go to push up pillows against the headboard. When he was satisfied, he extended his hand to her. "Come. I will tell you."

She went, ardent as the bride she still was, eager as the lifelong wife she planned to be. Against his chest, she curled beside him and kissed him. His lips were warm and giving. But as she drew back, his eyes went dim as he fixed them on middle space and recalled morose things she knew he never wished to tell her. In the early-morning chill, he pulled up the covers to their chests.

She waited.

"My wife was a distant relative. I'd known her since we were children. She, a few years younger than I, grew up an only child of indulgent parents. They were well-to-do, from a tradesman's family which had prospered in the last century. Unlike the Armstrongs, they did not gain a title. That was something Francesca wanted.

"And she wanted it badly. She'd had a lady's education, finishing school too. A London Season with a grand wardrobe unrivaled by any other. Jewels, courtesy of her papa. Encouragement to entertain all the gentlemen who wished to court her."

When he stopped, focused on that last with narrowed, flinching eyes, Verity asked, "And you were among them?"

He sucked in a breath. "Oh, yes. I was among them. She was beautiful. Stunning, with auburn hair the color of autumn and eyes the bright green of malachite. She was tall and voluptuous, enticing in low-cut silks. A feather on the dance floor and a witch in a card game. Her favorite drink was Scots whisky, and she could down a good bit of it and never show the effect. I often wondered how she survived the day afterward. An iron stomach, she said. An iron woman, I came to learn.

"She chose me. I was honored. I'd won over all those other swains. She was twenty. I was twenty-two. My father cautioned me against marrying so young, but I was determined to have her, beat the others, and take her home with me to my bed."

He shook his head, and it was a dreadfully long interval until he took up his thoughts once more.

"We were happy. I thought so. We lived in London—that was my father's and my arrangement. I would begin to take over business there, and he would continue to administer the mills here in the north. We did well that way. We prospered. I was able to help increase our sales and our profits. By a year later, I was eager to return here, but she refused to come. We argued. I came north alone.

"When I returned to London three months later, she was very different. She'd built a social set all her own. With those women she knew from school and those she'd met, plus all those men who had courted her, she was well occupied. Each night, she was out. Each afternoon, she was gone to tea or an at home.

"After a full fall and winter of this, I told her we would return here. She refused. I went north alone again.

"We went on like that for a few years. She had such social connections that her popularity contributed to our business success. She told me and wrote me about that often. It justified in her mind what she did. And what she did was cause rumors. Subtle but there. She was seeing other men. Quite a few, all at one time. My father had even asked if such a thing were possible. I was dismayed, to say the least. I wrote and told her she must stop her London whirlwinds. I was building a new mill, and my father was ill. I could not go south myself. Instead, I told her to come north for the summer and winter to live with me. Again, she refused.

"When we were married, her father had given her a cottage in Richmond as part of her dowry. I learned she used it as a second home. Fed up with her refusal to come north and interested in ending her behavior, which by then was notorious, I went to London, only to learn from servants that she lived primarily in Richmond. I went there. Confronted her.

"Only to see that she had company. Croyden was in residence with her. Everyone in Richmond knew it, and she did not care to hide it. Nor did he.

"I told her she must come home. Close up that house. Again, she refused. her father had recently died, and she'd inherited significant money. I had never wanted it. Nor did I then. But she told me she intended to use it to support herself. And she would use it for whatever she wished. I knew what she wished and wanted no part of it. I left and came north.

"The rumors continued…and the number of men increased. One month it was Croyden. The next it was someone else.

"I abolished her allowance. I cut half the London staff. The rumors were…disgusting. To say the least. She only increased her escapades. She went to Cornwall, rented a house there, and took Croyden and another man with her.

"My father encouraged me to divorce her. Knowing what it takes to get a divorce, I was aghast. The rumors of that would be as bad as what I currently heard. I went to her in Cornwall and told her I had begun divorce proceedings.

"She told me she was pregnant. I…I could not believe it. When we were first married, we were intimate often. I was surprised she had not conceived then, but subsequently I assumed us both barren. Later, when I knew she was familiar with other men, and she still seemed never to have gotten with child, I thought my conclusion correct—that she could not bear a child.

"But she laughed and said I was wrong. Though the child was not mine, she said that, legally, I had no choice. When the baby was born, she would write my name in the parish register as the father. She laughed, that wild, triumphant laugh she had when she'd won. 'After all,' she said with a sneer, 'you are my legal husband.'"

Miles paused, then climbed down from the bed. "Forgive me. I cannot sit still for the rest of it."

He found his banyan, tied the sash, ran two hands through his hair, then paced the room.

Verity remained seated, pulling the covers to her neck, stunned at the perversity he'd encountered.

At length, he stopped before the window and, in a deathly quiet voice, went on. "Later that summer, she wrote to me. *It is for the last time. I am at term, and the doctor tells me I will not have the strength to write more.*

"I assumed she implied she was about to give birth." His words were so grave, she knew he would never speak them again. "I wrote to her. I asked after the child…"

He hung his head. "She died six weeks later. She'd left a will in which she gave her father's money to me, but the cottage in Cornwall she gave to Croyden."

"And the baby?" Verity asked him, wanting to know and yet not.

He ran a hand across his mouth. He took a breath. Shook his head. "There was none."

What?

"I requested the doctor's death certificate be sent to me. It was very clear. She died of a growth in her stomach. If at first she thought it was a child, she later learned it was not. She died of it, lying to me at the end."

He whirled to face her. "That's why I burned the London furniture. That's why I never thought I'd marry again. Or want another ever again. But then, as time passed and grief died, I wanted more. I wanted normality, friendship, and a companion. I didn't know how to find one and took an advertisement. And then suddenly, there was you."

She was aghast at what he'd suffered and proud of how he had saved himself. "I am honored you've told me."

"I've learned to live a new way. A better way, Verity. You have brought me that." He approached her then, and the man who gazed down at her was different. Larger. Easier in himself. With the integrity of one who had acted as wisely as he could in his own best interests and with the mettle of one who had survived the disasters visited upon him by one without ethics or morals.

Revealing all this to her, he was a greater man. The finest she'd ever known.

He extended his hand, his gaze serene as he sought hers. "Come, my dear. Time to have a cup of weak tea and a few biscuits, isn't it?"

She rose out of bed and went into his embrace, grinning. "And all this time I've been avoiding eating breakfast, you've known why."

He wrapped the bulk of his banyan around her. "Each day I value you more."

"As do I," she told him, and yearned now to begin to paint him as he truly was.

Chapter Sixteen

V ERITY CLIMBED INTO the family traveling coach with Mary and Pip two hours later that morning. Jessup was in the box with a stable boy at the rear. Miles had filled her flask with whisky and handed it over with a flourish. He did not ask if she had her gun, but she winked at him and patted her reticule.

He chuckled and handed her up into the cab. "You are well prepared, as ever. Off you go, my dear. It will be good for you to see your home again. You've been working on the house too much. I fret that you overexert yourself."

"I am well." She worried that he'd taken her statement about her mother's miscarriages more severely than she. She had experienced no cramping or bleeding. Nothing was amiss. He had also been reluctant this morning to make love to her, but she had persuaded him. He had been as gentle as ever he was. She had no discomfort and had told him so. "You will not worry about me, please! Jessup is the best driver. The coach is well sprung and like riding in a cloud. And my aunt will treat us all like royalty."

"Leave me!" He grinned and stepped back on the drive as he gave directions to Jessup to mount up. "I shall see you in three days."

She blew him a kiss.

What she saw in his beguiling eyes was a new flame of affection burning there. The silent endearment thrilled her anew as

Jessup snapped the reins and the horses trotted away.

THAT AFTERNOON, AS Jessup drew the family coach into the yard before her aunt's cottage, Verity was filled with a triumph. She returned now a different woman. When she had lived here, she was the daughter of the clerk who kept the books for many owners of different mills. Now she was a married lady and the wife of an owner of mills that were competitors to her father's previous ones. Her attitude toward her old neighbors and friends was still as fond. She was not overblown with pride, but happy. Serenely happy. She was who she was. A name change or a new honorific did not signify in that regard. Nonetheless, many might perceive her differently because her status might induce them to bow or scrape. But she hoped they would welcome her as she had been—a girl who'd grown up with them, and who valued them and always would.

She had left her home for mixed reasons, and in a manner most unusual. But she had made excellent choices. She married a good man of fine character. And despite the fact that he had not yet declared he loved her, in so many ways that mattered, he did. And she loved him.

That alone made for a fine return home. She had made a happy union. Now she got to share her bounty with her last remaining relative in this world.

"Hello! Hello, my girl!" Great-Aunt Agatha struggled to the stoop of her cream stone cottage. Leaning on her cane, she waved from her little green doorway. "Hurry! I long to hold you."

Pip wiggled to be free. She adored Aunt Agatha too.

Verity climbed down with a helping hand from Jessup and rushed to her aunt's open arms. "Good afternoon, my dear. Oh, I am so happy. You do look well!"

Pip scampered around Aunt Agatha's feet.

"Ha! You always did see the world in cheerful yellow!" The silver-haired woman reached up to bring her down into her embrace. Short and plump, Verity's mother's maternal aunt was a sprightly seventy-eight. "Come here, Verity. Stand back. Let me see you. Truly see you!"

Verity stood at arm's length and waggled her brows at the woman who had been as much a mother to her as her own.

"Ha! I see it. I do! You rascal! Married and already with child." She cupped Verity's cheek with a palsied hand and grinned at her with cloudy blue eyes. "You do bloom. Oh, come inside. This is your maid, I gather. Welcome, girl. Do catch that dog. She remembers me, the good little thing. We shall talk. We will!"

She hooked one arm through Verity's, but spoke to Jessup. "You and your man will bring her luggage inside. Put all upstairs in the loft bedroom. I sent word to the blacksmith in town yesterday. He has the best rooms. Fraser he is, by name, and he will stable the coach and put up you and your man above his smithy."

Verity turned to Jessup. "Mr. Fraser is a fine man, Jessup. You and William will have good accommodations. Do avail yourself of whatever you both desire at the White Horse Inn, too. The payments are mine, of course."

"Aye, ma'am." He pulled his forelock and continued on with his duties.

Aunt Agatha led her and Mary into the hearth room of her cozy home. "You must be tired after your trip. Do sit. I have tea ready, and good shortbread and minced biscuits."

"I have looked forward to your delicacies."

"Have you, girl? I bet you have more so now that you're *enceinte*. Sit, sit!" She waved her to one of two old, lumpy Chippendale chairs near the fire. "I will pour and plate the refreshments while you put up your feet!"

Verity removed her pelisse and put it on the coat rack, then took a seat. Mary marched behind Jessup and William, who took the trunk and two valises up the narrow stairs.

Her aunt busied herself with serving this and that, then eyed Verity with keen old eyes. "You must tell me all. I know you are happy with this man. A stranger, no less. An arranged marriage in the oddest way, but nonetheless good for you. For him too, I imagine?"

"It is so, yes, Aunt."

"I will not intrude to ask for details which are not mine to ever have. And your letters provided some assurances of his value. But now you must look me straight in the eye and convince me that your husband is kind to you."

"I assure you that he is a gentleman in the finest sense of the word. Someone you will respect. He works hard at his business and seeks to grow it."

"And did he marry you to do that? Oh, not in the sense that he needed a windfall of a dowry. But he did ask for some small bit."

"Yes, three hundred pounds. But he never took it. No, what he wanted was a companion."

"Don't we all!" said the lady who had been married all too briefly to a young man killed months after they wed in the wars against the American colonies. "And money? Tell me why he stated he wanted that three hundred."

"He did not really want it or need it. Besides, three hundred is miniscule when one speaks of dowries, eh? I did not have anything worth comment. Or did not until this mysterious inheritance." She watched her aunt nod without any other emotion, and certainly none to indicate she knew the source of the money. "The three hundred pounds Miles asked an applicant to possess was one he required in an attempt to winnow the number of women who might apply. He wished for one with some education and some background which assured him of a good companion."

"Well! You are that. I am truly happy for you, and I long to meet him."

"You will find when you do that you love him as I do."

Her aunt narrowed her eyes. "Love him. Do you?"

Verity pressed her lips together. She'd let that slip. "I do."

"And what of he in return?"

"I think so."

"I see." Her aunt stirred her tea, then focused on Verity's figure. "You have proof aside from…?"

Her pregnancy. "I believe so."

"And you understand his reasons for failure as yet to declare his affections?"

Dear me. She should have prepared herself for so intimate a discussion. "I do."

"Good! Then you are here to show your old friends and neighbors that you are well married."

That led to a discussion of those Verity had left behind. She shifted in her chair. "The reason why I've come to fetch you is that, yes. But I also wish to talk with Charles Whitley and tell him about my intentions to increase funding for Goodwood House."

"More money for the house? My, my."

"Yes. I can afford to give more, and I will. I must tell Whitley how I wish it used, too."

"I saw him Sunday. He presided at services. Never fails, good man, you know. He is happy to receive you. Poor fellow was not happy, however, when I told him you had married."

"He should be happy for himself that he has found another. Besides, he knew I never would marry him."

"Why, I do not know. Would you tell me?"

"Oh, Aunt. He is kind and sweet, but I did not care for him as a wife should." *Mostly because when I stood in his parlor and cried because I could not help Amanda, he all but admitted to me that he'd known what was happening to her and hated himself because he could not persuade her to leave.*

In May, before Verity had left for London, her aunt had asked the same question, and she had answered the same way. But the wise woman had then asked, "Why marry a total stranger? Is the problem here so horrendous you must take on such a challenge?"

Verity sat taller with memory of her answer. The challenge was and remained exactly as awful as it had been.

Her aunt stared at her for a long minute. Finally, she broke her gaze and nodded in acquiescence. "Very well."

Verity would say no more on that issue. Never.

Her aunt smiled and turned to another subject. "Mrs. Felix Bainbridge wishes to call here on you."

Katherine Mordant, Verity's childhood friend, married six years ago to a tutor in the newest Bradford primary school, was an acquaintance whom she would be delighted to welcome. "Marvelous. When?"

"Tomorrow. She asked if noon was a good time. I told her you intended to visit at Goodwood, so she suggested that hour."

"Yes, we will have tea with her, then we can go to town."

"Also, Miss Durrant asked about you and bids you come say hello to her if you have time."

"The seamstress. Does she do well?" The villagers were not rich, but the woman was reasonable in her prices and very skilled at her work.

"She does. She has new work from many fine ladies, and she's prospering."

"As she should." Verity would visit briefly.

Pip came bounding down the stairs then and jumped up onto Aunt Agatha's hassock for a scratch under the chin.

"The papers announced your nuptials and added news of your honeymoon in Brighton and your arrival in York," her aunt announced with deadly calm. Pip settled to rest, her little nose near Aunt Agatha's feet.

"My, my. So well publicized," Verity said, and tried to smile. Yet her teacup rattled in her hand. She put it to the table. "I do not merit such notoriety."

"You married a viscount, my dear. A rich man of business, too. That is news to many here. You must realize all would wish to know the details."

"I don't want them to."

Compassion softened her old aunt's features. "I know, darling. I know. But when you are in town, you will be greeted by those who have full knowledge of your status and where you live."

Verity was out of her chair, pressing her palms to her skirts. "I am forearmed, then. Forgive me, Aunt. I will go upstairs and see how Mary is getting on with the packing."

As she reached the bottom step, her aunt called her name and made her pause. "My dear niece, I see you do not wish to speak of *him*. But I must. This once. He is not a man to leave you alone, Verity. We knew it after Amanda died. We knew it after your father died. He is persistent."

Verity summoned her resolve. "Never fear, Aunt. I am prepared."

Her aunt stood, her legs wobbly, as she leaned upon her cane. "My sweet girl, you were always brave. But Thomas Frobisher is a devious devil. You alone uncovered that. He will not forget it, no matter his silken words to you. Do be aware that your husband, his name, his title, and his wealth are impressive, but are they enough to thwart the ambitions of this creature?"

"They must be. I am well and truly gone from his sphere, Aunt."

"I pray you are right."

"I'M SO PLEASED I could call upon you." Katherine Mordant, now Mrs. Bainbridge, hugged Verity when she appeared at noon at Aunt Agatha's cottage door.

"Do come in. I'm so happy to see you." Verity grinned at her friend, but she noticed how pale and thin she was. "Aunt Agatha was so happy to see you as well."

"And I was delighted to see her. I visited my parents a few days ago and went to church."

Verity's aunt appeared at the door to the common room and hobbled over to greet Katherine. "Mrs. Bainbridge, so happy you are here."

"Thank you, ma'am. I cannot stay long. My mum has taken poorly the past few weeks. She does not speak well, and struggles for words. I dashed out this morn to come visit, but must return."

In truth, Katherine did not look well herself. Verity expressed her sorrow at the news of her mother's ill health. "And your father? I hope he is well."

"Not very, no. He was employed by the earl for his whole life."

The earl. Verity sat straighter. She hated the very mention of Thomas Frobisher. "Your father, as I recall, is no more than fifty years of age. Always hardy. Has he taken ill?"

"He is forty-two and ill, not so much of body. But of mind. Hope gone."

"I am sorry to hear that." To ask was to probe, and Verity did not wish to be indelicate. "Has he been to consult with the doctor or asked the apothecary for a remedy, perhaps?"

"There is no cure. None. I am sorry. This is not fine of me. I did not come here to pass my troubles on to you. I came to offer you my best wishes for your marriage."

"To welcome you here is an honor and joy, Katherine." Verity grew worried about her friend, who looked so bedraggled. Her once glossy chestnut hair was dull. Her brown eyes clouded. Her hand shook as she spoke. "But we are here to listen, and clearly you must tell the tale of what has happened to your family, my dear. This concerns you. And greatly so."

"I wanted to be bright and happy when I came. Not talk of this." Katherine sniffed back tears, and her chin trembled. "But my father's dismissal makes my mum's illness hard to bear."

"Of course it does," Verity said. "And you ten miles or more away. You cannot be at your mother's beck and call and not with your husband."

Katherine shook her head. "We will have to take them in. I

don't know where to put them. Our cottage is small, and Felix sleeps poorly. He is so beset with his own unruly little students."

Verity had seen other villagers deal with poor working conditions, poor health, and poor prospects all her life. She had had a wonderful, protected existence and knew sympathy for those afflicted and never cured any of their conditions.

"I do not understand." Aunt Agatha rapped her cane on the wooden floor. "Your father was the Earl of Marlton's gardener. Had been all his life!"

"Indeed," said Katherine. "He was dismissed by Marlton last month."

"Good heavens!" Aunt Agatha was aghast. "Was he pensioned?"

"No, ma'am."

Mordant had worked for Thomas Frobisher and for his father, the fourth Earl of Marlton, ever since Verity could remember. Not to be pensioned after a lifetime of service to so well-to-do a family was cruel. But then…Verity thought the deed typical of the man who did anything he wished to anyone.

Her aunt chewed over the character of Thomas, the fifth Earl of Marlton, with damning words. "He is a scoundrel. A misfit. A rogue. What did your father say? What happened?"

Katherine winced. "My father will only say he discovered the earl…"

Agatha and Verity glanced at each other.

Agatha went forth. "Doing what?"

Katherine swallowed. "In the orangery."

Agatha scoffed. "Tending a different sort of flower?"

Verity could not breathe.

Her friend gasped as tears appeared and rolled down her cheeks. "Yes. You know this of him?"

Verity rose to fetch a handkerchief from her reticule sitting under the far table. She returned to hand it to Katherine, an arm around her shoulders as she said, "We do. Yes."

"Many do," her aunt quickly added. "This is not the first time,

Katherine. The man needs to be put in leading strings and controlled like the child he is."

If Aunt Agatha only knew no ties could hold him.

"And so, Thomas dismissed your father because he recognized the girl." Verity did not ask. She did not need to.

"Father does not wish to say!" Katherine was screeching now, beside herself. "Why would he ruin a young girl's reputation? He cares nothing of the earl's! He's seen him with women before… Oh, my. I should not say!" She clamped a hand to her mouth.

"Have you discussed this with the vicar?"

Verity shot a look at her aunt. The lady knew a few facts about Marlton's proclivities, but not enough to stop her from asking such a question. For Charles Whitley would be able to do nothing. Even if he wished to. Which he did not. He got his patronage from Marlton. His very living would be destroyed much like Mr. Mordant's had been. Thomas Frobisher— Marlton—did as he wished. Destroying women as a daily pastime. Now, men too.

Katherine shook her head. "No. I hate to. My father would hate it too."

"Well, my dear girl," Agatha said, "it's not like the rest of the world does not know your father has been sacked. They'll wonder at the cause."

"Marlton has let it be known that my father killed his award-winning roses."

Verity scoffed.

Katherine swung her attention to her.

Verity put up a hand. "Katherine, believe me when I say that the excuse Marlton has put out for this dastardly deed is the very symbol of what he himself has done. I would wager that most in the village will get the analogy."

"He has done this before?" Katherine's voice rose an octave.

Agatha frowned at her. "Had you never heard of his tendencies?"

Katherine rolled a shoulder. Her defense was a raw admission of more. "I…I suppose I have. Yes."

Dear God. Frobisher had groped Katherine? Or worse? How many had he violated?

Verity clasped a hand to her throat. "He must be stopped."

Aunt Agatha spun to her. "How? Have you any idea?"

Verity opened her mouth.

But Katherine was quicker. "And if he is, what does that mean for my father? No. No! You cannot make Marlton a laughingstock. He will not come to heel. He is an *earl*. Untouchable!"

Verity took her friend in her embrace.

"Promise me, Verity. Promise me! You will say nothing to anyone!"

She gave her that promise readily.

She had escaped Thomas Frobisher, the evil Earl of Marlton. But many were not as fortunate as she. Not as willing to flee. Not as able to cope or thwart or even to discern what was happening to them.

She would do something to end his reign of terror. But she had no idea how.

Chapter Seventeen

VERITY STOOD BEFORE the vicar's small gray flint and red stone house at the end of the main street of the village. She'd walked here alone. Mary had started with sneezes and sniffles last night, and Verity had sent her to bed with a hot brick for her feet. Mary had argued to go with her, but Verity simply pointed her toward bed. Then she re-braided her own waist-length hair and wound it up over her crown, then put on her hat and her new forest-green walking suit. She'd gone downstairs to find her aunt, who was bent over, complaining that her hips ached badly today. Encouraging her aunt to rest her bones, she picked up Pip to accompany her to visit with Charles Whitley.

Her business with him would not take long. Her fury at his care of his flock would predominate. She anticipated she'd offend him by ranting and raving, so she tempered her desire to do that. But he could be stubborn. After all, he was the third son of a lord, reared in the ways of privilege, priggishness—and the injustices of *noblesse oblige.*

At her third set of knocks on his front door, he swung it open. Smiling after first sight of her, he then went stiff, as if prepared for battle. Good for him. He had few real defenses when it came to the issues she would raise about his slighting of women and disregarding of the rights of good men.

They exchanged pleasantries. She refused tea. Eager to get on with her business, she set her small reticule upon the nearby table. She ordered Pip to remain in her lap and removed her gloves. Then she launched into a discussion of her support for Goodwood House.

Whitley was quick to provide details of what he'd done while she was away. "With your funds, we've added more bedding in the loft and better portions of porridge for breakfast. We've placed two of our healthier women as maids. One to Miss Durant, the seamstress. The children have shoes. Two of them have never had shoes, and their feet are deformed. However, the cobbler has done right by them, and they now walk instead of limp."

"Mr. Gray always did have a fine product. I'm glad to hear of better conditions for everyone."

Whitley had sat by his large fireplace, and in the light from a good fire, he benefited from the glow with a rosier complexion. His flaxen hair formed a thinning cover to his pate. He was as lean of body as before, yet his face resembled a young rabbit with chubby jowls. "Shall we go to Goodwood now? You can see how clean and bright it is. I'm very proud of it."

"Before we visit, I wish to broach a few matters that concern me."

He folded his long hands in his lap. He cocked his head in such a way that she questioned if he feigned nonchalance. "Very well."

"Tomorrow morning I return home and—"

"So soon? Terrible. You won't stay for Sunday services?"

"No. I won't. My aunt goes with me for a visit."

"How good of you to take her with you. She'll like that."

For all his faults, Whitley did care for some of his flock some of the time. "Yes, she'll enjoy herself with us, I am sure."

"She talks of you all the time. I will miss her. How long does she remain with you?"

"As long as she wishes, though she speaks only of staying through the harvest festivities."

"Does she not wait to help with the birth?"

Taken aback by his mention of her condition, Verity paused. Men rarely brought up such with a lady who was not in their family. "I do not think so."

"Forgive me. I cannot help but see you are…" He indicated her form.

"Yes, I am with child." She could say that to anyone with the joy and pride in her heart.

"Congratulations," he said with honest gusto.

"Thank you. We are very pleased."

"I am certain your husband must be. He is good to you, is he?"

"Indeed, he is," she said, noting that his concern for her sounded real.

"He…he advertised for you, so I hoped he might be—"

She cut her hand in the air. Pip jumped up. She would not discuss particulars of the way in which she and Miles had met. "My husband is the finest man I have ever known."

"Oh. Yes. Well. I know you'll have a lovely babe who has the gleaming blonde hair and green eyes of the family." If he meant her hair and eyes, yes, her mother looked like that. But her father had brown hair and eyes. The man groped for words, didn't he?

"Thank you. He or she could have the black hair and darker eyes of my husband's."

"Of course he could. She…she could. Of course."

She took a breath, focused on telling him what she needed, then leaving to see the house. "I will tour Goodwood by myself this morning."

"Oh, but why?"

"I desire to go alone."

"But…" He ran a hand over his balding scalp. "I can show you. Accompany you in your condition, I mean."

"I go alone, Charles."

"If you insist."

"I do."

He waited, examining her features. "As you wish."

"But tomorrow morning, before I return home, I should like to visit Goodwood again. Briefly. With you." She wished to see staff and residents in his presence.

"Marvelous. Two visits. Love to have you. Cook will be happy to see you. Josie the maid, too."

"Today after the tour, I wish to review the account books."

"The…account books?"

She nodded. "Yes. At home. Where are they?"

"I…I have them here."

"Well, then. I'd like them, please. I will return them to you tomorrow morning."

He stared at her. "There's naught amiss with them."

She arched her brows. "I didn't think there was."

"Oh, well. Yes, certainly. Not a problem."

"I am the major patron. Or I was…"

"Yes. True."

"I am entitled, Charles."

"Yes." He gulped. "You are."

She prayed there were no misappropriations of the money. If, after viewing, she suspected any, she could demand an independent audit. Whom could she hire? That was tomorrow's question. For now, she had to show him her intentions. All of them. "I wish to donate more, and on a regular basis, Charles."

"Now that is good news." He rubbed his hands together and truly smiled. "Very good news."

"But I wish to see the books. Only normal."

"Very much so. Yes. I hoped with your newfound wealth you may consider giving us more."

That floored her. *More? From my newfound wealth.* He knew. *How? How?* Aunt Agatha did not spread gossip. "Who told you that?"

"No one." He said it so quickly, she believed him.

Still…she would press. "That I had new wealth? Who told you that, Charles?"

He frowned and cast about. "I don't know. Gossip. Why?"

"It's important to me to know. Do think."

He shrugged. "I cannot, Verity."

Though he appeared befuddled, she did not trust him. "If you remember, do tell me before I return home."

He pursed his lips in thought. "I will."

"Now," she said as she petted Pip, "I do consider giving the house more money. I know you have need."

"Indeed, we do. We've two new girls in, both in need of home and hearth."

"Local girls?" She hated the many reasons why young girls might need to join as house residents. "From Bradford?"

"Oh, yes."

She frowned at him. "How old?"

"Fifteen. Sixteen, I think."

"Why?"

"What?"

"Why, Charles, have they sought asylum with you at the house?"

"They are in need of moral counseling."

"Because?"

He flinched. "Because, Verity, they have been loose in their ways, and their families have disowned them."

As ever, the girl was blamed for failure to adhere to a moral path. "They are pregnant?"

"Yes."

"And unwed."

"Yes."

"Who are the fathers?"

"I did not ask. I would not."

She glared at him. "Why not?"

"Well, I...I would not."

"I demand you ask them. Ask them, and if and when they tell you, I demand you require the men to send funds to the house for the next year equal to each girl's room and board."

"You cannot do that!"

She lifted her chin. "Oh, but I can."

"It is not done!"

"It is now." She put on her gloves. Picked up Pip. And stood. All business, she bade him good afternoon. "The record book?"

"Yes, wait here." He went to a large oak writing desk and extracted from the bottom door a large red leather-bound ledger.

"Thank you. Tomorrow morning, at nine. I return for you."

Then she left him, muttering to himself about how impossible her demands were and how he would try, definitely *try* to do all.

He'd best do more than *try*.

Verity marched into town, smiling at the power of her resourcefulness. Money might persuade, and titles might influence, but purpose of mind and heart had won the day!

GOODWOOD HOUSE HAD begun a century or more ago as the longhouse of a prosperous farmer. His son lived long but had no issue. At his death, his widow had decided to sell his land in bits and pieces to others. The house, of plank doors and undressed stone, was large, capable of housing twenty or more. When the parish purchased the house from Widow Goodwood, it was in fine condition to receive numerous residents, with rooms for two maids and a footman, plus one near the kitchen for a cook. For four years now, the directors of the house, who were all from the parish, had hired only a cook and maid. Townsmen did any of the work for which a man was required.

Verity was greeted at the front door by Josie, the twenty-two-year-old maid who had served here since the house opened as a charity.

"Good day, milady," the girl said, and bobbed in deference. "So happy to see ye, ma'am."

"You are kind, Josie. Do not be curtsying to me. We've known each other too long."

"Aye, ma'am." Josie was a pretty, brown-haired, blue-eyed, sprightly little thing. A little person, she was from Eccleshill and had asked for this job in the house. It was that way, she'd said to Charles and Verity, that she would earn her place in the world, gain respect, and not be laughed at by uncaring others. "Come along. You know yer way. Would you like a cuppa?"

"No, thank you. I'll not make work for you."

"'Tis no work, milady." Cook, Mrs. Salter by name, rushed out as fast as her chubby legs could carry her from the far kitchen. She wiped her hands on her huge apron and curtsied too. "We're thrilled, we are, t' see ye."

Verity grinned at them both. "I've come to look around, not be pandered to. Let's to matters of concern. You both look well. Healthy, well nourished, and well rested. You will tell me if you do not do well, aside from that, yes?"

"Aye, ma'am. Cookie and I are good of bone and mind, we are." Josie held her arms out for Pip, who squealed to be held by her old friend.

Cook scratched Pip's head. "We are, and the 'ouse is full to the brim. Little ones, too!"

"They're sweet, the li'l ones."

Verity had always liked the two women's attitudes. "And we've two new young ladies, I heard from Vicar Whitley."

"Aye, that, too," Cook said. "Good girls, I'd say, though ye know, most do not."

Verity nodded in agreement and said naught to that.

"Ye've got the house ledger?" Josie frowned at the book in Verity's arms.

"I do." She juggled the book and her reticule.

"Is aught amiss?" Josie reached out to help her balance the book and purse.

Verity smiled. "No, I'm just doing my duty."

"Oh." Josie nodded, but seemed to remain unconvinced at

Verity's need to see it.

"Do *you* think there is something wrong in the accounting?"

"No. But I wouldna know."

Verity glanced at Cook with a question in her gaze.

"Nor I, ma'am. Vicar Whitley pays our butcher and green-grocer bills every week. To the penny, it were. I know because if it weren't, they'd no give me wares."

"All good to know. So, if you don't mind, I'd like to look around. The vicar has told me he afforded the house new beddings."

"Aye," said Josie. "Clothing and shoes and all for comfort an' warmth."

"Please to go up, ma'am," said Cook. "The residents are in their class. Money is today's talk. As for me, I've stew on the fire. I'll return, if ye donna mind."

"I do not. Will you amuse Pip, Josie, while I take a tour?"

"Oh, yes." The girl giggled. "Have a bone for her, do ye, Cookie?"

Verity watched them go, Cook to her kitchen and Josie to the kitchen garden with Pip. Passing the closed room, once part of the longhouse's original stable, she climbed the stairs to the dormitory. The beds, thin but serviceable, were made with taut sheets and hand-worked quilts. Every possession of each resident was in a neat pile in a small cabinet to the left of each bed. The room was tidy. The wooden floors clean of dust. The handwoven rugs colorful and in place.

She went to one window and looked out over the hills. The trees and bushes had turned into a burnished palette of reds and oranges and yellows, edged by dark and serene green. All was in order here. The few worries she had dissolved.

Below, someone had come to call.

She heard Cook talking low with the visitor. A man. Whitley, Verity presumed.

Their conversation ended. Cook's footsteps marched away.

He climbed the stairs, one solid foot at a time upon the creaking floorboards.

She spun just as he rounded the landing to come full commanding height before her.

Not Whitley.

Not Whitley.

"Good afternoon, Lady Bellamy." His guttural male voice bound Verity like chains. The sound dragged her back to a salon draped in black for a funeral.

Her pistol. She should have it in her hand. But what good would it do to juggle the ledger, unclamp her reticule, and fish around for it? None. *None!* She'd have to use her wits here.

The man who stood before her took her breath as ruthlessly as if he ripped her lungs from her chest. Frobisher held his hat in hand and inclined his head, his soft brown curls relieving the sharpness of his cheekbones, his granite-brown eyes seizing hers like a hawk spotting prey. "My heavens, you are stunning in that dark green wool. Even more breathtakingly lovely than in Brighton."

Brighton? She flinched.

A superior smiled played at his lush lips. "You did not notice me."

Her eyes flashed wide.

"The dressmakers', my beauty."

A sound of outrage escaped her.

"Pip noticed."

She set her teeth.

"He had loved you well even then, I saw. One would be blind not to notice…even before one glimpsed your growing belly."

She would not flinch.

"Ah, my dear. How well an amorous man suits you. But we knew you were so charming that any man worth his salt would take you to bed often so that you'd soon be with his child. Miles Armstrong is a lucky man."

She wanted to shriek at him. But her throat closed. How she hated that he could so easily cow her.

He strode toward her, easy in his skin, louche and confident as only a man so excessive could be. "I heard you would come to call today. I longed to see you." His gaze caressed her breasts. "Your bounty, all to myself."

She found her strength and summoned the will to use it. She walked forward, giving him a wide berth.

He stepped in front of her and caught her by the shoulders.

She flinched at his touch. Her eyes watered, her stomach heaved, and she had to cover her mouth. She fought it. To be weak would gain her nothing against him.

"I have not forgotten you. How could I? You were nubile then. Voluptuous now." He inched closer, his mouth upon her forehead. His body heat enveloped her as he hovered over her. She retched at his cologne suffocating her. "You're fine. Just shock, eh? Breathe. As I breathe you inside me. I always did. I can taste you. Delectable. And you smell of a new perfume. Did he buy that? I don't like it. Mine will be a better complement. A musk to complement your own."

She shook him loose, her whole body vibrating with despair and anger. Headed for the stairs, she gasped when he shot two arms around her waist and settled his torso along her spine. His member was erect, and he rubbed it against her like an animal.

His lips against her ear, he breathed hotly on her skin. "He may have made you pregnant, but he can never make you happy."

She kicked backward.

He grunted.

Downstairs she heard Pip barking. Running, she dug her nails into the wooden boards. Pip hated him.

Verity kicked at him again and, this time, managed to break his hold.

But he caught her roughly. "I told you long ago I would have you one day. I meant it then, and I do now. Husband be damned. I will see to it he will not keep you."

She struggled.

Pip took the stairs, barking at the fiend she loathed.

"Christ, that dog!" Marlton groaned as he raised a hand to cup her cheek and turn her head.

But as he lowered his face to take her mouth and kiss her, she bit him.

"You *witch!*" He jerked her around.

She lashed out at him, wielding the ledger at him so that she struck him on the arm. "You will not have me. Ever."

He cupped his elbow, seething. "No? You think not? Ha! I will ruin him. You'll not want him."

"Money has no lure," she shot back.

"No? You like the inheritance!"

"What? *How—?*"

He hauled her against him. "Or is it by advertisement any man wins you, my pet?"

Pip growled and went for his trousers.

Marlton shook his leg to fling the dog free. "Get this damn thing off me!"

"Leave me alone!" She writhed.

He let her go, but grabbed for Pip. Failing, he kicked at the dog.

But she eluded him and snarled.

Verity ordered Pip to her side.

But he caught her again. "Perhaps, my sweet, if I burn down your husband's house. The kitchen garden fire was so small."

He had set the fire in the back garden? She spun free, hitting him about the head with the ledger. "Bastard!"

He stood away, arms up, and gave a sinister laugh. "Your kind of bastard!"

Pip whined, eager to attack him.

"Stay," she told the dog as she backed carefully toward the stairs.

"I care not what you think of me," he crooned like the very devil. "I am for you, my lovely girl. Only you."

She scrambled to pick up her growling little dog, then whirled on him, panting. "Before I am ever yours, you, Thomas Frobisher, will burn in hell."

Then she hugged Pip close, secured the ledger under her arm, and strode away.

⇶⇷

SHE SAT IN the traveling coach the next day, Pip in her lap. Silent. Mulling over the confrontation in the loft.

She'd slept last night, but awakened often to memories of Thomas, fears of Thomas, threats of Thomas to burn their house, ruin Miles, take her from him.

Her aunt had pestered her to talk. "I know something is amiss. Talk is the beginning of a cure, Verity."

"When I can, I promise I will, Aunt." For now, she had to keep it all to herself. Fortunately, her little dog seemed unhurt. She had so feared Marlton might have kicked the animal and hurt her. But Pip had curled near her, quiet through the night in her bed.

The little dog did whimper now and then as they made their way home to York. Pip was as harrowed by the confrontation as she.

She'd been foolish to think she would forever escape such a nefarious man as he. He had seduced and tricked her cousin Amanda into marriage and his diabolical games. He assumed she would be easily lured. And she had…nearly so.

Nearly so.

That was what shamed her.

Her naiveté.

To think he was blameless for the bruises she'd so often seen on Amanda's neck and arms. To take Amanda's word for their presence and not to think more deeply about their position and their number. How over the years, her marks increased in severity. How she moved so gingerly so very often. As if she too had been thrown against a wall.

As dusk fell and their journey wound down the road toward home and an end, so too did Verity's thinking. And she came to a conclusion.

She would tell Miles.

But what could she say without telling him the whole of the hideous story? He would think poorly of her. To have run from the problem. To run so far. To run into marriage, no less. An arranged marriage.

Miles had such a dastardly experience with his first wife, she could not sour his opinion of her. He would be outraged.

He would not learn. Not from anyone here.

This whole thing should be a secret. His appearance. A secret between Pip and her. That would be so much simpler than telling Miles the whole of her discontent.

But she would pay a price for that.

For there were sins of omission as well as those of commission. What she had done wrong was flee her problem. Flee the man. His proposition. His trap.

If she did not tell Miles the whole of it, she committed the sin of covering up her past.

And when she did, she feared she would kill the light in his eyes. Destroy the joy he found with her, through her. And she with him.

When that happened, she would destroy any hope he would ever love her.

Then what would she do?

Live her life without the very man whose breath made her own a joy?

He would never love her.

Yes, there was that chance. Small, large, she could not gauge. For this sin was not hers. Never had been. Yet many men saw women as the root of evil in such matters of sexual attraction.

Miles had blamed his wife for her proclivities. And truly, the woman had agreed to her liaisons. She should pay for her own choices. But she was not the only one at fault. She had met and fallen in with men who agreed to the same behaviors.

Yet Verity could not allow that belief to stop her from doing what was right.

Because if she did not reveal what horrors Marlton cast upon women and men, how could she live with herself? Bring up her child—their child—with the integrity necessary to live a fruitful and useful life?

She'd have to reveal all to the man she adored.

And if he could not love her after that, then she would leave him. Take her child. For she would not leave a babe with a man who could not see that humans were frail but strived to be better and often were. She would ache to have Miles as her true love and friend and husband for all her days. But she would not conceal her fears or foibles for fear of his ridicule or rejection.

Nor would she remain silent and give aid to anyone who deserved nothing less than total disgrace upon their name and being.

Chapter Eighteen

MILES HAD BEEN alerted by his gardener, who ran to the house to say the traveling coach rounded the long drive to the main house. He rejoiced that Verity arrived, and raced down the center stairs. The new footman was just opening the front door for him when Miles strode across the foyer and out onto the portico. Dusk cast shadows over the land, and he could not distinguish well his wife inside the coach. No matter. He himself opened the coach door, grinning in expectation. He'd missed Verity every minute she'd been away.

He spread wide his arms to welcome her, and in a flash, his delight died.

She gasped at sight of him and burst into sobs. She slapped one hand over her mouth, then fell into his embrace.

Startled, he clasped her close. She trembled, and he did too at the shock of her sorrow.

"Darling, what has happened?" He did not expect an answer. She was in no condition to speak. Behind her, stunned and shaken, her aunt appeared. He shot the lady a look of apology, more wince than welcome, and let the footman do his duty by her.

He carried his wife up the steps into the foyer and straight back into the small sitting room to which the butler and footmen usually retired while on duty. He kicked shut the door, sat her down, and clutched her to his chest. After dislodging her hat, he unbuttoned the collar of her pelisse and buried his lips in her hair. No words, no entreaty did he plan. She was too undone to talk, and so was he, realizing that whatever had befallen her, relief from it had come at sight of him.

She cried her heart out, her head tucked under his chin.

He stroked her back. Cursed his lack of a handkerchief and waited.

At length, she quieted and wiped her cheeks with her fingers. She gulped and burrowed against him.

"Would you like tea?"

She shook her head and let her tears fall a bit more.

In time, he asked, "Was there an accident on the road?"

"No, no."

"Did you have an argument with your aunt?"

"Never. No." She shivered.

He lifted her chin. My God. She was ravaged. "Shall I take you upstairs? Would you like to go to rest?"

"I want to sit here. With you."

He combed his fingers into her hair, escaped now as it was from her pins and flowing like gossamer over his fingers. "Can you unburden yourself to me?"

She cast her lovely green eyes over his features. The look took his breath away. She loved him. His heart swelled. He'd known it for days, weeks. For he loved her in return.

"I want to. I will. I...I just had such a terrible experience at home." Tears welled up in her eyes, and yet again she could not contain them.

He sighed and hugged her close. "Listen to me. I am going to take you upstairs to our bedroom. We'll get Mary to help you undress. I'll call for tea and a light supper for you. For your aunt, too. I will welcome her briefly. She's dismayed, poor lady, by your sadness."

"Then you'll come to me?"

"At once. I will see to all this, and when you are comfortable, you and I will talk."

HE STRODE INTO the main salon where Verity's Aunt Agatha awaited him. His footman had notified him that the lady had been shown to her bedroom and that she had refreshed herself, but had requested to see him as soon as he was able.

She sat in the cheerful room that his wife had so joyfully refurbished. Her features drawn, her silver hair pulled back in a tight chignon, she was meticulously attired in a complementary dove-gray and blue traveling suit. She met his gaze with sorrow in her own and made to rise.

He shook his head. "Please do not stand on any ceremony, ma'am. I am Miles to you."

She nodded and resumed her chair, her posture erect, her eyes welling with tears. "And I am Aunt Agatha to you, sir. I wish no other address."

"Thank you," he said with abject gratitude and went to sit opposite her near the fire. He noted on the table to her side sat an empty tumbler and a plate with a few crumbs of bread and pastry. "I see the footman has brought you a whisky and biscuits."

"All a woman needs after a long journey with a silent, brooding niece."

"Cook has hot soup and fresh bread for us in a few minutes."

She gave him a wan smile. "But first, how is she?"

"Mary is helping her undress and wash and get into bed." He took a huge breath. "Let me welcome you with all the fondness in my heart that I know Verity bears you."

"I knew you would do that, sir."

He folded his hands in his lap. "Please tell me all."

"She came to me day before yesterday so full of her usual vim and vigor. But there was more to her. She has blossomed with you, sir, in many ways. That she is *enceinte* is a thrill to her, because her mother had so many problems in that regard. For the manner in which you two met and married, this relationship is a marvel. I saw it in her demeanor as she came to visit me alone. I saw it as you greeted her tonight and took her to your heart in her agony. I am most happy, sir, for her and for you. Such regard in an arranged marriage is not the norm. I would say that you, as a viscount, know this. Your class does not marry for affection, but only for advantage."

"I gather from Verity that the unions in your family are based mostly on great fondness, one for the other."

"This is true. We are in business, most of us, clerks or managers. High or low, we marry for love. And we wed with full commitment to make that love grow and prosper."

"The finest way to live."

"It is."

"And to Verity's outburst? What happened, Aunt, that she is so distraught?"

"I will tell you what I can. It is not much. I know where she intended to go yesterday and what she intended to accomplish. Aside from that, I am without the facts, and she has told me nothing."

"Very well. I am confused. Please go on. What did she do? Where did she go? Whom did she visit that this is the result?"

"That first day she came, it was late. Dusk had come, and we settled in for a good chat and supper. Your men went to the smithy's with your coach and spent two nights, eating at the local inn. The next morning, I had a crippling ache in my legs. I often do. And Mary, her maid, had the sniffles. She is still not well. A congestion in the chest. I do not like it, Miles. She wheezes."

"I'll get a remedy from the apothecary."

The lady licked her lips and grimaced. "Our Verity suffers too. She should not. I wish I knew what happened but…what I do know is that with Mary and me unable to accompany her the next morning, she took Pip and headed for the vicar's and the charity."

"Goodwood House."

"Precisely. She walked. Not far, it is, and she promised to return in time for tea."

"And did she?"

"Oh, more than. It was near two o'clock when she appeared at the door. She had in her hand the account ledger for Goodwood. She looked…ashen. Frightened. And unable, or rather unwilling, to speak but a few words."

He pulsed with alarm. "Did someone accost her? Hurt her?"

"No. No. She was whole in dress. But not in manner."

"And Pip?"

"Quiet. Not her usual little self."

"I agree," he said, his heart hammering. "She seems watchful over Verity, but…different."

"Wary. On guard."

"Why?"

The lady stared him in the eye and inhaled deeply. "The vicar is not one who has a high opinion of women."

That confounded him. "But he runs that charity for those who need shelter."

"He does. But that does not mean he believes that women are capable of good deeds. And come to think of it, that reality came home to Verity when an old friend of hers visited us early yesterday morning."

"What happened?

"Verity's friend, now Mrs. Felix Bainbridge, married years ago, but her father is in poor health. Fired by his employer for witnessing something he should not have seen. Her father told the vicar and asked for his help. But he did not aid the girl's father, and Verity was not pleased about it."

"Would the vicar argue with Verity about that? So much that Pip must watch over her?"

Agatha shook her head. "I doubt that. But our girl can get a notion and sting ferociously."

"I've not seen that, but I don't doubt it. So then, you say she came home with the charity's account book. Did she look at it? I daresay she has the right to examine it, since she contributes to the house's upkeep."

"She did. Last night when she came home, she lit a fresh taper and took it to read, page by page. And although she would not speak to me of whatever disturbed her on her visit, she did tell me at the end of her review that she found nothing amiss in the records. She thought the records viable because, this morning, she announced we would come home early today. She would cancel her plan to go to Goodwood with the vicar. So we asked a neighbor to get us Jessup up from the smithy, and when he arrived, she had him drive to the vicar's and return the ledger to the vicar. 'Twas Jessup who handed the book over to Whitley. And nothing was said between the men, save the vicar's thanks."

"That's good." Nothing was terribly amiss. What an impasse. "But then...yesterday, she visited the house. What of her assessment?"

"She would say only that the house was neat, clean, and all in order."

"Servants are there. A maid and cook, is that right?"

"That's true. She told me she saw them and they were in good health and happy to see her. Beyond that, she said naught."

"There is more," he said, reflecting on this. "There must be."

"She will tell us in time. She is not one to keep secrets."

He thought of another cause of her distress. "Verity worries about the source of the inheritance."

"Aye, she wrote to me saying that."

"Did you speak of that with her?"

"Not in any detail, no."

He sat back. "Do you have any idea of who may have given her the money?"

The lady shook her head. "No. I do not write fairytales."

A woman's cry pierced the house.

"Milord! Milord!"

Footsteps pounded the stairs.

He shot up from his chair. Was that the maid? "Mary?"

"Milord! Ohhh, sir!" The maid careened to a halt in the doorway. Her eyes wide, she stood, white and shaking. "Sir! Come! Now!"

He strode toward her. "What's—"

"My lady, sir! Ohhh, sir. She's bleeding!"

⇸⟩⟩⟩⟨⟨⟨

VERITY CLUTCHED HIS waistcoat in her fists. Tears marred her cheeks. Fear stood dark in her wide eyes. "I won't lose this baby! I won't!"

"No, sweetheart. No. You won't!" He covered her hands with his own, chastising himself lest he lead her on in regard to a matter that he nor she nor anyone could control.

"I won't let him win! Not like this!" *She speaks of that vicar? God in heaven.* What had the man done?

"I know you won't." He wanted to promise her that. But how could he? "No one defeats you!"

"I must keep him," she moaned, and wrung the satin in the vise of her fingers.

"Listen to me, darling. You must stop." He tried to pry her nails from his clothing, but she would not budge. "You've got to rest. Please."

"No. No." She hung her head and shook it back and forth in misery.

He uncurled her fingers and urged her down to the pillows. "You must be calm. It's the way for you to recover yourself."

She let out a sob.

He soothed her as best his own breaking heart could summon. "The midwife's on her way. She'll help you. But you must not cry anymore. All will be well."

She lay back, her eyes wild. "Who is she? I don't know her. Get Aunt Agatha. She knows who my mother had. She'll get *her*."

"Your aunt's right here, my darling. Here. Look just there."

"You will be well, sweet girl." Agatha rose from her chair to put herself in Verity's line of sight.

"Get Mama's woman."

"Oh, my dear. Your husband has summoned one better than she."

Verity examined his face for truth of that. "She'll come?"

"Yes, she does. She does," he assured her, and she sank, drained of all her fury, to the bed.

✦

THE HALL CLOCK chimed half eight o'clock when the midwife, a Mrs. Scofield from York, appeared in the main salon. She had arrived more than an hour ago, introduced herself without embellishment, and asked to go straight to her patient.

She was a woman of ordinary height and ordinary features, dressed in simple cotton of reds and greens. Of robust health, she smiled at him with good cheer as she took the chair he offered her. Wearily, she included Agatha in her kind regard.

He held his breath to hear her diagnosis of Verity's condition. "Please, tell us if she has lost the child. I long to return to my wife to comfort her."

"Your wife, I am happy to say, sir, seems out of danger of losing the babe. A few drops of blood she had. But no more. I have examined her, and I doubt there will be more bleeding. However, she did tell me she had a trying time on her visit to her former home in Bradford."

"She did. She was frightened."

"Well, sir," she said as she folded her hands together and met his gaze with firm resolve, "she is resting well. But whatever she did there, whomever she saw there, she must not again. She is hale and formed well to carry a child, but it is not a good thing to so upset a lady during her time. She must be nourished in body and soul. Has she been with child before this?"

"No. We are newly married."

"This is her first. I see." She frowned, her delicate brown brows telling of her worry. "Often, a woman can lose her first babe. In so early a stage, her body is changing so quickly that she does not adapt well."

Agatha got tears in her eyes. "Do you think this is true of my niece?"

"I cannot say, ma'am. She has had a shock. It has undone her. The bleeding has stopped, but she must not endure such again. If she does, she will surely lose the child."

"I will ensure she remains calm," Miles murmured.

"I suggest a week's rest in bed. Good food, books to read. She tells me she draws and paints. She must do that. Express herself. Override her anxiety. But after bedrest, she must be up and about, in sunshine, walking, no riding, no journeys, and no worries. None. Whatever has disturbed her must wait until she is stronger and can see her way through the problem.

"I have told her this," the woman said to him. "She is not to fret or trouble herself with anything. She is to be happy, and prepare herself to deal with whatever upset her, but only in a week or two. Not before."

"I will see she follows your instructions," he said, relief winging through him.

"Whatever this is that upsets her, you are not to ask her about it. She must come to you. And if she does and you see her in distress over it, you will stop her. Assure her you can wait. This is most important. Or the babe will be lost…and maybe even she herself. Many a woman has bled to death in a miscarriage."

"I understand. I will trouble her for nothing."

"I will return tomorrow at noon and each day for five to re-examine her. We will pray she remains in good health. But if in the meantime she has a recurrence, you will send your man for me at once."

"I will."

Chapter Nineteen

“I WANT TO tell you everything,” she told Miles after the midwife left early in the middle of the night.

“I won't hear any of it. Not until you feel better.” He kissed her hand and would have left, but she would not let him go.

“Stay. Sleep with me here.”

“You need to rest.”

“I will do that better if you are beside me.” Tears threatened. “Please. Do not sleep elsewhere.”

“If I bother you, you will tell me to leave.”

“I will kick you out in a trice, sir.”

He laughed, but he undressed in his dressing room and returned to her to take her against him.

They slept that way, twined together as they had been each night since they'd wed, except now they did not make love. They slept peacefully side by side.

Terrified of losing the baby or of losing her own life, Verity followed the midwife's orders. Remembering scenes of her mother berserk over her own miscarriages, she did not move from the bed except for the necessities. She did not bleed, and she was grateful. Though she hated the silence imposed upon her, she found it possible to think of Marlton and put his assertive actions against her in perspective. She had no reason to see him again, and in that she found comfort.

Each morning, it was Miles who brought her breakfast. Each afternoon, he appeared with a tray full of weak tea and biscuits, eggs, bacon, potato dumplings, and a new passion of hers, apple tarts.

"My intention is to grow big and fat and you won't be able to find me amid all my stuffing!" she told him a week later, patting her middle.

"Do it. If it pleases you, I care not if you eat every apple in the shire's orchards."

"How come the preparations for the Harvest Ball?" It would be in four days, and she wanted to be well enough to attend and dance with Miles. She said nothing to him in that regard, for each time she said she'd rise, so did his alarm. She would refrain and bide her time.

"Very well. Lady Sayer takes command." The woman was a leader of York society of whom Miles had spoken often. That lady's husband was a longtime friend of Miles and his father. "She has in previous years. I told her you are indisposed and unable to continue to help her. She sends her regards, by the way. So does Mrs. Newhouse, who came to call with her husband earlier this morning."

Verity recalled Charlotte very fondly. "Do they still want to sell their mill?"

"Yes, they persist in trying to sell it to me, too. I told them that I would not be able to travel to Durham to inspect it anytime soon, because I will not leave you."

She smiled at him. "I hate that you are delaying your plans because of me. But I am honored that you are."

He stood then and bent to kiss her lips. "You are more important to me than any business venture, my darling."

She pushed back happy tears. "You are very good to me."

"As you are to me. Now rest. I leave you. I have a few meetings next week with those who are my final selections for shipping."

"That's wonderful. You've chosen?"

"I have whittled the candidates to two."

"I am so sorry I am not able to hostess those dinner parties you wished to have."

"My negotiations go apace without them. We have time for dinner parties, darling, when you are better."

MILES LED HIS four guests into the main salon. He'd promised them brandy, and each had readily accepted. All of them were leaders in York business circles. Three of the four—Lord Sayer, Mr. Canabry, and Mr. Ruckles—had come alone without their wives, as Miles had explained in his invitation to dine that his own wife was indisposed. The third man, Thomas Frobisher, the Earl of Marlton, was a widower and had been quick to accept, and responded to him that he wished Lady Bellamy a speedy recovery from whatever afflicted her.

Miles had been pleased that Marlton accepted his dinner invitation because he'd not met him in over a year. His younger brother, Phillip, was the one with whom Miles had opened negotiations for placing his goods on their ships to the New World. Marlton resembled his younger brother in height and coloring, but in his features and in his demeanor, he was more pointed. Abrupt. Nigh unto rude. Miles could not say he ever liked the man and, frankly, did not trust him. That was a shame, because he had strongly considered his shipping rates as viable.

"I understand, Lord Bellamy," said Lord Sayer, "that you have met Roger Newhouse. My second cousin's nephew. He sells his Durham mill?"

"Yes, of course. A fine fellow. Both he and his wife were here yesterday to call upon us. My wife enjoys their company greatly, as do I."

Sayer considered the brandy in his crystal tumbler. The older man regarded Marlton across from him with a wary eye. "My nephew tells me you may be interested?"

"I cannot say definitely, sir. I should like to tour the premises and will not do that until my wife fully recovers her health."

Across the room in the Chippendale, Marlton shifted one leg over the other.

Miles blinked. Had he detected that Marlton had covered a sudden look of satisfaction on his face?

"Oh, Bellamy," Sayer said apologetically, "my wife and I do hope your wife will soon be well."

"We think so, sir. In fact, we expect in a few weeks we can announce our good news."

Sayer and the other guests blinked and startled, nodding as they caught Miles's inference. They raised their glasses in a toast of congratulations. Marlton followed with his own elaborate salute, his dark brown gaze on Miles oddly feral.

They continued a polite discussion of the harvest festival, the weather, and the coming Christmas season until the conversation went to the natural end.

"I will leave you, Bellamy," Sayer said after Canabry and Ruckles made their excuses.

Marlton glanced about. "I too shall depart. But first, if you don't mind, I must seek the men's retiring facility."

"Certainly," Miles responded. "My butler can direct you." Suddenly struck by a cutting dislike for Marlton, Miles watched the man head for the hall. Hair on the back of his neck prickled.

But he shook it off and accompanied the three to the hall and stairs down to the foyer. The butler stood at the door with the gentlemen's coats across the hall table.

Canabry and Ruckles departed with great thanks for an enjoyable evening. Sayer awaited his coat.

"I say, sir," Miles said to Sayer, his dislike of Marlton provoking a heinous thought, "I have a question for you."

"Of course. Anything." Sayer shrugged into his greatcoat with the help of the butler.

"Did you refer your nephew and his wife to me as a potential buyer of his mills?"

"I did speak highly of you, sir. But I will tell you true and break a confidence, for you need to know the truth. There is another who instigated this."

"Who?" Miles asked, awaiting confirmation of ugly suspicions.

VERITY ROSE FROM her chair, her chalk in hand as she paused to reflect from a standing position her latest sketch of Miles. By far, it was the best she'd ever done. He smiled upon her from the paper as he did in life. This she would show to him.

He asked so often, and now, tonight, she would offer it up in pride.

She blew out the candle and turned to Pip, who lay in her pile of bedding in her studio. She had taken to lying there during the days. She limped from Frobisher's attack, but she did get better slowly. She, much like she and others who had fought with Frobisher, was bruised and sore. But she seemed to recover, and she was happy for it.

With a smile to the little dog, Verity padded in her slippered feet toward their bedroom. She discarded her robe upon the bed and thought to check the quality of the fire in the sitting room. Lately, since her confinement, Miles had taken to sitting in one of the chairs, and encouraged her to sit with him to discuss the day's events before they retired. She liked to check the fire before he came up. Tonight, it burned steadily but unevenly.

Flinging her long braid over her shoulder, she picked up a poker and stuck it in the blaze.

The snick of the door latch had her turning.

"Good evening, my sweet."

Her smile died as her poker rose.

From the other room, Pip growled.

Frobisher strolled near. He shot a glance at the door where Pip appeared, snarling and walking forward slowly.

The lines of Frobisher's smiling lips turned her stomach. "You do look recovered. Your husband said you've fared well."

"Get out."

He approached.

She held her ground. The poker rose higher.

Pip stalked him, but wavered on his paws.

Frobisher glared at the dog, satisfaction in his dismissive regard of the animal. To her, he crooned, "I had to see how you fared, dear one. I could not leave without the sight of you to warm me."

"I'll do more than warm you." She took a step toward him. "Get. Out."

He raised his palms. "I mean only to wish you well, dearest. I had no idea I'd so upset you weeks ago."

She held the glowing poker near as she could to his rich ruby satin waistcoat. "Shall I burn you?"

"You have already, dear one. Years ago, when I first saw you, I wanted you." He waggled a finger at her in the delicate muslin nightrail. The garment was transparent, but she did not move a muscle. To be shy or modest would gain her no ground with him. "I envy him. He sees you like that. Naked. He loves you. Plants a baby in—"

She darted forth, and the silk of his clothing sizzled.

He jumped backward.

"Marlton!"

She wanted to shriek her joy.

Miles had a gun. Pointed straight at Thomas's chest. He strode in and circled the man to Verity's side. The flintlock, she noted, was already in position to fire. "You will go or you will die. Which would you prefer?"

A flash of fear crossed Marlton's craggy features. His hands up higher, he tipped his head. "Of course, I shall leave you."

Miles strode forward, motioning his pistol for the man to

walk before him. "Go to bed, my love. I will return as soon as I throw out the slops."

⇒⇒⇒⇐⇐⇐

MILES FOLLOWED MARLTON to the door. Picking up the fiend's coat flung across the table, he threw it at him. "Go. Never come within sight of my wife."

"Oh, but we do need to finalize your shipping arrangements." His bravado, Miles noted, was to appear brave as Miles's butler and Lord Sayer looked on.

Miles extended his arm, aiming the pistol at the creature's heart. "Oh, by all means," he ground out, "do stay. We can finalize your funeral arrangements."

The butler pulled open the front door, then scurried backward, cowering.

Marlton tsked at Miles. "Really, sir! Would you rot in prison for my murder?"

"No jury in the world would convict me when they hear that you tried to ruin my reputation by deprecating my products to Gaylord and thence to the Newhouses. But worst of all, you attacked my wife in her bedroom. No, I would be found innocent."

"Ah, well." The man shrugged into his greatcoat and cast a quick, yearning glance up the stairs. "Gaylord preferred my money more than the exercise of his ethics. And the Newhouses?" He sneered at Sayer. "Very gullible. And there is no proof."

"Their word is enough. Get out."

Marlton arched a brow. "It's so good to see you adore this second wife. Francesca demanded it, but this one deserves it."

Miles pressed the pistol to his chest.

Marlton put up his hands, then turned and strode off into the night.

Chapter Twenty

"H E'S GONE?" SHE stood before the sitting room fire, her hands clasped before her. She had donned her winter robe of quilted green silk. Her expression was clear, focused. And she did not tremble as she had the night she returned from her journey. Though her calm appeared real, Miles did not expect it to be enduring. Not after what she had faced. Nor would he demand explanations from her after such a violent confrontation.

"He is." Miles went to her and took her against him, stroking her long braid down her back. "You are cold. Come to bed."

"No." She stood back. "No. You must hear this. I will tell you who he is and what he did to my cousin…and what he tried to do to me."

"Very well. Will you sit?"

She nodded, but remained standing.

Shaken by the man's virulence, Miles had steeled himself to this discussion with her by secluding himself alone in the salon for a few short minutes after Marlton left. Whatever that creature had done to Verity, she had paid enough for it. He would not add more.

He took the chair nearest her.

She stood, within arm's reach, standing and observing the fire in the grate.

"Thomas Frobisher, the Earl of Marlton, married my cousin,

my second cousin, when she was eighteen. Two years older than I, she was a beauty, and even though she was from trade, her father gave her a coming out. She was sought after. With long golden hair and grass-green eyes, she would have been the Season's diamond. That is, if she'd been of the upper class. And if her own mother had had a good reputation.

"Marlton was the leader of society and the wealthiest man in the area. He pursued her. She was overwhelmed with his courting. Honored."

Verity looked at him, but saw only the past. "She would do anything to ensure she married him. Anything. I know because she told me. Her mother, my own mother's first cousin, had abandoned her home and husband years before. Whatever the reason, it must have been scandalous, because my mother would never tell me. What she did say was that Amanda needed a friend. And I was that to her. I thought she was to me. But I was wrong.

"I first met Marlton the day before he married Amanda. Then and there in Amanda's parlor, he tried to seduce me. Frightened, I went to Amanda and told her. What he had done did not matter to her. She would have him.

"They married, and he took her to London. Brighton, too. A long honeymoon trip of months. When they finally returned north and Amanda invited me to go to Marlton Grove in Bradford, they had been married more than a year. I was to stay for a two-week visit, but within two days, I returned home.

"He came to me in my bedroom and attacked me. I fought him off. Screaming down the house, I set him off. I ran to Amanda and told her. Again, she did not care that he was of such bad repute. She had his name, his title, and his wealth. She did not care about my concerns. I could leave.

"And I did. I told my father. I did not worry my mother with it. She was ill, dying. My father told me she did not need to hear my tale of… She didn't.

"Everyone knows about his behavior. My aunt. The vicar. All the local women."

He could not believe the man's audacity. "Such arrogance."

"He makes a practice of seducing women. The younger the better. Comely. Naïve. Lured by his words and his money. Taken to his home and locked in his rooms."

"Does not anyone stop him?" It was a foolish question, because Miles knew few could.

"Over the years, I have heard of two girls who went to the high sheriff. Nothing came of their charges. Marlton pays them, you see. And if they become pregnant, he pays for a local midwife to abort them. If the women run away, he does not bother to find them to aid or to pay for the children."

The enormity of Marlton's appetites and sins lodged in Miles's stomach like stones. "And your cousin accepted his behavior?"

Verity lifted her shoulders in resignation. "She protested, I know she did. But not for long. She learned the laws and stepped away from any action. After all, by what legal basis could she object? Divorce can be initiated only by a man. Proof of adultery is meant for a man to bring charges of criminal conversation. Not a woman. And the chances of winning against a titled lord are so very small."

She stared at him, her anger stark and meant for Marlton and all the men who had defiled a woman, then had ignored them.

He had not brought divorce proceedings against Francesca. He had proof against her. But he had not done so. Notoriety had stopped him. Further disgrace, continued and rife, in courts and broadsheets.

But then he had come to terms with the fact that, as Marlton had accused him downstairs, he had never loved Francesca. Not really. After their marriage, he saw the extent of her self-indulgence. Her demands, her screaming fits, her enormous expenditures. What had been his infatuation with her had soured to revulsion. That had fueled her to take more lovers. Her bouts with syphilis had sent her to the countryside, where she dealt with the cures, such as she might. Then one day, she was afflicted by a growth she could not dispel or heal.

He rose to put two hands to the stone mantel. Francesca was gone. He had another wife, generous, caring, devoted to him, worthy of all the love he bore her. So long he had cared for her and had not told her.

He faced her, ready to hear the rest of her story, eager to declare what he should have said weeks ago. "Finish this tale. Then you and I will truly bury the past."

"I want to. But is it that easy?" She shook her head. "Marlton is…"

"Gone. I warned him to never approach you again."

"Is that enough?" Tears streamed down her cheeks, and she wiped them away with her fingers.

He dug from his waistcoat inner pocket his handkerchief, and she took it. "I will ensure it is." He'd hire guards. Men who were trained in pistols and knives. Boxers, knaves. Anyone from the rookeries with a skill.

He returned to his chair. "Tell me all you know." He needed to hear it, learn it, gauge it so that he could inform those he hired.

"What I have already told you is not worst of what happened between them. If Marlton had done it all along or if he began after they were married, I do not know."

"Done what?"

Verity stared at him, and her tears dried up. "He abused her. She came to visit us after my father died to offer her condolences. He had been buried in the churchyard, and she appeared by herself at the back of the church. She had bruises on her hands and wrists. Her throat, too. The black and blue marks were unmistakable beneath the white lace at her collar. I asked her about them. But I knew who had hurt her. She did not deny he had done it to her. 'No babies,' she said to me. 'He's angry.'

"I told her to leave him. She would not. She laughed, actually. Told me how she loved him. How good he was." Verity cringed. "In bed."

Miles felt his stomach churn.

"She told me he brought girls home to show her having sex with him and offered her to them as well. She agreed, she said, because she was his wife, and that was what made him happy."

"Dear God, Verity. The man is diabolical."

"Indeed," she said, as cool and serene as if she spoke of the weather.

"She died young. How?"

"Syphilis."

The revelation did not surprise him. The disease was so prevalent among men who took multiple partners and were indiscriminate about the types of partners they took. Often, those men's wives contracted the disease.

"After she died, he came to me and asked me to marry him. I refused. He said he would not take my answer as final. He kept coming to me. After my father died, I decided I could not bear to see him again. And I thought to leave home."

She faced him, proud and defiant. "I answered your advertisement. Wrote to you often. Began to hope I might claim a different life. A worthy man. And to my delight, I found you."

He went to her then, on bended knee. "I am so happy you did."

"You are not appalled that I came to you to escape someone?"

"Did I not advertise to find someone with whom I could change my own life?"

"Have you?" she asked, yearning in her words.

"I have. I have, my darling. I have married the most wonderful woman I could never have imagined or fashioned for myself."

"And I have you," she said, and her chin went up. She clutched his hand, then got to her feet. "Will you come with me?"

He nodded. "Or course."

She took him to the back room, her new little studio where her faithful Pip greeted him from her pile of bedding with a friendly wag of her tail. Poor dog—she too had suffered from the odious creature who had attacked them all.

Verity picked up one sketch from the pile of her drawings

scattered across her large desk. "Here, all you are to me. Better than any of my other impressions of you here…and the best man I am fortunate to have married."

He stared down at himself. The serenity on his face showed him what he had known for many weeks—he was the happiest he had ever been. She had brought him that. He had changed too. Believing that a woman might bring him joy and pride and triumph.

All the things a man could ever want.

All the love he had never had in such fullness.

The sketch in his fingers, he took her in his arms. "I love you," he whispered, and watched his words weave magic on her lovely face. "I have loved you for so long it seems I have loved you forever."

The smile on her lips lit up his heart. "You are my own true love, meant for me, I think—"

"Since the dawn of time."

She beamed at his response, and he led them to bed. There, he told her of all the little things that inspired his love of her. And she told him her fears had fled because of him.

Entwined they slept, secure in the knowledge that they had shared their heart's contentment with each other.

IF IT WERE possible, Miles and she were more attuned to each other in the days that followed. Free of their nightmares of the past, they went about their daily routines with laughter even more abundant than before.

Aunt Agatha noticed and commented.

Pip regained much of her former energy and pranced about behind Verity as she went about her day.

The new staff, including the new butler who'd been so startled at the confrontation between his employer and guest, fell into the rhythm of the house and the quiet, happy tone set by the lord and his lady.

New staff, all men of gruff appearance and agreeable manners, joined the household. Miles had recruited four men as guards for Verity. Sending an urgent request to London to his solicitors, he'd requested they interview and hire four strong fellows versed in attack and defense. Military veterans would be good. Men of unquestionable character would be best, but if others applied, they were to be sent to York, expenses paid for Miles to interview personally.

Just Friday, Miles had decided on the four. One man, William Stout, former corporal in His Majesty's Royal Artillery, pensioned out for loss of one toe and an eye, quick on his feet as a man with a full foot and sight. A second man, George Fremont—at six feet, nearly as tall as Miles—had earned pots of money as a bare-knuckle boxer. Punched once too often in the head, Fremont was still a hulk of intimidation. Though he could not read or write, he often appeared to notice nothing but his own shoes. The next two were brothers. Hamish and Henry Conners hailed from Dublin, and while they claimed a pristine background, their attitudes were gruff, their muscles so impressive, that the housekeeper had to stop the maids from asking for demonstrations of their might.

The addition of the four men to the household imparted a sense of safety. But only at first. As Verity began to feel more herself and go to town to shop, she looked over her shoulder and all about before she stepped anywhere. She could not stay at home for the rest of her life, and she was grateful for the presence of The Four, as all in the house now called them. But all servants, too, began to realize over time that The Four seemed superfluous unless the master and mistress were out and about, and the staff worried among themselves about the necessity.

Mary, Verity's maid, brought up the subject one afternoon as she helped Verity try on the new apricot French velvet gown that had just arrived from London's Marks and Dingall.

Verity knew what it was to be afraid of the unknown, the fear one could not explain but only predict with dreadful consequenc-es. She put a hand on the girl's shoulder. "Mary, you have heard, I am sure, about the confrontation between Lord Bellamy and a recent guest?" No one had told the butler, Finneas, to keep word of the incident to himself.

"I did hear, ma'am."

"Then you know that Lord Marlton has made advances to me and threatened my husband." As the girl opened her mouth, Verity raised her hand. "The four new men are here to protect us all. We do not trust Marlton. He is devious. My husband has warned all of you to be watchful of anything out of order, anything amiss."

"Do not," said Miles to the maid as he suddenly appeared in their sitting room, "take my warnings lightly. Be on guard and support each other in all things."

"I will, sir." The maid bobbed.

At that, Miles indicated she should leave them. "Return in a few minutes, Mary. I must speak to my wife." And when the girl was gone, he smiled at Verity and had her do a spin in the ball gown. "You, madam, will be the sensation of the evening."

She patted her rounding middle. The gown, flaring from waist to ankle, was cut very low and caught up beneath her larger breasts with a wide, darker rust ribbon. "I do hope I am the sensation who can dance and remain in her gown!"

"You will," he said as he took her hand and kissed it. "I'm sure of it. I've come with good news."

He had gone to town earlier to meet with gentlemen to final-ize the agreements for shipping Armstrong cloth abroad.

"And? Who is it to be?"

He had not told her details of the latest negotiations, only that Jameson and Company wished to redeem themselves after Lord Sayer had told them of the revelations at the dinner ten days ago. Verity had argued that they were not to be trusted with Armstrong products.

But Miles had wished to hear them out. "I have issues I must raise with them and get some satisfaction."

Still, she had stood for Bretton and Sons to win his business.

"You were right, my love," he told her now, "it will not be Jameson and Company. But Bretton."

"Good."

"In the end, Bretton had better rates, schedules, and assurances. But I have more good news. Shall we sit?"

"I hate to crush the gown."

"Shall I call for Mary to help you remove it?"

She was eager to hear it. "This will take time? Your news?"

He went quite serious. "It will. You must hear it now."

Concerned, she frowned, then took his hand to take him to the settee. "Tell me now. I will be careful I do not crush the velvet."

He held her hands in his. "I spoke with both Jameson brothers this morning before I called in Bretton. In that conversation, I told them frankly why the contract would go to Bretton. I told them Marlton admitted to me the night he was here that he'd criticized Armstrong cloth to them both and paid them to tell this to the Newhouses."

"Even though Gaylord Jameson still encouraged the Newhouses to go to you to buy their mill."

"Indeed."

"What did they say?"

"Gaylord regretted his actions deeply. He told me Lord Sayer told them of Marlton's attack on you here in our bedroom."

"You told Lord Sayer?"

"He remained until he saw me force Marlton to the cobbles at point of my gun."

"Dear me," she said, a mix of emotions running through her at the news.

"You must not be distressed, my darling. All is well. Jameson told me he tried to return the money Marlton had given him to malign our cloth."

"Money!" she scoffed. "Bribe, more like. Did Marlton take it back?"

"No. Is the man so evil that you could predict he would refuse his own bribe?"

"Of course." She shook her head in disgust. "Did Jameson keep the money?"

"No," Miles said with satisfaction hard in his dark eyes. "He even apologized for being so naïve in regard to Marlton."

"Would that they base their business agreements on fact and keep out of subterfuge," she said with anger.

"I told them their proposal and their rates were competitive, and I would have awarded the contract to them had they not been so unethical."

"Good." She was proud of Miles. "And what did they say to that?"

"Gaylord declares he has learned a very valuable and costly lesson. He vows to be more careful in years to come."

"But that they had lost the contract despite their new vows to reform?"

"Yes. I asked them, how could I trust them with my goods?"

"Exactly."

"Then Gaylord told me something more."

She waited, tilted her head, eager to know what it was.

"He said that in the same meeting with Marlton when he discredited our cloth, he told Jameson that you had come into an inheritance."

Verity's mind whirred. Miles understood she was in a quandary over the source of the windfall. She put a hand to her mouth.

"I see this strikes a bell."

"It does!"

"What?"

She shot from her chair. "Oh, Miles, I had forgotten… In all the commotion of the past weeks, I had forgotten what Charlotte Newhouse told me." She faced her husband.

"Go on."

"When she came to tea, she told me that Mr. Jameson said I had recently come into an inheritance. Jameson got this information from Marlton? That's…ridiculous. How would Marlton know or care? Why would he?"

"Is it another fabrication of Marlton's to upset you? I think it is."

"You discount it?" she asked, not a little surprised.

He peered at her. "Don't you?"

"I…I don't know. How would he know such a thing? The newspapers? I don't recall any word of it being printed. How could it? We never told anyone. Not a soul. I wrote to Aunt Agatha, but she would not tell it abroad. No. Marlton got word of it…but from whom?"

"I don't want you agonizing over this."

"I won't. Really…" She gave him a bright smile but didn't quite mean it. "Really. I won't."

"The money is yours. You do with it as you please. Whoever it was who gave it did so with intentions to improve the quality of your life. For that, we praise him or her. Whoever it was."

"Agreed."

But why improve someone's life unless you knew them? Or had done them wrong? Or…

"Verity?"

She faced him. "You are right. I will not be looking under every leaf and stick."

But she could question who, and why, her benefactor had given her so much, couldn't she?

Chapter Twenty-One

"YOU DO THE gown proud, my dear." Miles beamed at Verity and kissed her hand as Jessup slowly drew their carriage toward the stark, Palladian-style York Assembly Room. "I am delighted to introduce you to the world, viscountess."

She rolled her eyes and chuckled, pulling her rust velvet evening cape about her in the chill of the late September night. "I am honored, sir, and well you know it."

Through her window, she glimpsed the flames of evening bonfires set for the amusement of those who would not attend the ball, but frolic in the streets. People laughed, running past the carriage down the street toward the stalls at the end of the lane. For them, the price of bread had recently risen five pennies because the crop yield was not as bountiful this year as last. Whereas local noblemen and businessmen celebrated that the production of cloth in northern mills had gone up eight percent. For them more than the poor, the world looked peaceful and prosperous. Yet many rejoiced because Bonaparte, who had been exiled to Elba since April, was still there.

"You want to go celebrate with those in the streets, don't you, darling?" Miles arched his brows in knowledge of her desires.

"I do." She'd worn masks, raised her skirts in three-legged races, and danced around bonfires. "It's what I am used to."

"We'll go next year."

"But I will enjoy this here tonight." She'd been to balls in Brighton with him, but this was special because these were his associates and his neighbors, now hers. She climbed down from the coach and thrilled to the beauty of the staid Grecian columns around the entrance to the rooms.

For the briefest moment, she thought of the threat of Marlton. But she relaxed at once. Behind them, in the household's second carriage, sat The Four. Their diligent guards would not gain admittance to the ballroom, but they would take up spots at the front door and the rear servants' entrance.

"We will make our presence known, and we shall have our dance, then depart early. The word has gone out in the town that you are *enceinte,* my love. They will smile and approve of our early departure."

She squeezed Miles's hand. Tonight, she hoped they might resume their marital relations. The midwife had been to check on Verity earlier and approved it. "I've missed our intimacies," she whispered to him.

He kissed her hand once more. "As have I. We will go home to mark the harvest with our own gratitude for our own prosperity. Come now. Jessup stops."

Inside, Miles swept her down the receiving line full of earls and barons, the mayor, leaders of York businesses, all rich men and their wives, here to celebrate the richness of the year. She met so many, and frantically sought to commit their names to memory.

Fanning herself at the edge of the dance floor, Verity appreciated a reprieve from all the introductions. She could stand and enjoy the musicians. Yet in the lull, she searched for Marlton. Her hope that he had taken Miles's warning seriously fought equally with her fears that, as Aunt Agatha had said, the man would never give up.

Miles lifted her chin. His gaze was solemn. "Look at me, my darling. He is not here."

She shook her head. "Of course not."

"Word has gone out about what he attempted, and he will not show his face."

"No."

"The musicians begin a country dance. Shall we?" he asked with a grin, and she would not refuse him. Ever. Not anything.

"I know this set, and I have a problem." She inclined her head toward the chalked floor. "I cannot hop."

"And neither will I. We will lift a foot only. Now, shall we?"

They took the floor to begin the set with three other couples. They had not danced together since their honeymoon in Brighton, and Verity had so enjoyed it. She relished the movement to the music, bright and gay. Her husband, elegant and natural in his grace, was a marvel.

She managed to get through two of the three parts of the dance when she leaned toward him and said, "I hate to say this, but I must find the ladies' retiring room."

He went with her to the edge of a long hall where a line of ladies stood at the entrance to a room. "I will wait here."

"Good. Then we'll go home."

"We will." He waggled his brows at her.

She chuckled and made her way down the hall.

"There is such a long line here, Lady Bellamy," said one woman when Verity appeared next to her. "We have a lady here who is ill, and we've sent all who are in immediate need to the room beyond."

"Thank you," Verity said, happy for the recommendation. She hurried down to the end of the hall where a sign proclaimed it as the ladies' facility.

Inside, one lady stood taking her time arranging her skirts. Behind a folding screen, another lady relieved herself.

"They really should provide more for us," the woman who fussed with her gown complained. Then she bit her lips together and nodded toward a black cape the woman behind the other screen had discarded across the chair. "Some of us have more need than others."

Verity considered the screen and whispered, "Have you asked if she needs help?"

"I have." The woman shook her head. "She is *very* indisposed."

On a groan of frustration, the lady dashed away into the hall.

Verity went behind the available screen and picked up one china bourdalou. She took a few minutes, during which she heard the fall of feet and a snick or two. Apparently, the poor lady who had troubles must have emerged. Feeling fresher, Verity pushed down her skirts and rounded the screen, only to come face to face with Marlton.

He stood, arms crossed, looming over her in the cramped room. He wore black, all black. A high-collared frockcoat, simple cravat of ebony, and a huge domino cape. "Good evening, dearest. How lovely you are this evening."

In control of her surprise and her anger, she gave him wide berth and headed for the door.

But was halted by his hands to her shoulders.

She would not panic. She had escaped him before. Twice. Three times, really.

"Take your hands off me."

"Never," he said, breathing the word into her hair. "My God, you smell like flowers in May."

"And you, like refuse."

"Naughty. Naughty. By dawn, you will feel so differently."

"No chance of that."

"Ah," he said, and spun her around. One hand to her waist, he drew her near. With the other, he cupped one breast. "But there is."

Indecent pig. She strained away from him—and stomped on his toes.

He yanked her to him. "I will—"

She opened her mouth to scream.

But he clamped his hand over her lips. "Quiet! We do not want to hurt this babe."

She opened her mouth to bite him as she had in Bradford. But he perceived her move and snatched his hand away, then dug something from his pocket. She yelled for help. But he deadened her scream by jamming a handkerchief in her mouth.

She gagged.

"Now, this is what we shall do," he said, his voice raw as a seething savage. He leaned to one side to grab up the cape from the chair. "You shall wear this, and—"

As he draped it over her, she breathed deeply to keep herself calm. Just as he yanked the cords at the neck tightly, she wrenched free and charged for the door.

"Locked," he said, hauling her back against him. "Too bad."

He swirled the black domino around her form. Heavy and oppressive it was, and she understood its purpose was concealment. In it, she struggled to take a step. "You devil," she tried to say, but failed, her heart as leaden as the garment.

"You cannot run, but yet, oh so light. I shall carry you. A man taking home his wife for the evening."

She pushed at the wadded cloth in her mouth with her tongue.

He reached over, put a key in the lock, and turned it so the door swung open. With an ugly smile as he swept her up into his arms, he made the turn away from the dance floor and strode down the hall.

She did not squirm. She did not fight. But forced herself to think.

Think.

Miles will miss me.

Look for me.

And our men. The Four. Where are they? Two at the front. Two at the rear.

When Marlton took a set of stairs at the rear of the building, she had a spark of hope. Servants' stairs they were, narrow and bare. Dark, with the light of one window only.

Where are we going? To the exit where two of our guards are?

When she saw they emerged from the stairwell into a dank, hell-dark room, she saw the pile of coal. The coal cellar. And was there only one way in or out?

He set her down, swirled her to the wall, and wrapped rope around her wrists. Then he pushed her toward an opening in the far wall. To another set of stairs.

"Up this time," he told her. "You go first. Unwise to try to run, my pet, lest you lose that baby you so dearly desire."

She jerked away.

But he pressed his lips against her ear. "Break away and you might fall. But I shall catch you. Know I want this baby, too."

She startled. He wouldn't want the child. *Fiend.* He'd kill the babe.

He frog-marched her up the steps, his legs against hers in a disgusting erotic synchrony.

At the top, she sucked in cool night air. Her need for freedom ran through her like a bird on the wing. She shivered, somehow unafraid of him, only fearful for the loss of her baby.

"Yes. Now you see how determined I am to make you mine." He whistled, his attention toward the end of the lane. He'd arranged a private carriage?

But at once he was focused on her again, benevolent and malicious in his grin. "Mine, you will be. Made for me, you are. Just like Amanda."

Her instinct to hit him, hide, run from him died in that moment to the inquiry that suddenly possessed her. Somehow she moved the cloth in her mouth and spat it to the ground.

"Nothing…" She coughed and at last managed, "I am nothing like her."

He hovered over her and cupped her cheek in a feint of tenderness, his lips up in a rictus of pride and possession. "You are alike. The hair, the eyes, the shape of your face. Yet better than she, my girl, you are!"

"You're mad."

"For you?" He yanked her toward him and threaded his hands

up into her coif. With a jerk, he pulled down the wealth of her hair, leaving her pins gone, her tresses hanging over her shoulders. He drew her to him by winding the length of her hair around his hands. "Yes! All of you is mine! Always will be! Amanda was such a disappointment."

"You ruined her." She held back her nausea as he planted kisses down her throat.

"I did. Indeed, I did. In the beginning, she gave me as much grief. Like her, you will give in eventually."

"Never."

"Blood tells, my girl."

Her cousin had been his tool. "You ruled her. Hurt her."

"She liked it. You will too."

She bared her teeth at him, ready to bite or scratch. "No."

"You are her duplicate. My pet"—he gave a laugh that was a falsetto cry—"you are her *sister*."

His words froze her.

His smile was monstrous. "You are! Why did you think you inherited all that money?"

She fought for logic. "That…that's not true."

"She knew."

"You lie."

He gave a dastardly chuckle. "I'm afraid not, my pet! Where in hell is my man?" He glanced down the empty lane past the shops that were closed and dark for the night. Then he whistled again and returned to grin at her. "She told me. Her whore of a mother gave you away. Had to."

Her heart banged in her chest. *Oh, this cannot be true.* "No. No."

"A good trade. Your mother got a babe she could not bear. Amanda's mother gave you away to her cousin, your mother. Thus she got her freedom to go and fuck another man."

"You are insane."

"Even I could not make this up! 'Twas her father had the wealth. Ah, hell. Where is my hack?" He whistled again. He slackened his hold of her ropes for a second and…

"You?" She wrenched to fully face him and saw him in the firelight of a dozen bonfires. Townsfolk danced like shadows before the golden flames. "You told the Jamesons you knew of my inheritance!"

He stood staring down at her, his attitude superior, and snickered. "Of course. Confused you, did I?"

Oh, he was the most damnable creature.

Somewhere off, she heard a man call to his horse, and the animal's tack jingled.

"Amanda didn't tell you."

"But she did. Her father got a conscience and willed you a fortune."

"Makes no sense. Why would he—"

"Because he pimped out his wife. Gave her a taste!"

She stepped backward, appalled, her mouth open, shaking her head. "No. You're wrong."

"She liked the high life. More than he knew. But, turns out, he felt guilty. Silly bloke. Amanda took after her. Just like her. A whore."

"You fantasize."

He lifted her chin, ran his gaze over her, and laughed in her face. "Your call, my girl. I care not. Only that I will have you tonight. Dregs for your Miles when I'm finished. Do you think he'll want you after I've plowed your pretty depths? He didn't want Francesca. And let me say, she was a lovely bit in bed. Eager. Hungry. You will be too."

The man was ill. Whatever a doctor would call it, he was sick with his own importance. His own depravity.

A hack appeared, silhouetted in black against the bonfires' scarlet flames. The horse objected, nickering, snorting.

"Oi, guv!" the driver called. "Git in! Can't 'old the 'orse!"

The way the horse fought the smell of fire, it was for Marlton to yank open the door. But the handle stuck, and he pulled at it once more.

And Verity ran!

Straight for the end of the lane where a bonfire burned brightly. Her way lit by flames as high as she, she held her belly and prayed her new slippers would not skid on slops or droppings.

She reached the edge of the lane. Where best to run? In the fires' red flares she could see the cathedral towers glowing against the dark of night. Toward the river, more townsfolk celebrated. She turned left toward them and what refuge she could take among them. Three doors down, she panted. Out of breath, she stopped and sank back into a recessed doorway. Gasping, she fought to make no noise. She saw him at the corner. He came to a halt, cursed, and glanced around. She shrank backward. She heard his footfalls on the cobbles as he ran straight ahead.

Sure of her path, she darted out and strode fast as she could go toward the river. She'd get someone to run to the Assembly Room and fetch Miles. She had to.

She came upon a group of people dancing to the tune of a lone fiddler.

Running up to one woman, she begged her to help. "My husband, I need him. Please help me. I'll give you a reward."

The woman turned to gaze at her, and it was in her dazed eyes that Verity saw she'd been drinking. More than enough. Those with her, too, were drunk. They whirled around her, taunting her, yelling. "Reward?"

"Reward?

"I'll 'ave yer cape," said one.

"And I'll have your bobs," said another, laughing as she reached for Verity's ears and another tugged at her roped hands.

Verity shrank from one and yanked away from the other. And she whirled away. Only to see Marlton running toward her.

She took off, mindless of her ungainly jog. If she didn't survive, neither would her child.

She headed for another group who were laughing, dancing, drinking. She darted between two bonfires.

"Come now." Marlton was upon her, eyes wide with fright,

hands out, fingers curling, urging her to go to him. "You're safe with me."

She shook her head and stepped backward. The heat of a fire swirled round her.

"Don't be foolish, my pet. I love you. Your baby, too."

"*Verity!*"

She spun to the call of her husband.

Miles ran toward her. Opposite Marlton. "Come to me!"

"Never!" yelled Marlton.

She swerved, feigning a path toward the cathedral, but pivoting at the next corner toward Miles.

Marlton bellowed, and she heard him run after her.

She tried to pick up her pace, but she was so very tired. She slowed to a walk, her tears coming in hot waves, and felt Marlton lunge at her. She yanked away from his grasping hands. *Let me go. Let me go.*

Then she whirled straight into a wagon ablaze in errant flames. She took a step away, and felt his strong arms trap her. Her head grew hot. Something sizzled. She screamed, the smell of her hair on fire gagging her.

Marlton caught her in his arms and forced her to the ground. She fought. Oh, she fought. But he rolled her over and over, his own cape up over her head.

They rolled in the dirt, and those around them yelled and screamed at them.

He rose on his hands.

Scrambling away, she shrieked at the sight of him.

His hair was aflame. His clothes too. He struggled to push away from her, but he shrieked as the flames licked at him.

Miles caught up to her and grabbed her into his embrace. Someone threw him a coat, and he wrapped it over her head. "Safe. You're safe!"

Her head no longer on fire, she turned in Miles's arms toward Marlton.

They stood, mouths open, watching the man struggle to his

feet.

Verity, safe in Miles's arms, cried, "Water! Help him! Help him!"

One bystander did.

Then another. Another.

Someone threw Marlton a horse blanket to wrap around himself. But he could not.

Afire, he windmilled his arms, then sagged and fell to his knees. Succumbing to the flames as if he melted, he sank to the ground. A man ran forward and threw a coat over him. But it was to no avail. Marlton, his clothing caught, burst into a ball of flame. In a final fit of madness, he waved about, screaming, arms curled to his body, facedown.

He burned and burned. His clothing smoldered.

And he did not move.

The smell of his burned flesh filled the air. Revelers milled about, asked each other details, and mourned the tragedy before them.

No one dared touch him. He was gone. Gone. She and Miles waited, sentinels to his demise as the flames that killed him waned and, finally, the fire brigade came. Three men, one to roll him over, one to examine him, one to pronounce him dead.

Chapter Twenty-Two

S HE SAT IN the chaise longue in her studio, her hands lax in her lap, her inks and pencils and oils untouched. Gazing at the sun as it crossed the sky on this October morning, she was content to do nothing. Only think.

Her shock over the tragedy of Marlton's death at the harvest celebration was offset by the firm knowledge that the fright had not affected her baby. She was still pregnant. The midwife had come each morning for a week to examine her. Each time, she had declared Verity well. For that, she gave herself bright assurance each morning she awoke to check and then tell Miles that their child was still safe and secure in her care.

The fire, thank heavens, had not touched her skin. Her clothes had been singed by the flames. But her greatest loss was her hair. She'd thought for many years it was unfashionably long. But the flames that caught her unawares as she backed away from Marlton had taken the majority of it. She was happy she still had some of it. She now sported very short curls that, according to fashion plates of the last decade, resembled those of Napoleon's first wife, Josephine.

Verity received no one, though many had called to express their concern and hopes for her well-being. She'd received good wishes from both Jameson brothers, Lord and Lady Sayer, and Miles's associates.

News of her abduction and Marlton's death had appeared in many newspapers throughout the Realm. From the publisher of the *Fleet-of-Heart Chronicle*, Germaine Hammond, and her aunt, Lady Peregrine, came lengthy letters full of good wishes, as well as a large box of sugarcoated almonds from Fortnum & Mason in London. Germaine had also run the story in her newspaper. Miles and she received copies of the latest issues, and to their surprise, Germaine had run a small piece about their expected arrival in the spring. The *Fleet-of-Heart* newspaper was prospering and included not only news of engagements and marriages, but also the *Advice from Lady MatchMaker* column penned by an anonymous woman. She wrote a wry piece each week on the arts of attraction. Verity, Miles, and even Aunt Agatha had chuckled over her tidbits of how to find—and care for—a worthy mate.

Verity laughed, and made it a point to do so often. But for a limited time each day she allowed herself to ponder what occurred that fateful night of the ball—and it tormented her. In that one hour on days like today, when the sun shone through her studio window, she could promise herself a bright future and recall the horrid statements her attacker had made. She had told Miles that night he brought her home from the debacle what accusations Marlton had made. Not all of it. Not word for word. But enough that Miles was very concerned she not challenge her health.

"Please do not dwell on anything he said or did until you are rested and ready to discuss it all." He had kissed her hand and told her to rest. "Your aunt wishes to see you, too. Only to assure herself you are whole."

Aunt Agatha had come to her bedside, tears in her aging eyes, and told Verity she had never trusted Marlton. "He always had a cruel look about him."

Verity had agreed. And so it was that two weeks passed before she finally felt willing to take up her daily responsibilities. She hired a new upstairs maid, referred to her by the local registry. She responded to two letters from Mrs. Newhouse, both long past due. She wrote to Germaine Hammond, too, and congratulated her on the growth of popularity of her matchmaking newspaper.

She did not attempt to draw or paint. Her compulsion was to paint Marlton, and she recoiled at the injustice of such a claim to her precious time. She would not honor him so. Not now. Not soon. One day she would, because she wished to explore his inner self, and only through ink and paint could she fully view the character of his soul. For now, it was enough that she thought of him. And that, despite all that he'd done and all that he'd been, she mourned his passing in so frightful a manner.

She also began to notice that Miles regarded her in a careful manner. As if she would break. Fine porcelain. Too delicate to cope with such aggression and anger as Marlton had presented to her.

She surmised that Miles suspected a rift in her heart and it was caused by something Marlton had said that night. Truly, she had doubts about herself engendered by Marlton's attack on her and by his declarations of her parentage. She had trusted her parents, loved them both quite deservedly, and could not fathom that they had lied to her about her relationship to them. It tore her self-assurance to shreds that she might not be who she thought she was. Try though she might to cast off the questions, she could not.

Eager to banish whatever devils she grappled, she also wished to put to rest whatever now haunted her husband. She decided to tell him all about that evening and begin the process of healing whatever remained amiss between them…and within her own heart.

At breakfast, she had risen from the table—their old romantic finger-play resumed in playful manner. The butler had just delivered to her a letter from Charles Whitley, the vicar in Eccleshill. Verity had written him last week and asked him a favor. She hoped he had found what she needed.

To her husband she turned and asked him to come to her that

afternoon. By then she should have read and accepted whatever Whitley had found—or not—in the parish registry. "When you have finished your work for the day, Miles, please come talk to me."

"About what's in that letter?"

"And more."

"I will," he said with concern knitting his brows. "But if you decide against it…"

"I won't. I feel well. It is time."

He came to her as the clock in the hall struck one. His eyes were somber as he sat opposite her in their sitting room in the matching Chippendale. Since the abduction, he had been as caring as before, but at night, in bed, he held her close to him and stroked her back until she fell asleep. The threat of losing the baby had kept them both from expressing their love intimately in the past two weeks. That she understood.

"I want to make us whole again," she said to open their conversation. "I know you have been cautious with me, and justly so, but I fear a wall goes up between us. I am not certain if I have built that or circumstances did, but I want us back as we were."

He reached across to take her hand and led her to come sit in his lap. The nearness of old brought tears to her eyes.

"I know not either, but we will become as one again. I am sure of it. First, I will confess that I am tortured by the fact that I did not protect you from him that night. If he had hurt you… Oh, forgive me. Do, please." He paused, cupped her cheek, and struggled for words. "I am horrified that I did not look for you sooner that night. That I thought you safe and foolishly underestimated the evil nature of that man."

"Stop. Please do not torment yourself. You did all you could to protect me. The Four were on guard. But none of us knew the cunning nature of our foe. He followed us in Brighton. Was in a dress shop in London. He even set the fire in our Brook Street garden! All those other nefarious statements to the Jameson brothers and the Newhouses and the Sayers! He was too sly for us, for anyone. Forgive yourself, Miles. Rid yourself of this. You were watchful, protective, and loving. I could ask for nothing more."

He kissed her lightly then and gave her a quick but reassuring smile. He noted the crushed paper in her lap. "Talk to me, my darling. Tell me all."

She began with the description of that night with finding the ladies in the two retiring rooms. How it seemed as though Marlton had entered the Assembly Room through a lower door, perhaps the coal cellar. How he'd most likely hidden in the ladies' room until she appeared. How self-assured he was throughout.

"He took a chance that I might not appear at all, even in that room, but then, he most likely had a second plan. He was prepared with capes to conceal who we were, with ropes for my hands, and even a handkerchief to stuff in my mouth. As well as hiring the hackney coach and stationing him near the Assembly Room."

"But you saw your chance and escaped him."

"I did. All the while, I was so focused on remaining calm that I was able to think rather clearly."

He cupped her cheek and kissed her eyes. "Your saving grace."

She bit her lip and met his gaze frankly. "I do think every day of his statements that I am not my parents' child. It rocked me."

"Such a thing would disturb anyone."

"He seemed to know that it was an agreement between my mother and her cousin, Amanda's mother. That my mother accepted the fact that she could bear no child and so to gain one, she would accept her cousin's…" Verity could not utter the word "bastard." "How do you think they could have arranged that?"

"If she were nearby and the child were born and kept in secret, then spirited to your parents' home, it could be done."

"And if that were successful, then the birth registry in the parish books would have to read that my mother gave birth to a girl with a birth date. But would not anyone in town know if my mother was pregnant? And so too that my mother's cousin was pregnant at the same time?"

"They would not have had to be in the same term of development. Didn't you say your mother would miscarry at different points in her pregnancy?"

"She would."

He threaded his fingers through her short curls. "Then who would know otherwise? Who would ask if this newest babe were not her own? She would be so glad, no one would have the heart to question her, would they?"

"That could be true."

She took pains to open the letter in her hand. "This came from Charles Whitley this morning. I wrote to him last week. I asked him…I asked him to look into the parish records for my birth."

Miles caressed her cheek. "Listen to me, my love."

She gulped back a sob. What she was about to reveal could make or break their union.

"Verity, darling, I know not what this is, but I can guess. Whatever this says, the words change not a thing about how I adore you. I advertised for a new companion. You are more than my friend. I advertised for a new wife. You are more than my partner. I told myself when I advertised that if I could love this person, I would be most blessed. If I loved you, I would be the happiest man alive.

"But I am more than happy. You have brought me bliss. A friend, a helpmate, a lover. You are more than my spouse. You are my love. My only true love.

"And what you are, my darling, is more than as you began when a babe. You have a character filled with generosity and gratitude, humor and delight in others and in the glories of this world. I love you, in your fullness, as you are. As you will always be, my dear wife and my lover."

She kissed him then, her lips a declaration of how much she had come to love him. They clung to each other, anew in their union as they had never been before.

She could not hold back her tears. "I thought I was this only child of older, kindly parents. Two people who worked hard and went to church, believed in each other and brought me up to be honorable."

"Darling," he said, "you are all of that."

"But if I am the daughter of a woman who had…liaisons, then who is my father? Do I know him? Do I care to?" She shook her head.

"Tell me what is in that letter, Verity."

"Charles checked the parish records for February 10, 1790."

"And?" Miles urged her on with a gentle smile.

"A daughter was born to my parents on that day in the village of Eccleshill. She was baptized Verity Ann Carr three weeks later."

"You are theirs. And they are yours. In the eyes of God."

"I am." She nodded. "I am. And I will temper myself to honor that and them by focusing on that for the rest of my days." She would not ask if her parents had lied to her, nor worry that some taint came to her in her blood from strangers who, in truth, gave her nothing of worth that counted as character.

She put the letter to the table and settled against her husband's sturdy chest. "The only remaining matter is this award of so much money. Marlton said Amanda told him it was her father who set aside an inheritance for me. Why would a man who had been abandoned by his own wife give a child of hers by another man an award of so very much money? Does that not seem beyond the pale?"

She watched Miles then as he stared into middle distance. At length, he said, "If the man had any compassion for the innocent, he would do that."

He gazed down at her, and her heart stopped in sorrow. "Miles…"

"When my wife told me she was pregnant with another man's child, I was filled…consumed with so much rage that I could have killed her."

He appeared so broken, she could not bear it.

He stared at her. "Francesca was a woman who knew her own mind. She had chosen who she was. But a child of hers, any child of hers, could not. And I feared. I feared, Verity, that when she gave birth, she would kill the babe.

"Oh, not by her own hand, although perhaps that might have been possible, too. I cannot say now for certain. But I do know that she had never been pregnant and she had never wanted to be. So when she told me she expected a baby, I was ready to kill her that instant. To put my hands around her and...end our misery in that one time when her own body, which she used so indiscriminately, had failed her plans.

"And as the urge to take her life drained from me, I was filled with one grand desire to take from her the life she would never value. The one she would never cherish. The one she would destroy by her selfishness and her careless pride. I wanted that baby. I did."

Verity's heart swelled with admiration for this man, this noble man who would take a child not his own to save the babe from disaster.

"I told her so. She laughed. Oh, the wickedness of her. She laughed. I did not care. I told her to have the babe, and let me know when it was born. I would send a wet nurse. I wanted him or her. I wanted that child to know he or she was wanted."

Miles blinked and looked at Verity again as he had not for the past few minutes. "If your mother and father wished for a child so dearly, why would they not welcome a babe when they had the chance to save that child for themselves, for their love and care? Why would they care who had created the babe, or in what circumstances? Why would they not care to love a child who needed it?" He smiled at her through unshed tears. "They would take the baby and make of him or her what love and care can make of any child."

She had not taken to heart any mark against her character if she believed Marlton's tale. Illegitimate as she might be, she did not feel as though she was.

"And why is it that I don't condemn myself if I am illegitimate?" She marveled at that question and the fact that she had no answer.

"That is for you to ponder, my darling."

She regarded him. "You are a wise man, sir."

"You praise me too much, madam."

"I think not. You would have saved a poor child even though the world would find you blameless to ignore the babe. I find you remarkable, my darling. And I am once more grateful that I have answered your advertisement for a wife."

"You fascinate me, Mrs. Armstrong," he said against her lips. "You see the good in everyone all the time."

"Then we are a very fine match, husband. For you are the finest man I know."

"Do I take it, then, that you and I are now able to await the birth of our own child with clear minds and hearts?"

"Without fears for tomorrow and with full knowledge that we answered advertisements for spouses who have become the loves of our lives."

Chapter Twenty-Three

February 28, 1815

VERITY SMOOTHED THE gossamer-soft cheek of her daughter and gently rose from the bed to lay her in her tiny crib. Eight days old, Marguerite Armstrong was named for Verity's mother, and resembled that lady in her serenity. The child only nursed and slept. For a baby so young, said the midwife, this was a godsend.

"Enjoy it while it lasts," the midwife had told her and Miles.

For herself, Verity enjoyed the triumph of having given birth within nine hours.

"Also unique," declared the midwife.

Verity covered her baby, rearranged the bodice of her simple muslin gown, and strode into her studio.

In the past two weeks, she had reconciled herself to the unknown of her origin.

She had talked with Aunt Agatha, who was the only person who might have an inkling of the truth. But the lady declared she'd had inklings that Clarice, Amanda's mother, gave away her illegitimate babies.

"There were many?" Verity had asked, astonished at the possibility of a mother giving away a child.

"At least two times she was pregnant, came to term, and

afterward, the children seemed to disappear. How or why, she would never say. Nor did her husband. Poor soul."

"Was my mother ever pregnant at the same time as Clarice?"

"Yes. But I cannot recall how far along she might have been." Her aunt had taken her hand, her rheumy eyes full of sorrow. "What good would it do to think of such a thing? That a mother gives away her child and gives it to another who…" She swallowed.

Who then takes up that baby as her own. Forever more.

In that moment, Verity ended her inquiry, resolved to be finished with the questions that she would never answer. Instead, she would accept that she had been loved and cared for, brought up in good spirits by kind hearts.

So too did Verity decide in that instance to cease her questions about the source of her inheritance. She'd been given it. She would use it. The source was anonymous and would remain so.

She had so much to rejoice in. Her child. Her husband. Her loving husband.

Her finished portrait of Miles now hung on the far wall. She tipped her head and smiled at him.

To display it had been his idea. She still appraised it with a jaundiced eye, looking at it often and thinking that one brush of his cheek could have been better done. Another of his frockcoat bore too much impasto. She could paint another, correct both, but for now, her rendering of Miles still brought a smile to her lips.

"Tell me not you wish to redo that," he said as he made his way toward her with a grin and open arms.

"I would not dream of it," she said as she leaned back against him and enjoyed his kiss to her cheek. "I will sketch Marguerite instead."

"A fine idea," he said, and led her toward the settee. "I've a question for you, madam."

She knitted her brows. "Sounds serious. What is it?"

"I have a letter this morning from my banker at Child's in

London."

"Ah." She settled into the cushions with feigned surprise. "What does he say?"

"Verity." He sat down beside her and focused on her with an umber intensity.

His look had her trying to suppress a giggle. "Yes, darling?"

"You must not fake innocence in this."

She picked at the delicate skirts of her gown. "Never, sir!"

"You sent the sum of three thousand pounds to my solicitor—and I do quote—'with the hope my husband finds it used as the purchase price of Newhouse Cotton Mills in Durham.' Verity," he said, and picked up her hand to kiss the back, "your inheritance is to be used in ways *you* find gratifying."

"This is. I sent for a complete inventory of the items for sale. Included are warping mills, winding machines, bobbins, and gears. All set near a water wheel and a waterfall of twelve feet! They employ two hundred weavers of cambric, all of whom live in the local cottages. Most own their homes, and if you buy the mill, they will continue to live well, doing what they do best. Mr. Newhouse was not very efficient, and the weavers worked for less and less pay each year of the past four. If you inspect the mills, think them worthy, and want them, why not buy them?"

He sat back with wonder in his gaze. "You always surprise me."

"More than that, dear sir, I wish to please you."

He nodded. "I know. And so is it my own desire to please you."

"So what do you say, Miles? Will you go look them over?"

"I will. In a few weeks' time. I will not leave you and Marguerite just yet. But if those mills are not up to snuff, if I must invest too much to make them profitable, I will not buy them."

"Agreed. Do not throw good money after bad."

"But if I do purchase them, I will do so with one hope."

She grew concerned. "What is it?"

"They will be owned by you. You will run them; you will

administer them."

She smiled at him, honored and skeptical of her abilities. "Oh, I question I am capable, Miles."

"You are the most capable person I know. Diligent and well informed of the challenges."

"I confess I am thrilled at the prospect. I will think it over, but I will not assume control just to please my pride. I did learn much from conversations with my father about proper administration of factories and those who worked in them. And I do understand the personal challenges of those who work in mills. But that does not mean I am the best choice for manager. Perhaps my role is one of consultant. Whatever I decide, that is for the future. Today, make me one promise. That if you like the facility, you will buy it."

"I do indeed."

"Good." She beamed at him. "When you return from your inspection, I'll require a complete report of the properties and the employees."

He grinned. "My dear wife, you shall have each detail."

She caressed his cheek. "And after a final analysis, we can plan our first spring ball."

He chuckled. "We're hosting a ball, are we?"

"Indeed. The first of many to show the world that two people who did not know each other the day they married could discover happiness beyond compare."

"Through the fine assistance of Germaine Hammond and the *Fleet-of-Heart Chronicle!*" He bent to take her lips.

She virtually purred beneath his kiss, "And through trust and love one for the other."

"Till the end of time."

Fleet-of-Heart Chronicle
Serving London and environs

NUMBER 19—Volume I.
Monday, March 6, 1815.
Price Sixpence Halfpenny
Published Mondays and Fridays

WANTED: Matrimony!

Frustrated in your search for domestic tranquility? Search no more!

Place your advert with the *Fleet-of-Heart Chronicle*!

News sheet now totally devoted to marital bliss.

Find happiness in a trice!

Affordable!

Exclusive. Confidential.

The strictest honour observed!

March 3, 1815

Lady Retires from Her Search for love!

Lady F—of Manchester, who advertised last month,

announces she has received so many applicants to her marriage proposal that she is no longer in doubt as to her choice for a husband. All others need not now send their resumés. Her marriage is set for next week in her home. Thank you!

March 2, 1815

Dear Mr. Hammond,

I apply to you to find my wife! She has left me and absconded with my two sons and the shop's income from last week. I understand that you are in the business of finding spouses, and I earnestly seek you to do this, as I do not have the funds sufficient to hire Bow Street Runners to accomplish this task.

My wife is my height, of healthy stock, fair hair and good teeth. She speaks well, reads and writes the King's English, although she is obviously too handy with her hands!

Find her, send her to me with the boys, and I will send you the reward.

Is Two Pounds sufficient?

I seek your urgent reply.

G. Roberts, The Battery, Canterbury, Kent.

March 1, 1815

To all Gentlemen who Qualify for my Very Fine Hand:

I am a spirited young lady, 22 years of age and of good family from Dover. I have waited in vain for the approach of a lover to suit my fancy and I am willing to taste the connubial joys with all due speed. I will happily bless you, sir, with my hand provided you are at least five feet six inches, well proportioned, athletic make, face inclined to the virile and no indications of a Dandy. My intended must be gallant, loquacious and not awkward or ill-mannered. He should be a gentleman by birth, rich, as I will make him proud. I have been in Manchester and in London Society too. I am possessed of a large fortune, which I will happily share. I am lovely to behold, and as God has blessed me with humility, I say I am an excellent match to any worthy man.

Letters should be sent to G. Hammond, Publisher, 140 Fleet St., London with all due speed, as I am in haste to marry the first man who fulfills my needs.

March 2, 1815

RESPONSE to '*A Spirited Young Lady by a Gentleman who Hopes to Qualify for Your Hand*':

Miss, I thought it prudent to send this public answer to your public address, as if I do not please you, I may someone else. You write that you have long waited in vain for a man who suited your taste, and have described the spouse you require. As I flatter myself I am that man, I trouble you here with my description. Five feet six inches in height is your requirement. I have six and two. An athletic make you request. I am of broadest shoulder and well-muscled calf. My attire, especially my breeches, are always all the crack, never of the foppish Dandy. My face is that of Adonis, attracting many admiring glances. As for my abilities at conversation, my mother will tell you that

I am loquacity itself. She has taught me during daily tea from age five, the art of amusing another. I never want for words, though I may at times lack ideas. For my birth, Mama does hint that my sire may have been closer to a coal porter than the viscount, the man whose name is in the church birth registry. But she is prone to her special brand of humor. (You will love her! She does live with me.) She and I are thrilled to read that you possess a large fortune. We will happily help you spend it appropriately. It is helpful to note that you are attractive. However, I must admonish you, should you and I marry, you must remain forever after virtuous and faithful. I would spare not the rod on a flirtatious woman. Mama would demand it! You say you have waited for a man for overlong. I hope you are not too old and that you have kept the most precious flower of your charms for me to pluck. I am eager to possess you.

Adored Miss, your able and willing servant, I am…
Mr. W. F. S. Of Norwich.

March 1, 1815

Desirous of a Husband!

I am a young lady, aged 25, fresh as a flower, and endowed with good manners, graces and sound education, and I wish to marry a man of moderate temperament. I have lived in Paris for many months and have a very handsome *trousseau*. I speak excellent French and German and though I have but a moderate fortune, I bring robust health and sobriety to this union. As a consequence of the disasters which have befallen my parents now that Napoleon Bonaparte has returned to Paris, I seek marriage to an Englishman or Scotsman which will afford me peace and quiet in the countryside. I assure all applicants that I wish to welcome children to my marriage and to do so quickly and in earnest hope of many progeny!

I await speedy replies as I am most eager to wed.

Letters to G. Hammond, Publisher, 140 Fleet Street, London

Births

Delivered safely of Viscountess **Bellamy, the former Miss Verity Carr, a daughter to her and her husband, Viscount** Bellamy, born February 20th this year in their home in Yorkshire.

THE END

About the Author

Cerise DeLand loves to write about dashing heroes and the sassy women they adore. Whether she's penning historical romances or contemporaries, she has received praise for her poetic elegance and accuracy of detail.

An award-winning author of more than 50 novels, she's been published since 1991 by Pocket Books, St. Martin's Press, Kensington and independent presses. Her books have been monthly selections of the Doubleday Book Club and the Mystery Guild. Plus she's won nominations and awards for Best Historical of the Year, Best Regency and scores of rave reviews from *Romantic Times, Affair de Coeur, Publisher's Weekly* and more.

To research, she's dived into the oldest texts and dustiest library shelves. She's also traveled abroad, trusty notebook and pen in hand, to visit the chateaux and country homes she loves to people with her own imaginary characters.

And at home every day? She loves to cook, hates to dust, goes swimming at least once a week and tries (desperately) to grow vegetables in her arid backyard in south Texas!